BLACKWOOD

BOOK ONE

SUNNY MAWSON

Blackwood
Book 1
By Sunny Mawson

❀ Created with Vellum

To everyone who ever said I couldn't. You lied.

PROLOGUE

16 years ago

"Alpha, there's no one left. They're all dead."

"Keep searching. We can't give up," he replied. *There must be survivors,* he thought. *An entire pack wiped out? It couldn't be.*

"I'm sorry, Terry. We've searched everywhere. They're all gone."

He sighed, "Leave me."

"Yes, Alpha."

The leader of the Greystone pack wandered through the devastation. He had never seen anything like it. In war, you never killed women and children, but this was not war, this was personal. The Blackwood Pack had very few enemies. They were the elite warriors and enforcers of the werewolf community but stayed out of conflicts and wars, only stepping in when the elders requested they do so. Attacking Blackwood was insane and didn't make any sense.

Suddenly, he heard faint whimpers coming from his left and he quickly turned to search for the small sound. As he got closer to the soft cries, he realized who he was looking at. He'd found the bodies of Blackwood's Alpha and Luna. Their mangled and torn bodies made him want to scream and kill someone. He heard the tiny whine again. It was coming from underneath of them. He carefully pulled the bodies off not knowing what he was about to uncover. What he found shocked him to his core.

A small wolf pup. But this was no ordinary wolf pup. The midnight blue of her fur told him this was Alexandra, daughter of Blackwood's Alpha.

Terry carefully picked the pup up and began to run as quickly as he could back towards the cars. He mind-linked his Beta, James.

"James, take over here. I need some time. Have everyone gather and burn the bodies and clean the area."

"Yes, Alpha."

Once he knew the path was clear, he quickly put Alexandra in the back-seat of his car.

As soon as the Graystone Alpha got in his car, the small pup began to howl loudly, clearly just finding its voice. He sped away from the group for fear that someone may find out about her. He set out to find a safe place to hide for a few days where he hoped that he could calm her down and get her to shift. A midnight blue wolf would definitely catch everyone's attention. He knew there was only one thing to do to protect her.

It was decided. The safest thing for Alexandra Blackwood was for everyone to believe she was dead.

CHAPTER ONE

Isabella

"Beep... beep... beep... beep"

Groaning, I reached over and turned my annoying alarm off. Monday mornings were evil. Especially at five am. No one should have to get up that early. I got up, stretched, and jumped in the shower. There was no time to waste since I had an hour drive to get to my seven am class. After showering in record time, I got dressed and ran downstairs. On my way to the kitchen, I was stopped by the last person I wanted to see. My "mate". Or so he says. Seeing that I don't feel any of the signs, I was pretty sure he was full of it.

"Where are you going little mate?" Chad asked.

"To class. The same place I go every morning. Perhaps you should try it some time. Oh wait, you did try it. And failed," I replied.

"You should watch that pretty, little mouth of yours, Bells. Just because we are mates, doesn't mean you can speak to your future Alpha that way," he snarled.

"First of all, don't call me that. Second, you are not my mate. We have been over this time and time again. Get it through your thick skull!" I yelled.

"Why you little..."

"Chad, Isabella, what seems to be the problem?" Alpha Terry interrupted him before he could finish.

"Nothing, Alpha. I was just on my way out to go to class," I sweetly replied with a smile.

"Go on then, sweetheart. Drive safe. And stop calling me that." he said, shaking his head.

"Sir, yes sir. Alpha!" *Phew! Saved by the Alpha!*

I picked up my bag and continued on to the kitchen, listening to the raised voices behind me get louder. What an idiot. I paused to try and hear what they were saying, knowing it was going to make me late. Oh well, that's what fast cars are for.

"Chad, I thought I told you to leave Isabella alone?" Alpha Terry asked.

"She is my mate, father," he replied angrily.

"We have been over this, Chad. You two do not share a bond. She does not feel the same things you feel. You need to reject her and move on."

"She is the perfect mate for me and the perfect future Luna for this pack! Why are you so against this?" he yelled.

"Do not speak to me that way! I am still your Alpha!" Terry roared at him so loudly the windows shook. "She is not the perfect mate for you! If she were, you would both feel the same connection. And you wouldn't be sleeping with every female willing to spread her legs for you. You seriously complain about her not wanting you when I can smell your latest conquest on you from twenty feet away?"

"I have needs, Father. You want me to reject her and move on? Fine, but remember that you asked for this." He sneered and stormed out of the room.

Terry got a distant look in his eyes, and I could tell he was mind linking with another wolf, most likely James, his Beta. More importantly, my dad.

Terry turned away from me heading toward his office. I knew I should've left for class, but something was making my hair stand up. A few minutes later, my dad walked into his office. I knew better than to listen, but I needed to. As quietly as possible, I tiptoed towards the door thanking the Goddess for my excellent hearing.

"What's going on?" Dad asked.

"We might have an issue with my son. I caught him harassing Isabella again this morning." Alpha Terry replied.

"Again?" he growled lowly.

"Yes, again. Chad also implied that he is going to reject her and move on."

"Finally. So, what's the problem?"

"I am worried about how he might carry out his plans. Not many people in the pack know about their situation. He's angry and could make a big scene out of this." Terry explained.

"What do you want to do?" he asked.

"I want to go ahead with what we planned in the beginning. Today is her last day of class. We both know she isn't walking at graduation. She already said she doesn't want to. We can make some calls to packs we have alliances with and see if we can send her to another pack for a while."

"I thought we agreed not to do this. My mate and I do not want our daughter sent away because your son can't control himself!" he shouted.

"James, remember who you are talking to. I do not want to send her away. She is my goddaughter; I love her like she was my own flesh and blood. I know that my son is an idiot and I wish there were something I could do about it. Right now, we need to think about what is best for Isabella. If he does something that embarrasses her in front of the entire pack, which I suspect he will do, there is no telling how they will react. She's never had much to do with the pack, for a good reason, but you know as well as I do they see her as an outsider because of that." Alpha Terry tried to calm Dad down. It took all the willpower I possessed not to burst through the door. My father's next words stopped me in my tracks.

"She is my daughter. We have raised her for the last sixteen years. It's not fair for us to have to send her away," he sighed.

I could feel the sadness in his voice. This wasn't what I wanted; I didn't want to leave. Why they thought I was the one that should leave was beyond me, especially when Chad was the problem. That jackass should have to leave.

"I know, old friend. And you both have done an amazing job. But for the safety of the pack, and more importantly her safety, we need to send her away. Just for a few months."

"Ok, do it. Make the calls. But if Isabella goes, I want her to go somewhere with the strongest fighters. Dark Sky in Washington, perhaps. Or Scarlet Creek in Ontario. Now, if you will excuse me, I need to go break the news to her mother," he replied dejectedly.

"Go tell Donna. I will call Dark Sky and let you know what they say."

I barely made it around the corner when my dad stormed out of the office. He paused, his back straight but his shoulders bowed with the weight of his disappointment. I watched him until he walked away before heading out to my car.

Fortunately, the drive was uneventful as my mind was completely distracted by what I'd just heard. Halfway through my last final exam, Alpha Terry's voice came through.

"Isabella. How would you feel about taking a trip?" he mind-linked me.

"A trip? I am always up for an adventure, Alpha. You know that." I did my best to seem excited when really, I wanted to scream and shout at the injustice of it all.

"Good. I want you home right after class to pack. You are to leave as soon as possible."

"What's going on? Why the rush?"

"Chad."

Duh.

"Oh shit, what now?" As if I didn't already know. My wolf growled in my head at the thought of that little shithead.

"I think he is planning something tonight. I am calling some of our allies

as we speak to see if you can visit for a while. Looks like the Beta at Dark Sky is in charge while their Alpha is away on business. I told him as little as possible about the situation, and he has agreed to allow you to stay there, at least until their Alpha returns. Now finish up and hurry home," he stated.

"Alright, I'll be home as soon as I'm done here," I replied.

CHAPTER TWO

Isabella

After Alpha Terry mind-linked me, I finished my final exam, turned everything in, and rushed out the door to my car. I was nervous about what Chad might be planning. That boy was dumber than a sack of rocks, but he was also conniving and manipulative. Whatever he was planning must be bad if Alpha Terry managed to convince my mom and dad to send me away. It was almost impossible to convince them to let me go to college and it was just in the next town over. Dark Sky territory was on the other side of the country. I briefly wondered if they would let me drive there. I did not want to leave my car behind for Chad to mess with.

Once I got back to the house, in record time I might add, I hurried to my room to begin packing. My parents and I lived in the pack-house. I hated living there, but it did have its perks. Like having the floor all to ourselves and private balconies.

When I got to my room, I quickly grabbed a couple of suitcases and began to pack. Alpha Terry told I would be gone for a few weeks, of course he told my dad different this morning, and I didn't know what the weather was like there, so packing a bit of everything made sense. At least to me. I had just finished packing some jeans when I heard a knock on the door.

"Who is it?" I asked.

"Your mother."

"Come in," I replied. I was surprised it took her this long to make her way here. Once she walked in, and I looked at her, I knew why.

"Mom, don't cry. It's not forever!" I cried.

"I am fine. I'm just going to miss you. We have never been apart, and I am not sure I am ready." she laughed lightly. "Did Terry tell you how long you'd be gone?"

"Only a few weeks. What did he tell you and dad?" I asked, playing dumb.

"Just that you should take enough to last the summer and we can ship anything else you might need to you. I think he was trying to say that you would be gone for a while without actually saying it."

"Oh, I didn't think I'd be gone that long." I muttered.

"I think he's worried about what Chad is planning and how the rest of the pack might react to things."

"I guess if I'm going to be there a while, I might as well take advantage of it." I shrugged. *It wasn't like I had a choice anyway.*

"That's my girl. Now, let's get you all packed up," she said, heading off to grab another suitcase.

"Thank you," I replied quietly.

We worked silently, side-by-side, until all of my suitcases were packed. We were able to fit quite a bit in there, more than either of us expected. With the clothes all packed, we headed to the bathroom to pack up "the essentials" which didn't take very long. My essentials ended up being pretty much everything in my bathroom. I wasn't really into makeup or getting glammed up. I preferred a natural look, only because I really sucked at putting makeup on. The most I ever did was some mascara and lip gloss. Kind of hard to mess that up. I keep watching those online videos that people do of makeup tutorials, but they might as well be painting renaissance masterpieces. No way in hell could I ever contour my face and have it look like that. As for my hair, it's long, down to my tailbone, and wavy, so it doesn't need much, just a really good conditioner and maybe some detangling spray.

After everything was packed, my dad came in with a couple of the pack fighters. They took all of my bags downstairs and loaded them into my car for me. Pack fighters helped keep the pack safe, patrolling the territory and enforcing the Alpha's rules. Terry and my dad must have been really worried if they were having these guys help out. All that was left for me to do was grab my purse and say my goodbyes. Hopefully, I would be able to get out of there before Chad pulled whatever stunt he was planning.

As I walked down the stairs with my mom and dad, I could see a crowd gathered in the living room. I stopped a few steps from the bottom where I could see Alpha Terry and Luna Karen arguing with their son. As if sensing me, Chad turned around and sneered in my direction. Never one to back down from a fight, I squared my shoulders, raised my head up high, and walked to where they were standing.

"Glad you could make it, little mate" Chad smirked.

"I have somewhere to be, Chad," I replied.

"I, Chad Stone, reject you, Isabella Greyson, as my mate and future Luna," he growled.

"*Finally.* I, Isabella Greyson, accept your rejection." I exclaimed. As soon as the words left my mouth, Chad fell to the floor, writhing in pain. The entire crowd was shocked into silence. I was even a bit stunned.

"Wow, all this time I thought he was lying when he said she was his mate," my mother whispered from behind me.

"Why isn't she in pain? How can she be standing there like nothing is wrong?" shrieked Andrea.

"Because I'm a witch." I snappily replied. No one liked Andrea. Well, some of the guys did. She had a certain reputation with the unmated males of the pack. Some of the mated ones too if rumors were correct.

Several people chuckled at that. After a few minutes, Chad finally stopped twitching and was able to get back to his feet. As soon as he did, Andrea was right by his side. He wasted no time in turning to her, tilting her head to the side, and marking her. The crowd went wild, and not in a good way. My father grabbed my arm and tried to force me from the room, but shock kept me rooted in place. As soon as he marked her, Chad looked up at his father and smirked.

"I have chosen Andrea as my mate and marked her as my Luna. The Alpha title is mine by right!"

"As your father and rightful Alpha of the Greystone Pack, I rescind your right to the Alpha title and bloodline." Alpha Terry growled. The crowd was immediately silenced. We had all heard stories of Alphas denying their children the right to inherit the Alpha title, but we thought they were just that–stories. If Chad thought me accepting his rejection was painful, he was in for a whole new level of hurt. It was a walk in the park compared to the pain of being rejected as heir to the Alpha title. He gasped and fell to the floor unconscious. Pack members began to mutter to each other, and it didn't take long before they were casting wary glances my way. Those glances and mutters quickly became glares and growls.

Alpha Terry turned to me and quietly said, "Go. Quickly, before he wakes up."

I nodded my head and left the room quickly with my mother and father. Once outside, we hugged and said our goodbyes as quickly as possible.

"Quickly, Isabella. You need to go before anyone comes out here," my father urged me, giving me a gentle push towards my car.

"Call us, every day. When you stop at night and before you get on the road in the morning," my mother pled.

"Of course." I nodded my head absently, still in shock.

"Isabella, we love you. Please know that and please be safe." My mother pulled me in for a hug, holding on tighter than normal. I felt my father's arms wrap around both of us.

"Be safe, sweet girl. We love you," he whispered. Pulling back, he gently unwound my mother's arms and pulled her to his chest as I slid into the driver's seat. They stayed that way as I drove off into the fading sunlight.

CHAPTER THREE

Tristan

Grumbling at the of the paperwork in front of me, I wondered how I was supposed to keep up with this for another six months. Jaxon couldn't get back fast enough for me. I knew he had to do his job as a council enforcer, but I seriously hated doing paperwork. Just as I picked up the first stack of papers, I was interrupted by the phone ringing. Saved by the bell, so to speak.

"Dark Sky, this is Tristan," I answered.

"Tristan, this is James Greyson, Beta of the Greystone Pack."

"James, how are you?" I asked.

"Not good, Tristan. Not good at all."

"What's going on? Anything we can help with?" I asked worriedly. I'd spoken to James several times in the past and he never seemed like someone who was easily shaken. The fact that I was hearing from him so soon after speaking with his Alpha set me on edge.

"You already are, friend. My daughter Isabella is on her way. She had to leave in a hurry tonight. It will be a few days before she gets there since she is driving." he replied.

"*Driving?* I thought she was flying up here and staying for a couple of weeks. What changed?" I demanded. We had offered to allow his daughter to visit for a short time, but I would not endanger my pack for her. Especially not with my Alpha gone.

"I know Alpha Terry told you a little of what was going on and why she needed to leave. Well, things escalated. Terry would've called you himself, but he is currently dealing with that issue now."

"What issue? I cannot and will not endanger my pack, James." I snarled.

"His son rejected my daughter and then proceeded to mark the pack whore in front of everyone and attempted to claim the Alpha title. Terry rescinded his right to the title and bloodline," he replied matter of factly.

"Oh shit. He actually did that? I mean, I have heard stories, but never for a second thought they were true." I blew out a quiet breath. Talk about a shocker.

"He had no choice. Terry is a good man and a great Alpha. Our pack would've been destroyed by that fucking idiot son of his. But back to my daughter, I hope I can trust you and Dark Sky to take good care of her. I realize the situation isn't ideal, but she never asked for this and she's innocent in all of this. She can't come back here, Tristan. Not any time soon. The pack is in turmoil right now and some are blaming her."

"Of course. We will protect Isabella as if she were one of our own. You know that. As for how long she can stay, that is up to Alpha Jaxon. He has the final say. However, he won't be back here for at least six months so she can stay for at least that long. Provided there are no issues, I don't see him making her leave." I stated. *Holy hell.* I'd met Alpha Terry several times and each time he had impressed me with his wisdom and patience. For him to rescind his only son's right to the Alpha title and bloodline shocked me. I'd met his son once and that was enough. I couldn't imagine what any of them were going through and I meant every word of what I said to James.

"Thank you. She is all we have. It would kill us if anything were to happen to her." he said quietly.

"James, you have my word as Beta, and as a friend, we will protect Isabella and welcome her with open arms. She will be safe here. I promise you." I said with conviction.

"Thank you. Please let me know when she arrives."

"I will. Goodbye, James."

"Goodbye."

As I hung up the phone, I couldn't help but wonder what made this girl so special. Alpha Terry had alerted me to the strange mating circumstances. How she was his son's mate, without him being her mate, was beyond me. That wasn't how it worked. Once Isabella arrived and I questioned her, perhaps we could do some research to figure out what had happened. In the meantime, it was back to paper-work hell for me. I wondered for a moment if I could get Evie to help me, then laughed at myself for even considering it.

CHAPTER FOUR

Isabella

Thank the Goddess for satellite radio. I would *not* have survived the long trip without it. Thanks to my late start the first day, I only got to Oklahoma City the first night. I made sure to call my parents and let them know where I was though. I didn't want them worrying too much. I asked them how things were at the pack-house, and they were very quick to change the subject. I just let it go and told them I would call them from Denver the next night.

Fortunately, the trip had been a relatively easy one. Long and boring, but easy. I stopped in Cheyenne, Wyoming the third night, and Missoula, Montana the next. I woke up early in the morning and decided to get breakfast at a little diner down the road from the hotel before getting back on the road. So glad I did. It was the cutest little mom and pop diner ever. Black and white checkerboard floors, red vinyl booths, and little jukeboxes on each table. And the best milkshake I have ever had. I couldn't resist having a milkshake for breakfast at such a traditional diner, I knew it would be good, and it did not disappoint. I finally made it to Washington and got off the interstate.

Thank the Goddess for navigation or I would never have found it. With tiny mountain roads, and massive trees covering every inch of terrain I didn't see any real landmarks. There probably wasn't even a mall. Following the directions, I pulled off the road into a long driveway that wound through the woods. I had to hand it to them, they sure knew how to pick a location. It was so beautiful here. I'd never seen so many different shades of green. Absolutely breathtaking.

My wolf was dying to get out and go for a run. *Soon, wolf. Soon.*

After about a mile, I finally pulled up to the gates. Fancy. Little guard shack and everything. And the biggest man I had ever seen in my life. He had to have been well over six feet tall, probably closing in on seven, and he was a good three hundred pounds at least. His face was screwed up in a scowl that would've scared off even the most hardened bad guy. Topped off with a shaved head and he was the perfect villain to any story. He looked like he could crush my car with his pinkie. Man, I hoped he didn't. I loved this car. As I pulled up to the gate, I rolled my window down.

"Can I help you?" asked Gigantor. The nickname I chose fit the man to a T. Even his voice was rough and gruff.

"Yes, I'm here to see Tristan Merritt. He's expecting me." I replied.

"And you are?" he asked in what sounded like a growl. Yep, gonna crush the car. I'm dead, I thought.

"Isabella Greyson," I said quietly.

Suddenly, Gigantor broke out in a huge grin. I was not expecting that. His face transformed like magic from angry and terrifying to happy and friendly. "Oh yeah. We've been wondering when you would get here. Welcome to Dark Sky. Go straight through the gates and follow the gray wolf. He'll lead you to the pack-house where the Beta is waiting."

"Thanks so much!" I grinned back at him. I guess you really can't judge a book by its cover. Hopefully, everyone else was just as nice.

I did as he said and pulled through the gates. As I did, I saw a large gray wolf waiting beside the driveway who had to be the wolf I was supposed to follow. He immediately turned and ran, and I quickly sped off to keep up. After several twists, turns, and forks in the road, we finally reached what could only be described as the most exquisite mountain hotel lodge looking building I'd ever seen. My jaw dropped so far I wasn't even sure it was still attached. The building was fantastic and huge, and I'd only seen the outside. It was at least four or five stories tall, built of some of the largest logs I'd ever seen, with an entrance that was a complete showstopper. Sweeping stairs led up to massive carved wood doors, but the columns were what drew the eye. They went all the way up to the roof line and held up the portico. The light fixture hanging over the entrance was probably bigger than my car.

Speaking of outside, several people were waiting for me. Swallowing nervously, I parked the car and slowly got out, stretching as I did. Time to meet the pack.

CHAPTER FIVE

Isabella

I could do this. *Breathe. Just breathe. And don't trip. Oh Goddess, please don't trip in front of these people.*

I squared my shoulders and walked up the steps to the front porch. Six people were waiting for me. Fortunately, none of them looked as scary as Gigantor at the gate. He turned out to be nice, so maybe these people were too. They looked nice, all with smiling and happy faces. That's a good sign, I thought. Shit, my nerves were going nuts. Once I reached the top of the steps, a "Mr. Tall-Dark-and-oh-so-very-yummy" stepped forward. I was pretty sure I could see myself liking it there from that very moment.

"Welcome to Dark Sky, Isabella. I'm Tristan Merritt, the Beta," said Mr. Tall-Dark-and-oh-so-very-yummy. *Guess I better lose those thoughts.*

"Nice to meet you, Beta Tristan. Thank you for letting me stay here." I replied.

"Oh my gosh! Can we please forgo the formalities and let me hang with my new bestie?" a short redhead squealed. "My name is Evelyn, you can call me Evie. We are now best friends. Get used to it." Her grin was infectious, and I couldn't help but smile back.

"Evelyn, let the girl relax before you attack her, please. And Isabella, please just call me Tristan. No need to be so formal." Tristan sighed.

"Shut up, Tristan. My new bestie, not yours. Now come, Bella. Can I call you Bella? Good. Come on, slowpoke. I'll show you to your room. Jack, you and Connor start bringing her bags up," Evie demanded.

Dang, this girl was bossy. She just got away with telling the Beta to shut up. Judging by the look of sheer exasperation on his face, she did this a lot. I wondered if they were mates. No, I didn't think so. She would've kicked both of our asses for him checking me out. And for me checking him out.

"Come on, Bella!" Evie shouted from the foyer.

"Coming." I called back. Everyone else on the porch gave me amused smirks as I handed my keys to one of the guys and hurried to the front door to catch up with her.

Once inside, I came to an immediate halt. *Holy crap balls.* If I thought the outside was gorgeous, that was nothing compared to the inside. The foyer was at least three stories high with massive log beams across the ceiling. Breathtaking.

Evie came back to stand beside me. "Beautiful, isn't it? It was a deserted ski lodge for the rich and famous back in the day. My parents put in a lot of work here. My brother has continued that. He pretty much let me do whatever I wanted with the design. I studied interior design in college," she whispered, not wanting to startle me.

I turned to look at her, slightly confused. "Your brother? Who is he? One of the pack builders? We had a couple in my old pack, but their siblings never got to design anything on their own." Maybe things were different here, I thought.

Evie looked at me for a minute with a bewildered look on her face, then she laughed. Hard. I'm talking holding her sides, tears running down her face, snorting. After five minutes of this, I had enough. I crossed my arms over my chest and glared at her until she finished. It took forever.

"Oh Goddess, sorry. I forget you don't know anything about our pack," she said, still giggling.

"I've been here all of twenty fucking minutes. How the hell am I supposed to know who your brother is?" I glared at her.

"Sorry," she replied, looking slightly ashamed. "My brother is Jaxon, the Alpha of Dark Sky."

Oh hell. I just cursed at the Alpha's sister. And called him a pack builder. Somebody freaking shoot me and put me out of my misery now.

"Don't worry, I won't tell him you called him the pack builder. Even though he kind of is. He's a bit of a control freak, so he doesn't like to have anyone else design things meant for the pack," she assured me. "Now come on, I will show you where your room is. And give you a bit of a tour on the way."

Evie showed me a bit of the first floor which was stunning. The kitchen was huge and completely modern. Didn't sound like it would work in a rustic lodge, but it did. The rustic log walls contrasted with the shiny stainless appliances and marble counters in a way I hadn't expected. The lighting was a mixture of old and new, or so it seemed. Recessed lights were paired with pendants lights fitted with old style bulbs. The dining room was massive, more like a ballroom, which Evie said it was used for as well. The living room was my favorite. Rustic wood, soft leather, huge antlers on the walls, a gigantic antler chandelier in the center of the ceiling, and the back wall was solid glass. Evie pointed out that the glass wall was actually doors that open all the way up to reveal the courtyard in the back. The second floor of the house held the pack offices, meeting rooms and the library. We skipped those with a promise to check out the library later. The third floor was where the fun stuff was. Two theater rooms, complete with reclining seats and snack bars, a large game room with multiple TVs and every gaming system and game you could imagine, and finally an arcade with pinball, foosball, air hockey, you name it. That had become my favorite floor of the whole house. Floors four and five were the bedrooms for the pack fighters and enforcers.

Moving on, we finally made it to the sixth floor. This floor housed the Beta, the Gamma, or third in command, and a few of the guest suites. It is also where I would be staying. The top floor belonged to the Alpha and his family, which currently consisted of the Alpha and Evie as their parents lived in their own home nearby.

"Are you sure I am supposed to be here? I don't mind staying where the rest of the pack stays." I told Evie.

She looked at me like I had grown horns. "We want our guests to be comfortable and safe. Besides, no bestie of mine is sleeping in gen-pop!" she remarked.

"Gen-pop? What are you, a prison rat?" I smirked.

"Oh shut it, you! You know what I mean. Besides, Tristan said that you were a VIP guest. That means you stay with us." She grinned like she'd just scored a major victory and stuck her tongue out at me. "My room is upstairs, on the Alpha floor. Only Jaxon and I are up there now that our parents have moved out." She walked me down the hallway and continued. "Now then, Tristan is in the room at the end of the hall. Luckily, the rooms are all sound-proofed, so you won't have to listen to him snore," she laughed. "Our Gamma, Cameron, and his mate Kayleigh are in the last door on the left. The other two rooms on the left are empty. Your room is the last door on the right."

We made it down the hall to my new room. Stopping at the door, I noticed it was solid wood with a beautiful carving on it. Two wolves, one a lighter color, the same as the wood on the rest of the door, and one a dark color, stood on top of a cliff under a full moon. Whoever carved them was extremely talented.

Noticing my interest in the carving, Evie told me that it was her brother who'd carved it. Apparently, it is one of several doors he hand-carved for the house.

Evie nudged me and I finally opened the door and stepped inside. The room was quite simply, beautiful. Dark hardwood floors, a four-poster bed, and a dresser with a mirror. On either side of the dresser were doors. The one on the right led to a massive walk-in closet, almost as big as my old one. The door to the left led to my bathroom. Thank goodness I had my own, and I didn't have to share.

The bathroom was luxurious. Two sinks with a makeup vanity in between, a massive walk-in shower all glass and tile. But the center-piece of the entire space was the biggest bathtub I had ever seen. I think you could swim in this thing. It was on the left side of the bath-room, underneath a large picture window. It even had water jets. *Wow.*

Walking back out into my room, I looked at Evie in awe. "I think I have died and gone to tub heaven. It seriously looks like someone dug through my brain and recreated my dream room."

Evie squealed and clapped her hands while jumping up and down. "I am so glad you like it! This is one of the first rooms I designed. Once Jaxon saw it, he loved it and said I could have free rein with the rest of the house," she said proudly.

Looking towards the door, I noticed my suitcases. I guess the guys brought them up while I was admiring my new bathroom. Sweet. Time to unpack.

Evie stayed and helped me unpack all of my stuff. We actually made quick work of it. By the time we were done, I was starving. My stomach decided to let Evie know this by sounding like a dying whale. Embarrassing. Luckily, it was almost dinner time. Evie left to go get changed, saying she would come get me before heading down.

I decided to take a quick shower since I had been in the car all morning and unpacking all afternoon. Not wanting to get my hair wet, I put it up in a bun and jumped in the shower. I didn't want to dress up too much, but I didn't want to look like a slob either. I finally decided on some dark gray skinny jeans, a snug fitting, cropped maroon sweater, and some black boots. Leaving my hair in its bun, I touched up my mascara and added a sheer lip gloss. Done. Nice, but simple.

Evie came back just as I was finishing up. We walked down to the elevators and headed downstairs. Thank Goddess for elevators. I would have hated to have to climb all those stairs every day. Although, it probably would have done wonders for my ass.

Dinner was pretty quiet. Thankfully. Tristan was there, looking as yummy as he did earlier. Evie made sure to introduce me to everyone. Beside Tristan was Cameron, the Gamma, and his mate Kayleigh. Cameron was tall, blond, and pale, while Kayleigh was short, had dark hair, and olive colored skin. They were a very striking couple. Evie sat across from Tristan, and I sat next to her. On my other side was Jack and next to him was his twin brother Connor. I could tell they were going to be fun. They were almost identical, but Jack had a small scar by his right ear. They were both pretty tall, but shorter than Tristan and Cameron. They had light brown hair, brown eyes, and a matching mischievous look on their faces. Across from them and next to Kayleigh was her cousin, Jade. She was tall, extremely thin, and gorgeous. Long, black hair, dark brown eyes, tanned skin.

Once dinner was served, I dug in. I probably made myself look like a total pig, but I didn't care. I hadn't eaten since breakfast, and I was starving. After I finished my second helping, I looked up and noticed everyone staring at me. "What? Never seen a girl eat before?" I grumbled.

They all cracked up laughing. "Never seen one eat quite so fast." snorted Jack. That earned him an elbow to the ribs. I smirked as he grunted and grimaced. "Rude," he muttered.

Once we had all had our fill of dinner, Evie, Jack, Connor, and I made our way up to the third floor. Evie wanted to watch a movie, Jack wanted to play some racing game, and Connor and I wanted to play air hockey. We all finally agreed to go play air hockey first and then video games.

After some very heated competition, meaning Jack and Connor fought over who cheated, Evie and I decided to head off to bed. My first day and I was loving it so far. I couldn't wait to meet the rest of the pack.

Once in my room, I grabbed my cell and called my dad. We talked for a few minutes before my mom demanded the phone. I couldn't help but laugh. Big, bad Beta being bossed around by a five-foot-tall blonde firecracker. Man, I loved those two. After assuring them that I made it safely, that everyone was nice to me, and that I was settling in just fine, I changed into my pajamas and crawled into bed. Snuggling under the covers, I smiled contentedly and quickly fell asleep.

CHAPTER SIX

Tristan

After everyone finished dinner, I went back up to my office to finish up some paperwork. I had patrol schedules to complete for the next two months, pack member profiles to update, financial reports to go over, the list went on and on. Luckily all I had to do for the patrol schedules was approve them since Cameron was the one to make them.

I finally caught up with everything after a few hours. It was time to head to bed, another long day was ahead of me. I planned on taking Isabella for a tour of our pack lands after breakfast, then I had a conference call with Jaxon after lunch to catch him up on everything. We'd had reports of rogues around our territory, but so far, no issues or attacks.

Taking the elevator up to the sixth floor, I made my way towards my room. The doors to Cameron's room and Isabella's room were closed. Thank goodness they were soundproofed. Cameron and Kayleigh did not know the meaning of quiet. I was halfway to my room when I heard the first scream. I stopped immediately to pinpoint where it was coming from. Isabella's room. There was no way I should've heard anything from there. I took off running as fast as I could down the hall. As soon as I got to her door, Cameron's door flew open.

"What was that? Are we under attack?" he asked just as Isabella screamed again.

I didn't stop to see if her door was locked. I kicked it in and prepared to shift and kill whoever was hurting her. But there was no one in her room. I looked over to see her asleep on her bed, thrashing around.

I rushed over to her. "Isabella, wake up! You're safe here. It's okay, please wake up," I said to her as I held her down to keep her from hurting herself. She continued to thrash in her sleep before stopping. I looked at her face and saw tears and heard her whimper.

Kayleigh came in once Cameron made sure no one was in danger. She quickly assessed the situation and hurried over to the bed.

"Let me help her, Tristan. Whatever she is dreaming about is obviously traumatic. We don't know what it is or who caused it, the last thing we need is for her to wake up to some man she just met pinning her down. I'll take care of her," Kayleigh said softly.

As much as I wanted to comfort Isabella myself, I knew Kayleigh was right. I got up from the bed and walked over to stand by Cameron as Kayleigh took my place. Instead of pinning her down, Kayleigh sat beside her and gently laid Isabella's head in her lap and began to lightly brush her hair out of her face. Knowing his mate was safe and had everything under control, Cameron motioned for me to join him in the hallway. I followed him out, gently closing the door most of the way behind me.

"What the hell was that?" Cam demanded. "How the hell did we hear her scream through the soundproofing in these rooms?"

"I have no idea. I'd just gotten off the elevator when she screamed the first time." I told him, confused as hell. "Whatever she was dreaming about, must've been awful." I shuddered.

"We need to get in touch with her father again. He has to know what this is about. We can't risk the pack if someone is after her," he stated.

"I'll call her father in the morning. I don't think we're at risk. James is a good Beta and a good man. He would not knowingly put another pack at risk without warning them." I replied.

"Not even for his daughter?" Cam asked quietly, making me pause and think. I didn't think James would do something like that, but people would do anything to protect their families.

"I don't think so, but I will call him first thing in the morning and find out," I said.

CHAPTER SEVEN

Isabella

I can't wait to open my presents, but mommy says I have to wait for people to finish eating. So of course, I sneak from table to table telling them to hurry! The kids hurry, but the adults just laugh. Do they not understand that the waiting is killing me? You only turn six once, people! Come on!

Finally, everyone is done, and I get to open my presents. I got new dollies, books, hair bows, dresses, shoes, so many pretty things. Mommy and Daddy even bought me a huge dollhouse for my dollies. It's so big even I can fit in it! Uncle Terry and Aunt Karen got me the greatest present ever! They gave me my own art studio! They also said I could paint on the walls! So cool. I can't wait to go in there tomorrow and paint new pictures.

After opening all of my presents, Mommy and Daddy tell me it's bedtime. I tried to tell them I wasn't tired, but a big, silly yawn interrupted me. Dumb yawn. They tucked me into bed, and I fell asleep thinking of my perfect birthday.

I woke to the sound of growling, howling, and screaming.

What is all that noise? It's so loud. Mommy comes running in my room, crying. "Quickly, Lexi, we need to hide you!" She whispers. I'm so scared. I can hear glass breaking and the sound of wolves growling and fighting gets louder. Mommy pulls me out of my bed and sprays me with something. Now I can't smell anything. Not even myself. She picks me up and runs towards the back stairs as quickly as she can. She runs down the stairs with me and out the back door into the darkness.

Wolves are everywhere! Attacking people. I begin to cry, but mommy hushes me and says we need to be very quiet. As soon as we get to the tree line, mommy sets me down and kneels in front of me. "Lexi, your father and I love you so much! I need for you to be a good girl and do exactly what I say. I need you to be very quiet and hide from the bad people. Can you do that for mommy?" she whispers.

"Yes, mommy. But I'm scared." I cry.

"Everything will be ok. You run and hide for mommy. Go, now Lexi. Quickly!" she tells me. I run as fast as I can until I hear a scream. My mommy's scream! "Mommy!" I yell out! Forgetting everything she just said, I shift into my wolf and race towards the fighting. I trip over something and fall down, tumbling over and over, hitting my head hard on the ground. My head hurts so bad, and my eyes go fuzzy. I try to look around, but I can't see anything. Then something heavy falls over me, and I can't stay awake anymore.

When I wake up, everything is quiet. Too quiet. I try to move but I can't. Something is holding me down. I whimper as the pain in my head comes back. Suddenly, whatever was on top of me is moved. A man is there. He seems shocked to see me lying on the ground. He gently picks me up and takes off running with me. As he runs, I look behind us and see what was laying on top of me. My parents. Dead. I try to scream but can't. Again, the darkness takes over, and I go to sleep once more.

Whimpering, I began to wake up. I soon realized someone was holding me, gently brushing my hair. I jolted upright, stifling a scream. It was Kayleigh.

"What happened?" I asked her, confused.

"You had a nightmare, Isabella. We heard you screaming from our rooms," she quietly responded.

"But I thought the rooms were soundproofed. How did you hear me?" I asked.

"I really don't know but you were very loud."

"I'm so sorry. I didn't mean to wake anyone. I'm fine now. You can go back to bed," I said, unable to look at her. I couldn't believe someone heard me. No one knew I still had nightmares. Not even Terry or my parents.

"It's all right. We were worried about you. Do you want to talk about it? Sometimes that helps," she said softly.

Not for me, it didn't. No one could know my secrets. Only a handful of people knew what happened and who I really was. No one else could ever know. "No, thank you. I'm fine. It was only a dream." I put on a fake smile hoping she would believe me.

"All right. Well, if you need anything, Cam and I are right across the hall," she said.

"Thank you."

Kayleigh quietly left the room, closing the door behind her. I went to lock the door, only to see that it was broken. What the hell?

"Knock, knock. It's me, Tristan."

"Hey, Tristan," I muttered awkwardly. This was not a conversation I was looking forward to.

"You ok?" he asked.

"Yeah, I'm fine. It was just a bad dream," I lied. "By the way, what happened to my door?"

"Sounded like more than just a bad dream," he sighed worriedly and looking a little sheepish. "Sorry about the door, I kicked it in when I heard you screaming. I'll have the knob and lock replaced in the morning."

"Oh, ok. I'm sorry I woke everyone and worried you. But really, I'm fine now. It was just a dream, and it's over. I'll go back to sleep, and everything will be great in the morning," I reassured him.

He sighed again. I was sure he could tell I was lying but thankfully didn't push it. "Alright, get some sleep. I will see you at breakfast, Isabella," he conceded.

"Bella. Call me Bella. Isabella is too formal. Goodnight, Tristan," I replied.

"Goodnight, Bella," he murmured before walking away.

Groaning, I shut my door and returned to my bed. Sitting on the edge, I wondered if I should even try to go back to sleep but when I saw that it was only one in the morning, I decided to take a shower and wash off the sweat from the nightmare before going back to bed. I felt sticky and gross.

Grabbing some fresh pajamas, I walked into the bathroom and turned on the shower. The hot water beating down on my skin felt amazing. Luckily, I had put my lavender body wash in there while unpacking. Lavender always helped me relax and sleep.

Once I finished showering, I went back into my room and checked my alarm clock to make sure it was set for the morning. I climbed back into bed, closed my eyes, and drifted off into what would I hoped would be a peaceful sleep.

CHAPTER EIGHT

Tristan

When my alarm went off, it was early. Well, it felt early since I had only gotten a few hours of sleep. I was worried about Bella. She told me that her nightmare was nothing but a bad dream, however, I couldn't help but notice that she couldn't look me in the eye when she said that. I'd hoped that her father would give some answers when I called him.

Stretching and yawning, I made my way to the bathroom to shower and shave. I turned the water on to heat up and grabbed a new razor. Being a wolf is great, but it does mean shaving more often since hair tends to grow quicker. Thank Goddess I'm not a female, I can't imagine having to shave my legs all the time.

After getting cleaned up, I quickly dressed in jeans and a t-shirt before throwing on my good boots and heading down to my office. I wanted to call James before breakfast. He answered after a few short rings.

"Greystone, James speaking," he answered.

"James, it's Tristan from Dark Sky. Hope I'm not calling too early," I greeted.

"Tristan, how are you? No, not too early at all. We're two hours ahead and I've always been an early riser. What can I do for you?" he reassured me.

"Good, good. I'm calling to talk to you about Bella. She's fine, so don't worry. However, I am concerned about something. As I was heading to bed last night, I heard her screaming in her room. Our rooms are all sound-proofed, so I'm sure you can see why I was alarmed. She had locked her door, so I had to kick it in. I thought she might be under attack. Turns out she was having a nightmare," I informed him.

"Damn it. I thought she was over those," James muttered quietly.

"What do you mean over them?" I questioned.

"As I said before, Donna and I adopted Isabella when she was six years old. We know nothing of her life before Terry found her. She has never spoken of her previous life to anyone. We tried therapists, nothing. Her nightmares began a few days after Terry found her. She had one almost every night until the age of thirteen. Then they stopped. Or so she claimed. I guess she just didn't want us to worry about her," he recalled.

"She has never told you or your wife what her dreams were about?" I asked him.

"No, not once. Terry spoke to her about them a few times, but he would never say what she told him. Only that she came to him in confidence, and he would not betray that confidence," he remarked.

"Do you think he knows something about her previous life?" I queried.

"That's something you'd need to ask him," he explained. "He never revealed anything to us."

"All right. Would you mind speaking to him again about Isabella's dreams and her past? See if there is anything at all he will tell us. I believe the two are linked in some way. If it helps, he can call me, or I can call him and speak to him about it," I offered.

"I'll talk to him, and one of us will call you back," he replied.

"Thank you, James. I will wait for your call," I said.

After hanging up with James, I headed to the elevator to go down to breakfast. The doors opened and I was pleasantly surprised to see Bella waiting inside.

"Good morning, Bella. How are you feeling?" I greeted her.

"Good morning, Tristan. Quite well, thank you. I hope you managed to get some sleep last night," she smiled shyly. I guessed she was still a little embarrassed about last night.

"I did, thank you. Did you?" I asked.

"Yes, I did. That is probably one of the comfiest beds I have ever slept on," she proclaimed.

"Good. I was wondering if you would like to go for a run after breakfast?"

"I think I will skip the run for now. I'm not familiar enough with the area, and that makes my wolf a little nervous. I hope you're not offended," she said quietly.

"I'm not offended. Just thought I'd offer. If you would like, we can take one of the jeeps out to tour the lands instead," I offered.

"Thank you. That sounds great," she replied with a smile.

CHAPTER NINE

Isabella

Breakfast was a much bigger affair than dinner the night before. At least fifty to sixty people were sitting at the giant dining tables when I walked in with Tristan. As soon as we walked in, they all stopped talking and eating and turned to stare at us.

"Everyone, this is Isabella Greyson. She is visiting us from the Greystone Pack, one of our allies in Texas. She's the daughter of their Beta. Please make her feel welcome," Tristan announced.

Everyone smiled at me and began murmuring hellos, good mornings, and welcomes. I relaxed and smiled back, thanking people on my way to the table. Evie was flagging me down to come and sit by her again.

Once I got to my seat, Evie asked me how I slept. I pretended not to notice the looks I was receiving from Tristan, Cameron, and Kayleigh.

"I slept great. The bed was so comfortable, especially after being on the road for a few days."

"That's great. I can't stand long road trips, so I don't know how you did it," she replied.

"Well, it wasn't easy, but I did like getting to see the country. I've never really traveled much," I admitted.

"Oh gosh. So, your first time going somewhere and you take a cross country road trip? You're braver than I am."

We continued with small talk as we finished eating. The food here was delicious and I had no trouble clearing my plate again.

After finishing breakfast, Tristan recommended that I change into some clothes that I didn't mind getting dirty and some mud boots. I guessed his plan was not just a tour.

Upstairs, I changed into an old pair of skinny jeans that fit like a glove, a Rolling Stones t-shirt I'd had forever, a hoodie, and my favorite pair of rain boots. I threw my hair up into a bun, grabbed my sunglasses, and hurried back downstairs.

I walked out the front door to meet Tristan and saw the biggest jeep ever. The tires on this thing were almost as tall as my head. *This tour should be awesome.*

Touring the Dark Sky territory with Tristan was interesting to say the least. I couldn't even begin to tell you how many times we got stuck. I was starting to think he was doing it on purpose with the way he chuckled every time it happened. By the time we got back to the pack house, I was covered head to toe in mud. The landscape was beautiful. We saw mountains, forest, and rivers, all pristine and untouched natural beauty. As much as I missed my parents and Texas, I could definitely see Dark Sky as a place I could stay.

The next few weeks went by quickly. I settled into pack life and made some good friends. I finally received my college degree in the mail and began to look for a teaching job nearby. Evie and Kayleigh were helping me with the search. The pack had a huge Fourth of July celebration with some of the best fireworks I'd ever seen. We had barbeques, we went swimming at the lake, hiked the trails throughout the territory, and tried to work on our tans. Before I knew it, summer was over.

I finally heard back from a nearby elementary school and after interviewing, I was hired as a first-grade teacher. I was nervous but so excited. School started after Labor Day, and I couldn't have asked for better students. It didn't hurt that they were all kids from Dark Sky. It took a few weeks for us to settle into a routine, but the kids were so much fun. I felt like I was learning just as much as they were. My principal checked on me every few days, making sure that I was doing okay. I'd been warned by college professors that I would be on my own when I started teaching, but this school was different. I was so happy I came here. My parents were even trying to set up a time to come visit.

Once school started, time really began to fly by. Before I knew it, Halloween was upon us. Growing up without many friends, I never dressed up or went trick or treating or went to parties. When I found out that the Dark Sky pack threw a Halloween costume party, I couldn't wait. Evie, Kayleigh, and I decided to go shopping for our costumes together.

The Saturday before the Halloween party, the girls and I went into town to find our costumes. We skipped the big costume shop and headed to Vintage Row to check out the cool vintage shops and clothes.

"I think we should coordinate our costumes," Evie declared.

Kayleigh looked at her like she had grown three extra heads. "Yeah, that is so not happening, Evie. I remember your costume last year. A lamb. You glued cotton balls to your bra and panties. Alpha Jaxon about had a heart attack. No way am I letting you have any control over my costume!" She laughed.

"Cotton balls? Are you serious?" I asked, shocked that anyone would do that.

"What? I looked good, girl!" Evie stated smugly. "Not that I would do it again. Jaxon threatened to send me to a convent."

Kayleigh and I howled with laughter at the look on her face. She looked offended that he would even suggest it.

As we browsed the racks in our third store, Evie gasped and squealed. "Bella, I have found your costume, honey! Get over here and try this on now!" she shouted.

"Oh shit, I'm scared," I said with a chuckle.

Kayleigh giggled, "Maybe you should start running now."

We both cracked up laughing as Evie shot us dirty looks. "Just come look," she demanded.

Kayleigh and I hurried over to where Evie was standing. She held up a small red and white outfit. When I took a closer look, I realized what it was.

"Little Red Riding Hood? Are you kidding me?" I laughed.

"Yes, Little Red Riding Hood. No, I am not kidding. This isn't your everyday Red costume; this is an H-O-T Red costume. Go try it on," she said sternly.

Knowing better than to argue with her, I took the costume and went to the changing rooms. I hurried and changed into the costume. Once it was on, I turned and looked in the mirror and gasped.

"Evie, there is no way in hell I am wearing this!" I shouted.

"Shut up and let us see," she demanded.

I opened the door slightly and peeked out to make sure no one else was around. I did not want anyone to see me in that outfit. Since I only saw Evie and Kayleigh, I opened the door wider.

"Holy shit, girl, if you don't buy that costume, I will!" Kayleigh gasped. "Either way, you are wearing it."

"Told you so." Evie smirked.

"My boobs and my butt are practically hanging out!" I protested.

"That's the point!" they both exclaimed.

What have I gotten myself into? I tried arguing with them, but when they both threatened to shift and kick my ass right there in the store, I gave up. Slutty Red Riding Hood it is. Goddess help me.

The day of the Halloween party Evie and Kayleigh both showed up at my door dragging a less than impressed Jade with them. Kayleigh insisted that Jade, her cousin, was the best at hair and makeup. Seeing as how every time I have seen Jade, she always looks flawless, I believe it.

The girls brought their costumes with them to get ready in my room. I was excited to see their full costumes. Jade was going as Wednesday Addams, which was perfect with her dark hair and dark eyes. Kayleigh was dressing up as an Egyptian princess. With her dark hair and olive skin, she looked like she'd just stepped off of a Hollywood movie set. Evie was smoking hot as a sexy devil.

Kayleigh and Evie did each other's hair and makeup while Jade worked on mine. By the time she was finished with me, I was stunned. I was shocked that she could make me look sexy and yet it didn't feel like I had a ton of makeup on, but my skin looked flawless. I had cheekbones and eyelashes for days. The smoky eye look that she had done reminded me of the online videos I watched and failed to replicate. Jade knew what she was doing, she had some amazing skills.

Once we were all ready, we headed downstairs. The guys had gone on ahead of us to help set up.

"Where is the party?" I asked again. Evie had told me when we were shopping but it went in one ear and out the other.

"At a club in town owned by one of the pack members," Evie replied. "It has several levels, but the bottom two are for shifters only. The top floor is for humans. Separate entrances keep things running smooth. We tell them it's a private member's only club."

"I've never been to a club before," I admitted to the girls. You could've heard a pin drop in the car.

"Never?" Jade said, shocked.

"No, I wasn't really that popular in my old pack. No friends to go with," I quietly confessed.

"Well thank the Goddess you moved here," Evie declared. "Those people are morons if they didn't want to be friends with you. You are amazing."

I smiled with tears in my eyes. I was fortunate to have met them.

"You cry and mess up my masterpiece and I'm kicking your ass," Jade said with a growl and a smile.

"These last five months have been the greatest. I can't wait to party with my besties tonight!" I exclaimed.

Once we got to the club, we hurried to the shifter only entrance.

The bouncer at the door let us right in. I was shocked to see how crowded it was already. Inside, we quickly made our way to the VIP section. There we found Tristan, Cameron, Connor, and Jack. Kayleigh made her way to Cameron, leaving Evie, Jade, and I to hang out with Connor and Jack. Tristan was busy talking to some of the servers.

"Holy shit, Bella, you look fucking hot!" Jack shouted over the music.

"Yeah, she does," Connor agreed.

"Shut up you two. I need a drink if I am going to make it through the night," I blurted out.

They all laughed at me. "Come on then, let's get you girls some drinks," Connor replied.

Jack, Connor, Evie, and I headed over to the bar to grab some drinks while Jade took off for the dance floor. At the bar, Jack ordered us each five shots. I would've been worried if it wasn't for shifters having a high alcohol tolerance. We finished our shots and then headed down to the dance floor, passing Tristan on our way.

"Bella, you l-look amazing," he stuttered.

"Thanks." I giggled. The shots had taken the edge off for me. "We are heading down to dance. Want to come with us?"

"Maybe in a little bit. I need to take care of some business first. Be careful. It's not just our pack here tonight," he warned.

"Always!" Evie shouted as we walked away. Tristan and I both shook our heads. If there was one thing Evie was not, it was careful.

Evie and I lost Jack and Connor on our way down to the dance floor, we didn't really mind though. Evie found a group of girls she knew, and we all started dancing together, having a great time. Jade made her way back over to us, bringing a tray of shots with her. Evie and I immediately downed several each before dancing again. This round of shots proved to be much stronger than the last ones and I felt the effects right away.

After several more shots, I decided to take a quick bathroom break. I let Evie know and took off in the direction she pointed to find it. I found the bathroom and luckily there wasn't a line. After washing my hands and touching up my makeup, I headed out the door, surprised to find the hallway empty, and back to the dance floor. Before I could get there, someone grabbed me from behind. The alcohol had dulled my senses and slowed my reaction, so fighting back proved more difficult than I expected. Whoever grabbed me was strong.

I kicked and screamed as I was dragged down the hallway past the bathrooms where he kicked open a door and threw me inside, quickly following me and shutting and locking the door behind him. He flicked on the light, and I knew instantly that I was in big trouble. The adrenaline flowing through me managed to wipe out some of the effects of the alcohol, but this guy was huge, and I had no idea what he wanted with me. He could be Gigantor's brother. No way was I getting out of here unscathed, and I frantically scanned the room looking for a way to fight back.

I spotted a broom and snagged the handle just as he came at me again. I swung wildly, screaming as I tried to fight him off. He grunted as the broom connected before he backhanded me, and I fell to the floor. I kicked my feet out, scrambling backwards as he came for me once again.

CHAPTER TEN

Jaxon

I finally finished my job for the council, and I made it back to the pack house only to find it empty. *Oh yeah, it's the night of the Halloween party.* I headed up to my room, but not before catching the faintest hint of the most amazing scent. It was sweet and more than a little distracting. Even my wolf sat up and took notice. Shaking my head, I quickly changed and headed out to the club.

Once inside, I headed over to the VIP section to surprise Tristan. As I walked up behind him, I caught a slight whiff of that amazing smell again. Before I could think any more about it, Tristan turned around.

He jumped when he saw me, and a huge grin spread across his face. "Man, am I glad you're back. Doing your job *and* mine sucks," he cracked.

We both laughed and chatted for a few minutes. Tristan informed me that Evie was down on the dance floor with the visiting female he'd told me about. According to Tristan's thoughts, she was a hot one.

I kept getting stopped on the way to the dance floor by pack members welcoming me home and making mention of the new girl. It felt good to be back. As I got closer to Evie, that amazing scent I kept catching a whiff of became stronger. It was like jasmine, honey, and mangoes. Mouthwatering.

I snuck up behind Evie and grabbed her by the waist, causing her to scream. She turned around ready to hit me but when she saw it was me, she smacked me on the arm and gave me a huge hug.

"I've missed you," she squealed.

"Missed you too, little sis." I laughed at her. "So, where is this new wolf everyone is talking about?"

"She went to the bathroom, but that was ages ago. She should've been back by now," Evie responded sounding worried all of a sudden.

We both knew how handsy some wolves could get after a few of the club's holiday drinks, so we headed toward the bathrooms to check on her. As we got closer, my wolf and I become more and more anxious. I could feel him pacing back and forth in my mind. That scent got stronger as well. Between it and my wolf going nuts, I could barely concentrate.

Evie was saying something to me, but I ignored her and kept walking past the bathrooms. Something was telling me to keep going down the hall. Suddenly, we heard muffled screaming and crashes from one of the storage rooms. I ran to the door and kicked it open. Inside was the most beautiful woman I had ever seen in my life. A rogue had her pinned to the ground as she struggled to get free.

I rushed in and grabbed the attacker throwing him against the wall. I was vaguely aware of Evie pulling the woman out of the room before I began to pummel the stranger's face. *No one touches her.* I landed hit after hit on the guy. He never had a chance.

Before I could kill him, which I most certainly had planned to do, Tristan and Cameron raced in and pulled me off of him. They called the security team in and had him taken to the pack prison. Tristan was saying something to me, but I shook him off. I needed to find the woman with Evie. Immediately.

I pushed by everyone and made it to the hallway where I found Evie comforting her.

The wolf in my head was screaming, "Mate!" and it was then I knew why I'd acted so crazy. As I approached, her head shot up while she stared at me with a shocked expression. I stopped in my tracks, not wanting to scare her.

Evie looked up at me and sighed in relief. "Thank Goddess you were here, Jaxon!" she cried. "Who knows what that monster would've done to Bella?"

I shuddered at the thought and saw red all over again. I wanted to walk out the door and find that rogue and kill him with my bare hands for touching what's mine.

"Bella, sweetie, are you ok?" Evie asked worriedly.

"Mine," she whispered, before fainting.

I sprung forward and caught her before she could hit the floor. Tristan stepped up to help me but was stopped by my growl.

"Oh hell," he muttered. "She's your mate, isn't she?"

I growled at him again until he backed away.

"Alpha Jaxon, I only want to help you. Let me pass so I can open the door. My car is right outside. I'll drive you and Bella home. Evie, Cameron, and Kayleigh will come with us," Tristan assured me.

I nodded my head and let him pass. He jumped in the driver's seat and took off once we were all inside. Cameron and Kayleigh sat in the front while Evie sat in the back with me, Bella on my lap. I refused to let go of her.

We made it back to the pack house in record time. As soon as the car stopped, I jumped out and headed inside to my room, Evie following closely behind. Once in my room, Evie stopped everyone else at the door telling them that I needed space. I gently laid Bella on my bed.

"She's your mate," Evie stated. I nodded, not looking away from Bella.

"You need to speak to Tristan," Evie sighed. "Isabella is here at the request of another pack. He could have some information you need."

"I will once she wakes up. I won't leave her alone like this."

I heard a soft moan coming from the bed. I looked over and saw Bella's beautiful green eyes staring at me.

"We need to talk," she said quietly.

CHAPTER ELEVEN

Isabella

I woke up in a bed that wasn't mine. It was strange, but it smelled delicious. The same wonderful scent I noticed at the club before I passed out. When I opened my eyes, I saw Evie standing next to the bed talking to someone. She was speaking with the most incredibly gorgeous man I had ever laid eyes on.

Damn, he was tall. What are they drinking here to get that tall? He had *to be well over six feet tall. Long legs, narrow in the hips and waist, broad chest, and shoulders, yum.* He had auburn hair, deep blue eyes, the most kissable lips, and a jawline I just wanted to lick. And he smelled like cedar, pepper, and musk. Strong, spicy, and delicious. This must be his bed I am currently laying in. He's my mate. *Holy shit! I have a mate. Please, Goddess, let me be his mate. Don't screw with me like this.*

I heard Evie telling him that he needed to talk to Tristan and that I was here at the request of my old pack. I guess that meant I needed to tell him the truth. The whole truth. I just prayed he didn't reject me.

"We need to talk," I whispered quietly. Both of their heads snapped in my direction.

"You're awake!" Evie exclaimed.

My mate slowly walked over to the bed and sat down next to me. "How are you feeling?" he asked, concern evident in his eyes.

"I'm fine. A little embarrassed that I fainted," I said with a nervous chuckle, "but fine."

"Don't be. You were attacked by a rogue," he growled angrily. "I can assure you; he has been caught and will be punished. No one touches my mate."

He said mate. He said his mate. I. Am. His. Mate. He is my mate. We are mates. Thank you, Goddess, you rock! Internally, I was doing the happy dance.

I smiled at him. It was probably more of a full-blown grin than a smile. I couldn't help it. After everything that happened with Chad, I didn't think I would get a mate.

"We should talk. I have some things that I need to tell you. Maybe we could go talk in your office?" I told him.

He frowned before replying, "Of course. We can go down to my office and talk. Need me to carry you?" he winked.

"I am perfectly capable of walking," I retorted. "But I would never pass up a piggyback ride."

He stood up and turned around. "Hop on," he said, laughing. *Hell yeah.*

As soon as I hopped on his back, there were immediate sparks. We both gasped at the sensation and then chuckled. Evie shook her head, laughing at us. She walked ahead of us and opened the door where Tristan, Cameron, and Kayleigh were all still waiting outside.

"Jaxon, is everything okay?" Tristan asked.

"Jaxon? You're Jaxon? A-Alpha Jaxon?" I stuttered.

Everyone got very quiet. "Um, yes?" he replied.

"Oh, hell. Thanks for the warning." I muttered, ducking my head in embarrassment. I can't believe I just asked my *Alpha* mate for a piggyback ride.

Next thing I knew, my whole body was shaking. No, actually his whole body was shaking which was making me shake. He was laughing. Loudly. Then the rest joined him.

"You didn't know he was Alpha?" Evie asked.

"No! How was I supposed to know? No one told me," I replied, still not looking up.

"It's alright, sweetheart," he comforted me, still chuckling.

"Whatever. Let's go talk," I grumbled. "You might want Tristan and Cameron to join us." I unlatched my legs and wiggled until Jaxon let me slip off of his back. I was embarrassed and uncomfortable. I hated having people laugh at me and I was not looking forward to this talk we needed to have.

Jaxon looked down at me, confused. "Trust me, you'll want them there for some of this," I assured him. He just nodded and told them to head down to his office. Evie and Kayleigh volunteered to go down to the kitchen and fix everyone something to eat. I was grateful for that since dinner felt like it was days ago.

Once Jaxon and I got to his office, we sat down on the couch. Tristan and Cameron were standing off to the side by the bookcases against the far wall.

"I need to ask you something. But first, I want to clarify a couple of things. I am not accusing anyone of anything. Nor am I saying anyone isn't trustworthy. Once you hear my story, you'll understand, but for now, please don't be offended by what I ask. This goes for all three of you," I pleaded.

They all nodded their heads and promised to keep an open mind and not get offended.

I took a deep breath and looked at Jaxon. "Do you trust them?"

"Absolutely," he replied.

"With your life?" I countered.

"Yes," was his response.

Taking another deep breath, I asked: "As your mate, do you trust them with *my* life?"

He gave me a questioning glance. "Without a doubt."

"Good. Because what I'm about to tell you, cannot leave this room. You guys cannot tell your families, the rest of the pack, or your mate, Cameron. To do so would endanger the lives of everyone here," I cautioned.

"Maybe we should all sit down so you can start from the beginning?" Jaxon proposed.

"I'm not sure what you already know, so I'll start with the story we tell everyone. When I was six years old, Alpha Terry Stone was returning from checking out a report for the council and found me on the side of the road. I was totally alone and abandoned. There were no records of a missing child so Alpha Terry's Beta, James Greyson, petitioned the council to adopt me. He and his wife were unable to have children. The council agreed, they adopted me, and I have been with them ever since."

I continued my story, "At the age of eighteen, Alpha Stone's son, Chad, informed his father that I was his mate. As you know, when you find your mate, you just *know*. Their smell is amazing, the sparks when you touch, wanting to be with them constantly. Chad felt all of these things. I didn't. We both allowed Alpha Terry to look into our minds to confirm what was happening. He did. I was Chad's mate, but he was not my mate. This was unheard of. Chad was livid, almost to the point of being driven crazy by it. I wanted nothing to do with him. He was still the same little shit that had made my life hell for the last twelve years. I did my best to avoid him. He began to sleep with other females in the pack, possibly hoping that I would get jealous. All I felt was relief that he was finally leaving me alone. This caused him to become more enraged. My father and Alpha Terry began to talk to other packs after Chad tried to ruin my birthday party in April, as he did every year. We knew that I would have to leave eventually. On my last day of college in June, Chad cornered me in the kitchen. Luckily, Alpha Terry managed to interrupt him and prevent him from doing anything. I was supposed to leave for class but eavesdropped on their conversation. Chad made some threats that his father had to take seriously. He spoke with my father and told him that it was time to find a pack for me to go stay with for a while. Alpha Terry mind-linked me in class and told me to come home and pack, that I was leaving that night. When I got home, I packed as quickly as possible, but it wasn't quite quick enough. Chad had gathered a crowd in the main room downstairs.

When I got down there, he made of show of rejecting me. I felt nothing. So, I accepted his rejection and rejected him back. He fell to the ground in pain. When he got up, he smirked at his father and me. He then proceeded to mark the pack whore as his mate and tried to claim the Alpha title. Alpha Terry immediately rescinded his right to the Alpha title and bloodline. To say we were all shocked, would be a massive understatement. Chad was in so much pain, I thought he was going to die. Alpha Terry ordered me to leave. My parents rushed me out the door and into my car, and that is when I drove here." I confessed.

You could've heard a pin drop in the room. I knew that Tristan knew some of this, but he didn't know everything. Cameron and Jaxon were both clueless. I watched Jaxon's face for any sign of what he might be feeling. He looked very calm, but judging by his white knuckles and shaking hands, he was anything but calm.

Jaxon slowly raised his eyes to look at me. He wrapped his arms around me and held me tight, just breathing in my scent. Gradually he calmed down, and the shaking stopped. Growing up, I'd watched my mother sooth my father in this same way, sometimes with a simple touch. I never thought I would be able to do the same.

"I'm sorry. I'm so sorry that you had to go through all that. You deserve so much more," Jaxon whispered.

I sat there, wrapped in his arms, and just relaxed for a moment. There was more to tell, but I knew that the three of them, especially Jaxon, needed a few minutes to process what they had just heard.

Cameron was the first to speak to everyone. "You said that what you would tell us could endanger everyone here. Am I right in guessing you haven't told us that part yet?" he asked.

I nodded. I tried to get up, but Jaxon tightened his arms and shook his head. I assured him I wasn't going anywhere, I just wanted to be able to see everyone as I spoke.

"Everything I've told you so far is the truth. With the exception of a few things. Terry did find me when I was six years old. It's true that the council had no record of a missing child my age. That's because the council was under the impression that I was killed along with the rest of my pack. Terry knew who I was. He lied to the council and told them he found me beside the road. He didn't."

I examined the expressions of the men in the room before I made the big reveal, my heart racing. "My name is Isabella Greyson. When James and Donna adopted me, they kept the middle name my birth parents had given me. I was born Alexandra Isabella Blackwood, daughter of Michael and Elizabeth Blackwood, Alpha and Luna of the Blackwood pack. My entire pack was brutally murdered the night of my sixth birthday. My parents died protecting me. Terry was my father's best friend. The council asked Terry and his pack to respond to reports of an attack on Blackwood. Terry found me, unconscious, underneath my parents' bodies. He knew that if news got out that I was still alive, whoever attacked my pack would stop at nothing to kill me. He lied to his pack and the council to protect me. I am the last of the Blackwood warriors," I confessed.

CHAPTER TWELVE

Jaxon

Well, that was a bomb I didn't expect. Isabella was a Blackwood. The *last* Blackwood. Holy shit. I knew what happened to the Blackwood pack, everyone knew what happened. My parents were at her birthday party. They left early to come back because we had reports of rogues near the borders. Everyone at the party was found dead early the next morning. Or so we were told.

"How do we know you're telling the truth?" Cam asked her.

I growled at him. "It's okay, Jaxon. This is pretty unbelievable," Isabella acknowledged, turning to face Cam. "My wolf. Blackwood wolves are special. I can shift, and that will give you all the proof you need."

"It's true. Blackwood warriors were special wolves. No other wolves looked like them. If someone joined their pack, their wolf would change to match the others. It's the only pack that did that," Tristan confirmed.

I glared at Cameron for not believing my mate. He at least had the decency to look somewhat ashamed.

"If you're ready, I can shift now," Isabella said gently.

"Absolutely not! No way in hell is my mate going to be naked in front of another male!" I roared.

Isabella giggled. "I won't be naked. Special looking wolf isn't the only thing Blackwood's are known for. When we shift, our clothes don't shred."

Well damn. "You're sure?" I asked. She just smiled and nodded. "Ok then. Go ahead, prove him wrong."

Isabella smiled at me and then began to shift. Her form shimmered and you could hear her bones cracking and breaking. It was a very quick process. One second, she was standing there, the next, a giant, midnight blue wolf, was in her place.

"Fucking hell! She is a Blackwood. I never thought I would see a Blackwood warrior wolf." Tristan blurted out.

"I'm sorry for ever doubting you." Cameron apologized.

Isabella kept her eyes on me the entire time. She was the biggest female wolf I had ever seen. She was only slightly smaller than my wolf, and my wolf is huge. She still had the same bright green eyes. They looked amazing next to her midnight blue fur. Quite the combination.

She whined quietly, bringing me out of my thoughts. I slowly approached her and held my hand out. She leaned her head forward and touched her nose to my palm. I gently ran my hand up her snout to the top of her head and scratched behind her ears. I swear she purred. I chuckled at the thought of a wolf purring. She must have thought I was laughing at her because she pulled her head back and glared at me before licking my hand and scampering back.

"Gross. That was uncalled for," I complained, wiping my hand off on my leg. Her wolf just huffed at me. "Ok, can you change back now? My wolf is getting a little antsy seeing you in this form," I informed her.

Isabella's wolf began to shake and shimmer as she shifted back to her human form. Sure enough, her clothes stayed on her as she changed back. That was a relief.

As soon as she was completely human again, I walked over and wrapped my arms around her, holding her tight.

"Your wolf is just as beautiful as you are, sweetheart," I whispered so only she could hear. My whole life I'd watched as the people around me found their soulmate. I wanted that connection more than anything. That instant feeling of knowing I'd found the one that was made for me.

When her shoulders started to shake, I knew that she was crying. "Sweetheart, what's wrong?"

"Jaxon, I... I need to ask you something." she stammered, stepping back to look up at me. "I know that I come with a lot of baggage. That my existence alone could be a threat to your pack. I'm truly sorry for that. But I need to know, are you going to reject me? If so, please do it now and get it over with."

"Why on earth would I reject you?" I demanded, utterly confused as to where her feelings were coming from. "You're the best thing that has ever happened to me. I've waited twenty-five years to meet you. I am not going to, nor will I ever, reject you."

Knowing that we needed to have a private talk about where all this shit was coming from–because that's precisely what it was, shit–I linked Tristan and Cameron and asked them to give us some space and asked if they'd bring us some food. They nodded and quietly left the room.

"Isabella, why would you think that I would reject you?" I asked, unable to keep the hurt from my voice.

I watched as she blinked once and the tears, she had been keeping at bay escaped and ran down her cheeks. I wrapped her up in my arms and carried her to the couch, cradling her to my chest.

"Please don't cry, sweetheart," I murmured softly. "I didn't mean to hurt you."

"You didn't. These aren't sad tears, they're happy tears!" she exclaimed. "I never thought I would find my mate. Not after every-thing that happened back home."

At the mention of home, and her old pack, I growled lowly. "I want to kill that ignorant fuck for what he did to you!"

"Don't," she pleaded. "He did me a favor."

I couldn't help but look at her like she was crazy. She calls that shit a favor?

"It's true. If he hadn't rejected me in the way that he did, I might not have ever had to leave. If I hadn't left, I never would've found you."

"True, but I still think he needs his ass kicked."

She giggled. I held her close, hugging her to my chest as her breathing slowed and evened out. I wasn't surprised that she fell asleep on me. She'd had quite the eventful night.

A soft knock let me know that Tristan had returned, hopefully with food. I was fucking starving. He set the food down on the table in front of me and nodded towards Isabella. I let him know that she was fine, and he quietly left us in peace.

After Tristan left my office, I ate my food, trying not to wake Isabella. She looked so peaceful sleeping in my arms. Once finished, I carefully stood up and carried her to the elevator to go up to my room. Evie was waiting just outside my office.

"Figured you'd take her up to your room," she shrugged when I glanced at her. "That costume won't be very comfortable to sleep in and she might not take kindly to you changing her while she's asleep."

"Good call."

Upstairs, I gently laid her down on my bed. She grumbled a little in her sleep and made the cutest pouty face. I couldn't help but smile. Evie carefully removed her shoes and costume. Little Red Riding Hood. That must've been Evie's idea. I chuckled to myself. I think I will keep that for later. I grabbed one of my t-shirts, handed it to Evie, and headed for the bathroom as she slipped it on Isabella. Didn't want her to think I was a pervert.

I made sure Evie was finished before coming back out. I thanked her and told her we'd talk to her in the morning. I slipped off my jeans and shirt, leaving me in just my boxers, and I crawled into bed next to her. I couldn't help but grin when she rolled over and threw one leg over mine and an arm over my chest, pulling herself closer to me. I wrapped my arms around her, kissed her forehead, and fell asleep.

The next morning, I woke up feeling content, happy, and very well rested. I opened my eyes and saw that my mate was still asleep. She was incredibly beautiful. I watched her sleep for a few minutes.

"Creeper," she said with her eyes still closed, and her mouth forming a little smirk.

I threw my head back and laughed. "I didn't think you were awake yet." I chuckled and kissed her forehead.

"Kind of hard to sleep with someone staring at you." She yawned.

"Well, get used to it. I'll be staring at your beautiful face for the rest of our lives," I vowed.

"I accept that." She sighed. "Now, are you going to kiss me good morning or just stare at me?"

I could feel my wolf strain to take over when she said that. We both couldn't wait to mark her and make her ours. I slowly leaned my head down and captured her perfect lips with mine, soft and sweet, just like I'd imagined they would be. I moved one hand to cup her cheek while keeping the other one firmly pressed to her back, holding her to me. I swiped my tongue against her lower lip, and she parted her lips to allow me entrance. Our tongues danced and swirled together in sync.

When we broke apart, both of us were panting. I knew if I didn't put a stop to things now, I would end up marking her, with or without her consent.

"Unless you want to be fully mated before breakfast, we should probably stop," I groaned.

"You're right," she said, still panting. "I would at least like for the pack to know that I am your mate before they find out we are fully mated."

I chuckled and kissed her lips. "Speaking of the pack, Tristan just informed me that they are wondering where I am. We should probably head down."

"Fine," she huffed, with a grin on her face. "Let me at least shower first."

"As you wish, princess," I smirked at her. That earned me a smack on the arm.

Since all of her clothes were still down in her room, Isabella decided to go there to shower and get dressed. I promised to meet her there after I showered and got ready. Kissing her goodbye at the door, I rushed to the bathroom. I didn't want to be away from her any longer than necessary.

As I neared her door, Tristan came out of his room.

"Hey man. How's it going?" he asked.

"Good. Isabella came down here to shower and get ready since her things are still down here. I want Evie and Kayleigh to move everything up to my room today." I informed him.

"Cool. When are you planning on introducing her to the pack as your mate?" he inquired.

"I would like to do that tonight at dinner, but I need to talk to her about a few things first. You and Cameron should join us," I insisted.

"Ok, want me to have the kitchen send lunch up to your office?"

"Yeah, that would be great. Thanks. We'll meet you guys down there in a few." I nodded.

"Ok. See you down there. I'll let Cameron know. I'll also have Evie and Kayleigh start packing Bella's things while we meet," he proposed.

I thanked him again and knocked quietly on Isabella's door. Not getting a response, I opened the door and went inside. I saw that her bathroom door was closed and could hear her humming inside. I sat down on the bed and waited for her to come out.

CHAPTER THIRTEEN

Isabella

After leaving Jaxon's room, I hurried downstairs. Luckily the elevator arrived quickly, and I didn't have to wait long. Once in my room, I went to my closet to pick out my outfit for the day. I wanted to impress my mate and have him be proud to introduce me to his pack. My favorite burgundy sweater dress and some knee-high brown boots would be perfect.

After laying my outfit on the vanity table in the bathroom, I took the fastest shower ever. With that done, I threw my hair up in a bun, brushed my teeth, swiped some mascara on my lashes and some gloss on my lips and called it good.

I opened the bathroom door to find Jaxon laying on my bed. *Damn, he is fine.* He sat up on the edge of the bed and motioned for me to come over. I did, and when I got near, he wrapped his arms around me and kissed me. His kisses are like fireworks and rainbows and butterflies and all things magical rolled into one.

He pulled his head back, way too soon for my liking, causing me to grumble in complaint. He just chuckled.

"We should head down. I'm sure you're hungry," he remarked.

"I am. Starving actually," I agreed.

"Good. Tristan is having the kitchen send up some food to my office. He and Cameron are going to meet us there. I want to discuss a few things with you regarding last night's revelations," he said.

"Oh, okay," I replied. I was worried. Even though he had a smile on his face, his tone was serious. I hoped he hadn't changed his mind about not rejecting me.

Jaxon and I headed down to his office. When we got there, Tristan and Cameron were already waiting for us. And they brought the food like Jaxon said they would. I think I could've eaten a bear I was so hungry.

Jaxon and I sat down on the couch and grabbed our plates. Belgian waffles with whipped cream and strawberries, fruit salad, bacon, and sausage. So yummy. I finished my food in record time, while Jaxon was taking his time. Tristan and Cameron were filling Jaxon in on a few things that he'd missed. While he was paying attention to them, I was paying attention to his bacon. While he was distracted by whatever they were saying, I snuck a piece and ate it. Tristan happened to see me out of the corner of his eye and laughed.

"What's so funny?" Jaxon asked him.

"Check your plate," he replied. *Damn it.*

Jaxon looked down at his plate and noticed the missing bacon. Ok, so I took more than one piece. I actually took all of it.

Jaxon looked up from his plate and growled, "Who took my damn bacon?"

"I did," I shrugged. "Should've been paying attention. Bacon is life."

I could see that he wanted to argue, but he knew I was right.

"Fine," he grumbled. "Apparently I need to keep a closer watch on you when it comes to food."

Tristan and Cameron chuckled as I just shrugged again. "At least with bacon."

"So, I did some thinking last night. Since you are the last member of the Blackwood pack, and you are the Alpha's daughter, that technically makes you the Alpha of the Blackwood pack," Jaxon announced. Well, I wasn't expecting that.

"The Alpha? Seriously?" Tristan questioned. "So, what happens if she joins our pack? Will that be the end of the Blackwood warriors?"

"I'm not sure. I think we need to call my parents back from their trip and fill my dad in on everything. He was close friends with your parents, Isabella. Maybe he would know something," Jaxon confessed.

"Maybe. We should also contact Terry and see if he can come for a visit. He was my dad's best friend. He might be able to help us out with this," I offered.

"Good idea," Cameron chimed in. "To keep suspicions down, perhaps he can come to visit with your parents."

"That's a great idea, Cameron!" I said. "I have missed my mom and dad so much! And Alpha Terry. Is that ok with you, Jaxon?"

"That sounds like a great idea to me," he replied. "I'll call my dad and get him and mom to head back today or tomorrow. You call your parents and Terry and see how soon they can get here. The sooner, the better."

"Tristan, go find Evie and Kayleigh and make sure they don't need any help getting things ready," Jaxon ordered. "Cameron, I want you to go over the patrol schedules. Beef up patrols for the next couple of weeks."

"Yes, Alpha." They both responded before heading out the door.

After Tristan and Cameron left, Jaxon and I made our phone calls. His parents were in Alaska, visiting his mom's sister. Jaxon had told me that his aunt was mated to the Beta of a pack up there. I listened as he called his dad and told him that he needed them to come back as soon as possible. He explained that there was a situation that he needed their advice on right away and did not feel comfortable discussing it over the phone.

"How'd it go?" I asked.

"He said it was no trouble and they would be back tomorrow."

"Oh, that's great news. I'm not sure my parents will be able to come up as quickly as that, but I will certainly try. I think I should call Terry first."

"Sounds good. He'd be the one to decide how quickly they could come up," Jaxon agreed.

I picked up the phone and dialed Terry's number from memory. I wasn't surprised to hear him answer in his usual gruff manner.

"Terry speaking."

"Hi, Alpha Terry. It's Bella."

"What have I told you about calling me that, young lady?" he grumbled.

"I know, I know. *Uncle* Terry." I teased.

"So, to what do I owe the pleasure of my favorite goddaughter calling me when she hasn't called me in all the time that she has been gone?"

"Oh, well, you see–" I began.

"I'm teasing, Bella. What's going on? Everything alright?"

"Of course it is, couldn't be better. I was wondering if my parents could come up for a visit, the sooner, the better. I have some news for them."

"What kind of news?"

"I found my mate."

There was complete silence on the other end of the line, I had wondered if we'd been disconnected.

"You what?" he finally managed.

"I found my mate. Like my actual, real, all mine, mate."

"Tingles, smell, all that good shit?"

"Yep."

"Holy shit, Bells. That's amazing! Of course, they can come up. Karen and I will too. I want to meet this mate of yours. Who is he?"

"Jaxon Daniels, Alpha of Dark Sky."

"Well, I'll be damned. I couldn't have asked for a better mate for you, girl. He's a good man. A damn good man. Comes from good stock."

"So, you'll come?"

"Damn skippy we will. We'll fly out first thing tomorrow morning."

"That's great news! I'll tell Jaxon. Now I better go so I can call mom and dad to get them to come as well. Just make sure that you eavesdrop on their call so you can insist on coming. We don't want them to know that I called you first." I giggled. "Bye, Uncle."

"Terry's on board with coming up here?" Jaxon asked.

"Yep. Now I just have to call my dad and get him on board. Which won't be too hard. My parents have been bugging me about coming to visit." I grinned.

"Ok, call your dad. Hopefully, they can come up in the next day or so."

"Oh, I'm sure they will. Especially once I tell my daddy that his little girl found her mate." I smirked.

"Maybe having them come up isn't such a good idea," Jaxon mumbled.

"Aw, is the big, bad Alpha afraid of a Beta?"

"Only when the Beta is his mate's father," he grumbled. I just laughed and picked up the phone to call my parents.

CHAPTER FOURTEEN

Jaxon

I let Isabella know that I needed to take care of a few things and she nodded her head absently, dialing her dad's number. I headed downstairs to the kitchen to let everyone know we would be having guests for dinner tomorrow. Once that was done, I headed back upstairs to check on Evie and Kayleigh and make sure everything was getting moved. When I got to Isabella's door, I noticed that the room was empty of her things. Smiling to myself, I went up to my room to see if they were up there.

Stepping out of the elevator, I saw Evie and Kayleigh heading towards my room.

"You ladies get everything?" I asked.

"Yep," Evie chirped. "Tristan helped us bring some of the boxes up. We have the last of it now. Did you have a chance to make space for everything?"

"No, not yet. I can do that now."

"Ok good. Where's Bella?" Kayleigh asked.

"In my office on the phone with her parents. She wants them to come visit so we can meet," I replied.

"I wonder how soon they will be able to come," Evie pondered.

"I think she is trying to get them to come up tomorrow. I want to speak to her father before I mark her, so the sooner, the better," I replied. I didn't want to tell anyone else why I was really waiting. Although, talking to her dad first does make a good impression.

"That's so sweet that you are waiting to talk to him first, Jaxon. Mom would be proud of you!" Evie exclaimed.

"Speaking of which, mom and dad will be home tomorrow as well. I already spoke to dad this morning," I informed her.

"Ok, I'll have a couple of the ladies go over this afternoon and freshen the place up for them," she replied. "Now, go make room for Bella's stuff."

I opened the door to my room and headed to one of the closets. When Evie and I redesigned the Alpha's quarters, we added his and hers closets so my future mate would have plenty of space. Of course, in the last seven years, I had started storing things in her closet that would now have to be removed. Luckily it was only a few boxes, nothing major. I grabbed the boxes and moved them to a corner of the bedroom until I could put them in storage somewhere else. Once that was done, the girls brought in Isabella's clothes and shoes and started putting them away.

While the girls were busy in the closet, I grabbed the boxes for the bathroom and took them in. I made sure that the drawers and cabinets on Isabella's side were empty and clean before heading back out to the bedroom.

"Evie, the bathroom boxes are in there, and her side is empty and cleaned out. I'm going to head back downstairs. Thanks for doing this!" I shouted, before heading out the door.

Isabella was just hanging up the phone when I walked back into my office. "All finished, sweetheart?" I asked.

"Yep. My parents will be here tomorrow, late afternoon. Alpha Terry and Luna Karen are coming with them. Do we need to do anything to get their rooms ready?"

"Nope. I'll have a couple of the ladies get them prepped in the morning. Evie is having some of them get my parents place ready anyway," I responded.

I walked over to where she was sitting in my chair, picked her up, then sat down with her in my lap. The sparks were so intense it felt like electricity running all over my body. She wrapped her arms around my neck and sighed.

Leaning down, I kissed the top of her head. She tilted her head back and kissed my jaw, slowly peppering me with feather-light kisses.

I moaned as she kissed everywhere but my lips. Finally having enough, I slid my hand up her back, grasped the back of her neck, and captured her lips. This kiss was like nothing I had ever felt before. Our mouths moved together like they were made for each other. The thought made me growl which caused Isabella to gasp. I kissed her even harder, forcing her mouth open and plunging my tongue in. I grasped her hips and spun her on my lap until she was straddling me, putting pressure where I needed it most.

I pulled back way too soon, Isabella whimpering in complaint, only to kiss across her jaw and down her neck. Kissing and sucking, I found the sweet spot along her neck that caused her to moan out loud.

"Soon, sweetheart. Soon you will have my mark here." I growled. "But we really need to stop now before I can't."

"I don't want to," she whined. "But I guess you're right. If we don't, my dad might be tempted to kill you tomorrow and I really don't want that to happen."

That made me laugh out loud. "Me neither."

"Come on, it will be dinner time soon. Let's go change and get ready."

On our way upstairs, I told Isabella that I wanted to introduce her as my mate to the pack tonight at dinner. I didn't want to wait. I wanted them to celebrate with us.

"Jaxon, don't you think we should wait until we meet the parents?" she asked.

"Do you want to wait? I mean, they'll be here in the morning," I shrugged.

"Yeah, I kinda do. I'd like for our parents to be here when we announce it."

"You do realize that everyone is going to know when we walk in together, don't you?"

"Maybe, but I still think we should talk to our parents first and have them be here when we officially announce it."

"All right, we can do that. We'll just make the announcement at dinner tomorrow."

When we got to my room, I told her I had a little surprise for her. I put my hands over her eyes and told her no peeking. I opened the door, ushered her in, walked her across the room with her eyes covered, and stopped in front of the closet.

"Ok, I did a little something this morning, and I hope you're ok with it. Open your eyes, sweetheart," I whispered.

I watched the emotions flit across her face. I loved it. She had no poker face whatsoever. She turned around to look up at me. "You did this for me? When did you have time to do this?"

"Well, I had a little help," I admitted. "Evie and Kayleigh moved everything up here and organized it for me this morning while we were in my office."

"Thank you, Jaxon. I love it!"

"I didn't want you to have to worry about moving anything. You sure you're okay moving in here with me?" I asked. "I know it might seem quick, but I really can't stand the thought of you not being here."

"Of course, I'm ok with it, silly," she giggled. "Wouldn't want to be anywhere else."

"Good, because there is no way I'm letting you stay anywhere else!"

"Possessive much?"

"You have no idea, sweetheart." I growled, kissing her neck.

I chuckled as she softly moaned and finally managed to wiggle her way out of my grip. "Uh-uh, mister. You start that, and we will never make it down to dinner," she chided.

"I'm ok with that," I smirked, stalking towards her.

"But everyone is waiting for us."

"They can wait." I growled again, reaching out to grab her.

"Oh no, you don't mister. You stop right where you are!" she demanded. "You are going to introduce me before you mark me, and you are not marking me until we know what will happen. You keep this up and waiting will be out the freaking window."

I grabbed Isabella by the waist and pulled her to me. I wrapped my arms around her and buried my face in her hair, breathing deeply.

"Sorry about that," I apologized. "My wolf is not happy that I haven't marked you yet. He knows why I haven't, doesn't mean he likes it."

"It's okay. I understand. Trust me, my wolf is practically panting right now," she admitted. "However, I need to change for dinner, and you should too."

I leaned down and kissed her gently on the lips. "You know they already love you, right?"

"I know. I just want to look like I care about what they think because I do. I'm going to be their Luna. That freaks me out a little. From the time I found out that I was Chad's mate, but he wasn't mine, I thought I would never have a mate. I just don't want them to be disappointed," she whispered.

"They couldn't be disappointed in you if they tried. You are perfect. Strong, independent, smart, and unbelievably gorgeous," I assured her. "I feel so incredibly lucky to have you as my mate, and I just met you. They've had months to get to know you. I'm more than a little jealous of them right now."

"I'm pretty sure that I am the lucky one," she replied, kissing me softly.

"Now then, go pick out something to wear. I'm going to shower really quick, and you can have the bathroom when I'm done. Unless you care to join me," I winked cheekily.

Isabella just laughed and swatted me on the ass as I walked away.

I showered as quickly as I could, not wanting to spend any more time away from my mate. Even though she was just in the next room. *Our room.* That thought made both me and my wolf very happy.

When I came out of the bathroom with nothing but a low-slung towel around my hips I couldn't help but stop and watch Isabella as she stared at me. I could almost feel her eyes on me as they traveled up my body.

"Like what you see, sweetheart?" I mused.

"Do I ever," she groaned. "Remind me to thank your momma tomorrow."

I couldn't help but laugh. "Will do. Now go before I take you right where you are. I can practically hear your naughty little thoughts," I said.

CHAPTER FIFTEEN

Jaxon

After Isabella ran into the bathroom, I heard her lock the door, like that would stop me if I wanted to get in. I grabbed some jeans, a button-down shirt, and some shoes from the closet. After getting dressed, I laid down on the bed and waited for Isabella.

I must've dozed off waiting, because the next thing I knew, I felt the bed dip next to me and her lips lightly brush across mine.

"Don't tease me, sweetheart," I groaned, opening my eyes. She was a vision to behold. Her green eyes shining down at me, her long brown hair hanging around her face and covering both of us.

She smiled at me, leaning down to press her soft lips to mine once more. My hand slid up her back to her neck to hold her in place before she could pull away as our lips moved perfectly together. Isabella's tongue brush softly against my lips and I gladly parted my lips to deepen the kiss. She moaned, and I quickly rolled us over, so I was on top and back in control, making sure to keep my weight off of her while hovering above her. I slid my hand down her arm and tangled our fingers together. Isabella's other hand cupped my cheek before sliding to the back of my head. She grasped my hair and tugged on it, causing me to moan loudly. Kissing down her jaw and along her neck, I made my way to that sweet spot, sucking on it lightly which caused her to moan even louder.

"Jaxon," she panted. "W-we sh-sh-should s-s-stop."

"Don't want to," I groaned. I stopped kissing her neck but didn't move. "Just give me a minute, sweetheart."

"I think I need one myself," she admitted.

After a few minutes, I finally managed to calm myself down enough to move. I rolled off of Isabella to lay by her side. I hoped that Terry and my dad had some answers for us. I didn't know how much longer I could wait to mark her.

"You ok?" she asked.

"Yeah, I'm good. Sorry about that," I apologized. "You have no idea the effect you have on me, sweetheart."

"Pretty sure I do." She laughed. "Come on, let's head down to dinner. Just let me check my hair really quick."

"Fine, but you look positively edible," I replied. Isabella blushed and stood up from the bed. I sat up and watched her walk into the bathroom to touch up her hair. Once she was finished, I grabbed her hand and we headed for the elevator to go downstairs.

Isabella couldn't stop fidgeting in the elevator. She picked at her dress, fussed with her hair, checked her teeth. If she weren't so nervous, I would've laughed out loud. Instead, I just pulled her close to me, wrapped my arms around her, and kissed the top of her head. She took a deep breath and I felt her relax.

"Just breathe. There is nothing to be nervous about. They are going to love you," I assured her.

"I know, I know. I just can't help it," she whined.

"I will be right beside you the entire time," I promised.

The elevator doors finally opened, and we stepped out. Isabella sighed and let go of my hand, taking a step away from me. We could hear voices coming from the dining room. Tonight, we were having dinner with the warriors in our building and some of the elders of the pack. All in all, about a hundred pack members. Once my parents returned, and Isabella's parents arrived, we would have a party with the entire pack to celebrate our new Luna. Hopefully, I would be able to mark her before then.

As we stepped into the dining room, everyone stopped talking. I could feel Isabella tense up beside me.

"Evening everyone. I'm glad you could all join us for dinner tonight," I began. "As some of you know, I returned a few weeks early from my council duties. I got back late Friday, just in time for the annual Halloween party, where some of you were definitely having a good time." Laughter erupted, and fingers pointed at those who had obviously made fools of themselves.

"I want to thank my Beta, Tristen, for stepping up in my absence and taking care of the pack. I'm sure you all have met her by now, but for those who haven't this is Isabella Greyson. She has been staying here for a few months, taking a break from those southern temperatures. I thank you all for making her feel welcome here. I hope that she likes it enough to continue to stay with us." I paused and gave her what I hoped was a reassuring smile and then announced, "Now then, let's eat!" Everyone cheered and began to fill their plates.

After dinner, Tristan and Cameron wanted to speak in my office and go over some reports he had received from Cameron. I asked Isabella if she wanted to join us.

"No, you guys go ahead," she declined. "I'm going to go hang out with the girls for a bit before bed. I'll meet you upstairs."

I nodded my head and gave her a smile before she headed off to find Evie, Kayleigh, and Jade. Cameron and Tristan followed me to my office.

"Ok, what's up?" I asked.

Tristan nodded at Cameron to tell him to go ahead.

"I got some reports back from the patrols," he stated. "We've had some signs of rogues near the borders. Nothing more than usual until today. Five separate patrols reported signs of rogues crossing our borders. Normally they get to the border and go around without crossing it. I think they might be searching for a weakness."

"Jaxon, I don't think this is a coincidence. You find your mate as she is being attacked by a rogue and now, we have five separate reports of rogues crossing our borders. We haven't had problems with rogues in years," Tristan continued.

I growled loudly, causing Cameron and Tristan to bow their heads. To say I was pissed would be an understatement.

"What if they aren't rogues?" Cameron asked.

My head snapped up. "What do you mean?"

"Like Tristan said, this is too much of a coincidence and I don't believe in coincidences. You find a woman being attacked by a 'rogue' and she happens to be your mate. Now we have groups of them attempting to cross our borders. I think it's all related. I don't think we are dealing with rogues at all, I think we're dealing with another pack. A very clever one," Cameron offered.

Once he finished, the room was silent as Tristan and I thought over what he had just said. It made sense, but who? Who would want to invade our pack? We're allies with all of the surrounding packs.

"Who? We have alliances with the surrounding packs," Tristan said.

"I don't know," Cameron admitted. "I can't think of any pack that would risk going to war with us. Which is what will happen if this is another pack entering our territory without permission. Did anything happen on your council trip that could warrant this?"

"No. Everything was routine. Training a new Alpha that took over when his father died, checking up on a couple of packs under council evaluation. Routine," I replied.

"The packs under council watch, could this be them?" Tristan asked. "Maybe they're unhappy having you check up in them."

"No, I don't think so. They understand why they are being watched. Plus, this was their last evaluation. They passed with flying colors. The last thing they'd want to do is draw negative attention to themselves," I answered.

"Alpha," Cameron began, "I think maybe we need to consider that this is related to your mate." As soon as he finished, Cameron lowered his head exposing his neck as a sign of respect. He knew that I would be pissed at what he was suggesting.

"I want patrols doubled. Send scouts out, teams of four, to find where these rogues–or whoever it is–are coming from. All warriors are to be notified. I want all pack houses on a curfew for everyone not trained. No one is to be out after dark without permission and an escort. I will not have anyone in my pack hurt." I commanded.

"Yes, Alpha," Cameron and Tristan responded.

"Tristan, I want guards for Isabella. At all times, even in the house. Teams of four. If she leaves to go anywhere, that doubles. No questions, no excuses. I also want guards for her family when they arrive tomorrow. I'll make sure that Evie sets up a room here in the house for my parents. I want them close for now," I demanded.

"Yes, Alpha. I'll get right on it. It will be taken care of tonight. Do you want guards in the hallway tonight?" Tristan asked.

"Yes," I answered. "I will not take chances with her."

"Understood. I'll make it happen. Anything else?" Tristan asked.

"No, that's all," I replied.

As we left the office and walked out in the hallway, I could hear Tristan and Cameron whispering behind me.

"You really think someone is after our Luna?" Tristan asked Cameron.

"I'm not sure," he admitted. "But it's what makes the most sense to me. I don't believe in coincidences. I hope I'm wrong."

"Me too, Cam. Me too," Tristan replied.

"You two do realize that I can fucking hear you, right?" I said angrily. "Cameron, go talk to the warriors and get the patrols set up and the scout teams. I want the scouts out as soon as the sun rises. At least five teams. Preferably more. I'm going to send out messages to the other pack houses and select Isabella's guards. I'll see you in the morning."

After Cameron left, we headed across the hall to Tristan's office. I paced his office while Tristan sent messages to the other houses in the pack regarding the curfew and new restrictions.

"All done, Alpha," Tristan looked up me from his desk.

"This is bullshit. I want to know who the fuck is behind all of this."

"And we will find out. We have the best scouts and warriors of any pack, you know this. Now stop wearing holes in my carpet."

"The minute you find anything out, and I do mean anything, I want to know immediately," I said with a growl, unable to stop my wolf from coming forward.

"Yes, Alpha," Tristan replied, bowing his head slightly.

CHAPTER SIXTEEN

Isabella

After dinner, Jaxon went to talk to Tristan and Cameron, so I went up to the entertainment floor to find Evie and the rest of the girls. I finally found them in one of the theater rooms, arguing over which movie to watch. Evie wanted to watch The Notebook, Kayleigh wanted to watch Valentine's Day, and Jade wanted to watch Crazy Stupid Love. Gag. I hated chick flicks.

"Ladies, ladies. Thor. Tom Hiddleston and Chris Hemsworth," I stated. "Any argument is invalid. Now shut up and let's turn the hotness on." Evie groaned while Kayleigh and Jade laughed.

"Fine," Evie muttered. "But I get to pick the next movie."

"Not if you're picking some cheesy chick flick," I declared.

"The Notebook is not cheesy!" she shouted.

"But it is a chick flick, and I don't do chick flicks," I sassed.

"Ok, settle down girls. Let's watch some hot guys," Jade broke in before Evie could reply.

We all settled down onto the low couches to watch the movie. I loved me some Tom Hiddleston and Chris Hemsworth. So hot. Not as hot as Jaxon though. I hope he isn't going to be too long.

I made it about halfway through the movie before I started yawning and nodding off. Next thing I knew, Jaxon was picking me up off the couch to go upstairs. I could tell that he was agitated, but I couldn't make my mouth work to ask him what was wrong. I just snuggled closer to his chest and relaxed. As I did, I could feel some of the tension leave him, but definitely not all of it.

Once in our room, Jaxon laid me down on the bed and headed into the bathroom. I knew if I slept in my clothes, I would wake up uncomfortable. I stood up from the bed and stumbled to my closet to change. Too tired to do anything else, I just stripped off my clothes and dropped them on the floor before putting on some pj shorts and a tank top. After I changed, I headed back to the bedroom.

"I thought you were sleeping." Jaxon murmured, walking over to wrap his arms around me.

"I was, but I woke up on the way up here and knew if slept in my clothes I would be unhappy about it later," I mumbled into his chest.

"You could have slept naked," he suggested with a smirk.

"I'd smack you for that comment, but I'm too tired," I yawned.

"Then let's get you to bed," he said, picking me up and carrying me.

Jaxon laid me down under the covers and slid into bed next to me. He wrapped an arm around my waist and pulled me closer to him. Even as sleepy as I was, I knew he wasn't completely relaxed.

"What's wrong?" I whispered. "You seem awfully tense."

"We can talk about it tomorrow," he answered. "You're tired. Get some sleep, sweetheart."

"Are you sure?" I asked, trying, and failing, to stifle a yawn.

"Yes, I'm sure. Now close your eyes and sleep," he chuckled, kissing the top of my head and squeezing me slightly.

I kissed his chest and snuggled into him, enjoying the warmth and security as I drifted off to sleep.

The next morning, I woke up to an empty bed. I couldn't help but feel disappointed. I reached over and felt his side, and it was still warm, so I knew that he'd been here recently. I sat up, rubbing my eyes, and stretched. I couldn't sense Jaxon anywhere in the room.

I decided to take a shower and get ready for the day. Jaxon's parents would arrive soon, as well as my parents and Uncle Terry and Aunt Karen. I grabbed my clothes and headed into the bathroom to shower. After showering and drying off, I quickly got dressed and began to dry my hair. With that done, I threw it up in a bun and brushed my teeth, added some mascara and lip gloss.

After finishing in the bathroom, I put my boots on and opened the door to go downstairs. I was surprised to see Gigantor and his equally large friend standing outside the door.

"Morning," they both said.

"Bella, just call me Bella. And good morning, Gigantor and friend. What's going on?" I asked confused.

"Gigantor?" the friend muttered.

"Sorry. I didn't know your friend's name, and when I saw him for the first time, I called him Gigantor in my head since he was the largest man I had ever seen," I embarrassingly admitted.

They both laughed.

"Gigantor, I like it," Gigantor chuckled. "The name is Grant. This is Thomas. We are part of your guard, Bella."

"Guard?" I questioned. "What guard?

"Alpha Jaxon can explain. He is in his office," Thomas answered.

"How many guards are there?" I asked, getting more and more pissed by the second.

"Um, four," Grant replied.

I cocked an eyebrow at him in disbelief. For some reason, I didn't believe him that there were only four guards. I just stared at him until he finally broke.

"Four guards per team. There are four teams. We are with you for six hours, and then the next team relieves us and takes over. If you leave the pack house for anything, the guard team doubles," he finally admitted.

I glared at Grant and Thomas as they hung their heads. *Oh hell no.*

I do not need guards. I especially don't need four guards in the freaking pack house. I turned and headed for the elevator to go down to Jaxon's office so he could get a piece of my mind. He was going to have to call them off.

My new security guards followed me into the elevator silently. Not a single word was spoken as we headed down. When the doors opened, I stomped out and over to Jaxon's office, throwing open the door without knocking. I barely noticed when Grant threw out an arm to stop the door from coming back and hitting me.

"Guards, Jaxon? What the actual fuck! Why do I have guards in the freaking pack house? You expect me to run?" I asked, shouting.

Jaxon looked up in shock.

"Grant, Thomas, wait in the hallway," he ordered. "Tristan, if you would give us a moment, I need to explain some things."

They left as instructed, followed by Tristan who gave me a sympathetic smile. I didn't bother responding to it.

"No, I don't think you are going to run, sweetheart," Jaxon began. "I was hoping to be back upstairs before you woke up so I could explain everything to you."

"Well, we can see how well that worked out for you," I glared at him.

"Yeah. I promise I have a good reason for assigning you guards. I received reports from our patrols that rogues have crossed our borders this weekend. We have had reports of them near the borders, but not crossing them, for the last few months. Now quite suddenly *you* get attacked by a rogue, I find out you are my mate, and rogues are crossing our borders. Too much of a coincidence for me to take a chance. You are mine to protect. The most important person in my life. I cannot and will not take any chances when it comes to your safety," he explained.

"You think these rogues are after me?" I asked, concern growing in my mind.

"I don't know. Cameron suggested that perhaps we are not dealing with rogues, but with another pack. I'm not sure what to think of that.

I just know that I will not allow anyone to get close enough to harm you. I'm sorry you don't like having guards, but they stay until we figure out what's going on," he replied.

"Fine. I will deal with the guards. But do I really need eight guards when I go to work? The schoolhouse is on pack grounds," I complained.

"Yes. I told you I won't take chances. Sorry, but they stay," he apologized with a shrug.

I walked over and sat in Jaxon's lap at his desk. I wrapped my arms around his neck and kissed him lightly on the lips before snuggling my head into his chest.

"Sorry I yelled at you," I apologized. "I was a little upset when I walked out to see Gigantor one and two standing outside our door."

Jaxon chuckled. "Gigantor?"

"Have you seen how freaking huge they are?" I gestured towards the door.

Jaxon laughed. My stomach decided this would be the perfect time to announce its presence.

"Sounds like someone is hungry," Jaxon said, tickling my belly.

"Stop it." I laughed. "I am hungry. Carry me downstairs."

"A please would be nice, sweetheart," he teased.

"Nope, you assign me guards without telling me, you have to carry me whenever I want," I teased right back.

He stood up and threw me over his shoulder and headed for the door.

"This is not what I had in mind, caveman!" I yelled, squirming around.

"Should've specified, sweetheart." He chuckled.

Damn him. Tristan, Grant, and Thomas started laughing as soon as they saw Jaxon walking out the door with me over his shoulder. I glared at the three of them causing Grant and Thomas to stop. Tristan had no shame and kept laughing, so I flipped him off. That made him stop laughing but caused Grant and Thomas to start back up.

He carried me all the way to the elevator before setting me back on my feet. We all chatted and laughed as we walked into the dining room. Jaxon greeted a few pack members that were having their breakfast as we made our way through the room. At first, Grant and Thomas weren't sure where to sit, but I assured them they should sit by us.

CHAPTER SEVENTEEN

Jaxon

Isabella and I finish our breakfast quickly. I almost felt bad for Grant and Thomas for having to eat so quickly, but I had to go back up to my office to meet with Tristan and Cameron again. I asked her if she wanted to come with me, hoping she would say yes.

"No, not right now," she declined. "I'm going to go help Evie get the rooms ready for everyone arriving today. I'll stop by in a little bit, okay?"

I hid my disappointment. "That's fine. Please don't leave the house without telling me first."

"I won't," she promised. I pulled her to me and kissed her hard before letting her go find Evie. Grant and Thomas already had their orders to follow.

Tristan and I made our way up the stairs to my office to wait for Cameron. He was gathering the reports from the previous night's patrols. Tristan and I were both quiet until we walked in the office door.

"I was thinking this morning," he began, "that we should have your dad and Alpha Terry pull the council reports from the attack on the Blackwood Pack. Maybe we can all go over them together and see if we can find anything someone may have missed."

"Good idea. I want to see the reports for myself anyway. I am going to have them pull all of the Blackwood files, not just the ones about the attack. There has to be something in there that will give us an idea of who attacked them or just point us in the right direction," I agreed.

"Morning guys," Cameron greeted as he walked in the open door, shutting it behind him.

"Morning. Anything from the scouts?" I asked right away.

"Nothing yet. I sent them out this morning at dawn. As soon as I hear back, I'll let you know." he responded.

"Good." I nodded. I filled Cameron in on our plan to have the Blackwood files pulled.

"That's a good idea. Perhaps we can also get their financial records and any business transactions they made in the last year before they were attacked. Who they were doing business with might give us some clues." he pointed out.

"I knew I kept you guys around for a reason." I grinned. They both chuckled.

The three of us worked on reports and schedules for the next hour or so, trying to work out any problems that came up. Luckily there weren't many, and we finished quickly. Tristan and Cameron left when we finished to go help prepare for the arrival of our guests. I decided to take advantage of the quiet and work on the pack's finances for a while.

The pack owns several businesses, including a logging company, a construction company, a private security company, as well as a few other smaller businesses. I had lost track of time while working and didn't look up until I heard a soft knock on the door. Isabella peeked her head in, smiling at me.

"You planning on working through lunch?" she asked.

"I hadn't planned on it, just lost track of time working," I admitted. "I was hoping to finish up all the pack business before our parents arrive."

"Well luckily for you, you have an amazing mate. I brought lunch with me," she smiled bringing a tray in with her.

"Yeah, she is pretty damn amazing," I grinned. "Thank you, sweetheart."

We sat on the couch in my office and ate lunch together, laughing and talking and getting to know each other. We played Twenty Questions, asking each other about all of our favorite things.

"What's your favorite movie?" I asked Isabella.

"Oh gosh, I don't know. I have so many."

"You have to choose one."

"Steel Magnolias. I love that movie. It's so funny and sad and just the best." she sighed. "What's the toughest thing about being Alpha?"

"Shit, asking the tough questions now." I paused, thinking about what to say. "Probably trying to live up to everyone's expectations. My father was a great Alpha and a great man. To know him is to love him and respect him. He did so many great things as Alpha. They are pretty damn big shoes to fill."

"Oh, Jaxon. You don't know how much your pack loves and admires you, do you? For months now, all I've heard is how great you are. How much you do for your pack. How fair you are and how you are always there to listen to them and talk to them. I think you've done a great job of filling those big shoes."

I reached over and wrapped my arms around her and pulling her to my side. "You don't know how much that means to me, sweetheart."

I loved learning more about her. I especially loved how she laughed at some of my answers, head thrown back and holding her sides. The sound of her laugh made me smile, not just on my face, but my whole self was happier.

We had been sitting together, cuddled up on the couch, talking for a couple of hours when Tristan knocked and said my parents would arrive in about thirty minutes and Isabella's parents, along with Alpha

Terry and Luna Karen, were about an hour out. Isabella and I headed upstairs to change and get ready, the new guard team following silently behind us. I couldn't wait for my parents to meet her. I knew they were going to love her.

CHAPTER EIGHTEEN

Isabella

The more I learned, the faster I was falling for him. He truly was a great man and a great Alpha. Occasionally I would catch him staring at me like I was the only thing he could see. It made me blush every time. Spending time with him was definitely my new favorite way to spend time.

Once we got upstairs, we each headed into our closets to change. I wanted to make a good impression with his parents. He said that they would love me but looking nice can't hurt. I wanted to at least look like I had made an effort.

Walking back out into our room, I saw that Jaxon had already changed. He looked up at me and smiled, stepped forward, took my hand, and kissed me softly before we headed downstairs.

I was so nervous about meeting his parents. I kept fidgeting with my clothes and hair in the elevator. Jaxon gave my hand a small squeeze, and I glanced up at him.

"Calm down, sweetheart. They're going to love you," he assured me. "In fact, don't be too surprised if my mom hugs you and cries."

I laughed and attempted to take some deep breaths to calm my nerves. I knew that Jaxon's parents would like me. I was just worried about what they would think when they found out who my real parents were. His father was friends with my father. He knew what had happened to my family, to my pack. Before my mind could race away with my thought process, I leaned my head against Jaxon's chest and breathed in his scent, forcing myself to relax. He chuckled and wrapped his arms around me, holding me tight.

When we stepped out of the elevator, I saw Tristan, Evie, Cameron, and Kayleigh waiting for us. Tristan opened the door for us to all go wait outside. Once outside, the men began to talk about pack business, so Evie and Kayleigh pulled me to the side to chat while we waited.

"You look great, Bella," Evie gushed.

"You really do," Kayleigh agreed.

"Thanks. I am so nervous," I admitted.

"Don't be. Mom and Dad are going to love you. They have been waiting for Jaxon to find his mate. Heck, you're doing me a favor," she assured me.

"A favor?" I looked at her confused.

"Yep. They will be so excited about you that they will lay off me not having a mate for a while," she replied. We all laughed loudly, causing the guys to turn and look at us. I shook my head and kept joking and chatting with them. I was so glad they were here. Evie could always make me smile and relax.

After a few minutes, Tristan got word from the gate guard that Jaxon's parents had just arrived. Jaxon motioned for me to come and stand beside him. Evie and I both walked over and a minute later, a black SUV pulled up.

I felt so much more relaxed after chatting with Evie, I'd have to thank her later. As his parents parked, he wrapped an arm around my shoulders and pulled me to his side. Smiling up at him, I wrapped my own arm around his waist. I loved the way he kept staring at me until the car door opened.

The first thing I saw was his mother stepping out of the car laughing at something his father had said. They reminded me of my own parents, full of life and love. When they got to us, Jaxon stepped forward, sliding his hand around to grasp mine, and gave his mom a quick hug and shook his dad's hand. They both hugged Evie and said hello to Tristan, Cameron, and Kayleigh.

"Dad, Mom, I would like you to meet my mate, Isabella Greyson. Isabella, these are my parents, Robert and Kathleen," Jaxon introduced them. Sure enough, his mom let out a squeal and grabbed me in a hug, squeezing me tight.

"Please excuse my wife, Isabella. She's very excited to meet you, we both are." Robert laughed, trying to pry her off of me. I laughed and patted her back, it didn't bother me at all.

"Your parent's flight got in early. They're almost here," Jaxon leaned down to whisper in my ear. I tried not to get nervous again but couldn't help it.

I glanced up at him and saw that his eyes were glazed over. Looking around I saw that his dad, Tristan, and Cameron all looked the same. He must've been telling them that we wanted to talk in his office after all of this.

I tried to pay attention to what Kathleen and Evie were saying, but I couldn't help but be distracted. My parents would be here with Terry and Karen any second. What would they think? Would they accept Jaxon and the fact that he is my mate? Jaxon gave my hand another squeeze and just like that my mind was calm.

I could hear the cars with my parents, Terry, and Karen coming up the drive. Out of the corner of my eye, I saw my guards nod and immediately head off, I assumed to join the other guards. I looked up at Jaxon, a questioning look on my face and he smiled, just shaking his head.

I smiled in return and tilted my head back as he leaned down to give me a kiss. We both looked over as the two cars come to a stop. My parents stepped out of the first one, and Alpha Terry and Luna Karen got out of the second one.

As they all walked up the steps towards us, I let go of Jaxon's hand and raced forward to hug my parents. Everyone laughed as I leaped at my dad and he stumbled back, grinning wildly. Jaxon waited a couple of minutes before stepping forward to greet them.

"Beta and Mrs. Greyson, welcome to Dark Sky. I'm Jaxon, the Alpha of Dark Sky," he greeted them before turning to Terry. "Alpha Terry, Luna Karen, welcome to Dark Sky. We thank you for coming."

I turned my attention back to my parents. I couldn't help but smile, I was so excited and happy they were here. I'd missed them so much. Jaxon stepped up behind me, wrapping his arms around my waist.

"Alpha Jaxon, thank you for having us here," my mom replied.

"Please, call me Jaxon. You're my mate's parents, there's no need to be formal," he requested. They both nodded their heads in approval.

"Jaxon, it's a pleasure to meet you. Thank you for inviting us here. I'm James, this is my wife and mate Donna," my dad said.

"The pleasure is all mine. Having you all here makes Isabella happy. I'd do anything to make that happen." They both smiled at me, clearly thrilled.

"I'm sure you're all tired after traveling today. Your bags are being sent up to your rooms now if you would like to follow. Take some time to relax and freshen up before dinner," Jaxon addressed every-one. They all agreed and headed inside. I saw Robert pull Terry aside to speak to him.

"Evie, will you, Kayleigh, and Kathleen show Karen and my mom to their rooms please?" I asked.

"Of course. Right this way." She gestured towards the elevator.

Jaxon and I headed up the stairs behind the other men to Jaxon's office. Once inside, Jaxon asked everyone to have a seat. I pulled the desk chair around to where the couches were.

"So, anyone want to tell me what's going on?" Robert asked, looking around at everyone. "I have a feeling that I'm missing something."

I nodded my head to Jaxon, indicating he should go ahead and tell everyone everything.

"Dad, there is something we haven't told you about my mate. If it's ok with you, I'm going to let her show you." Jaxon explained.

"Show me? Alright. Go ahead, dear," he replied, clearly confused.

I stood up and took a few steps away from everyone, so I'd have plenty of room. I smiled at Jaxon, Terry, and my dad before looking at Robert.

"Please understand that the only people who know about this are in this room, except for my mom and Luna Karen. I know that seems strange, but I think you'll understand in a few minutes." I explained. Robert nodded his head slowly, slightly confused.

I closed my eyes as my body began to tremble and shift.

CHAPTER NINETEEN

Terry

As soon as she shifted into her wolf, Robert's jaw dropped in shock. If it weren't such a serious moment, I'd have laughed at him.

"Holy Shit!" he shouted, jumping out of his seat. "Tell me I'm not going crazy, Terry."

"Robert, calm down. You're not going crazy. Bella, shift back please?" I calmly requested. Bella shifted back and when Robert saw that her clothes had not been shredded by the shift, he dropped back into his seat, practically shaking.

"Robert, I know this is a shock, but I can explain," I began, looking straight at him. "The night the Blackwood pack was attacked was Bella's sixth birthday. You and Kathleen were there, Karen and I were there. Bella is my goddaughter and Michael was my best friend. You and Kathleen left early to get back to your children and pack because of reports of rogues. Karen and I left just after sunset. We had to get back to deal with some pack business. From what I understand, the party continued for several more hours. I got a call from the council around midnight. They told me that there had been a report of an attack on Blackwood." I paused and shook my head. "I actually laughed. Who would stupid enough to attack the Blackwood warriors? The council rep finally convinced me that the report had merit and they needed my pack to investigate as we were the closest. I took James and the majority of my fighters with me to check it out. When we got there, it was complete and total devastation. Everyone was dead," I paused to look over at Bella. Seeing that she was curled up in Jaxon's lap and he was comforting her, I continued.

"We searched for hours. Every building, every room. Not a single survivor. They slaughtered men, women, and children. And we couldn't find any evidence of who did it. Whoever attacked, they were smart about it. Took out the security room and all of the video surveillance. My men searched the woods surrounding the territory looking for survivors and any clues. After a couple of hours, we finally admitted to ourselves that they were all dead. I told James to have the men gather the bodies so we could identify them. As I walked away, I heard a small whimper. I made sure that no one was around and listened until I found her. She was under her parents' bodies, in wolf form. I knew who she was right away, of course. I also knew that if anyone knew she was alive, whoever attacked would stop at nothing to finish the job. I picked Bella up and ran for my car. I told James I needed some time and asked him to let Karen know that I would be back in a few days. I headed away from both of our territories into Louisiana and stopped at a hotel the next morning. I paid for a few nights and made sure that no one saw me take her inside. We spent the next few days there, talking and crying. I explained to her that if the people who killed her parents knew that she was alive, they would come after her. I explained that we needed to lie about who she was and where she was from, only tell people that she didn't know. I took her home after that and contacted the council telling them that I found a small child in Louisiana. I told them that if they couldn't find her parents, my Beta and his mate would adopt her. They couldn't have children of their own. She's been with us ever since," I finished.

I kept looking back and forth between Bella and Robert. Bella was still curled up in Jaxon's lap and I could hear him whispering to her, comforting her. I knew that what I had said was hard for her to hear. It had to be. She'd been through so much in her life. I hated rehashing everything, but Robert needed to know who she was and what was going on.

I could also see that Robert was completely shocked. He kept opening his mouth, only to close it again and shake his head. After a few minutes of doing this, he finally stopped and just stared at Bella.

"How could I not see it?" he asked. "She looks just like Elizabeth. But with Michael's hair color and a little taller."

"She does," I quietly agreed. "You understand why no one else knows? Why we kept this a secret?"

"Absolutely," he replied. "We need to contact the council and see about getting the Blackwood files. I have a friend there that I trust. He won't ask any questions, and he won't tell anyone what we are asking for. I have used him in the past to help out with problems that required discretion."

I looked over at Jaxon, and he nodded his head.

"Call him. Tell him nothing other than you want to see the files. Don't give him a reason. Just make sure that he doesn't tell anyone who is asking for the files or even that someone did ask for them." I advised.

"Make sure when he sends you their files, he sends all of them, not just the ones on the attack. We need any files pertaining to Blackwood Pack. That includes all financial records, real estate transactions, everything." Tristan added.

"Of course. I'll call him now." Robert replied, heading towards the phone.

Jaxon stood up, his arm around Bella. "I'm going to take her upstairs to rest for a bit. We'll see you all at dinner."

"Thank you, Jaxon," I replied as they left the room. Now to wait and see what Robert's friend had to say.

Tristan, Cameron, and I sit quietly while Robert spoke to his council friend. After a few minutes, he hung up and turned around to face us. "Ok, everything is good to go. He's going to box everything up and overnight it to me in the morning. We will have it all here in just over a day."

CHAPTER TWENTY

Jagger

"Alpha, a call came in requesting the Blackwood files."

"From who?" I demanded.

"Robert Daniels, the former Alpha of Dark Sky."

"Did he say why?" I asked.

"No. Wouldn't say anything. Just asked for every file related to Blackwood. Not just the attack file."

"Interesting. Send him everything he asked for. Keep me posted," I ordered, hanging up on him.

I knew having a spy in the council would pay off. I couldn't have anyone finding out that my father was responsible for the attack on the Blackwood pack. If they did, my entire pack and everything I have worked for would be destroyed.

"Kade, get in here!" I shouted. Kade strolled in, taking his sweet time. *Infuriating bastard.* He's lucky we were childhood friends. I would kill anyone else for acting the way he does.

"Yes, Alpha?" he asked.

"What is the latest on our scouts? Have they managed to find out anything else?" I asked.

"Not yet. Dark Sky is locked up tight. I think they might be smarter than we thought and putting two and two together." he replied.

"Damn it! Is it confirmed that their Alpha found his mate?" I asked.

"Not confirmed, but it looks that way. His parents came home early today. The Alpha and Beta of Greystone also arrived today with their mates. It looks like the Beta's daughter is the one who will be Dark Sky's new Luna," he responded.

"Interesting. Greystone's Alpha was good friends with Blackwood's Alpha, wasn't he?"

"Yeah. Best friends. Greystone's Alpha was the godfather for Alexandra Blackwood," he replied.

"Why would they be requesting the Blackwood files? Why now? After all these years?" I wondered aloud.

"Who knows?" he yawned, looking bored.

"Well, find out! Now!" I yelled, snapping him to attention.

CHAPTER TWENTY-ONE

Jaxon

Hearing Terry retell the story of what happened to Isabella's birth parents and pack was obviously rough on her. I walked her up to our bedroom and urged her to lay down on the bed. She kept a tight grip on my shirt to prevent me from leaving her. I scooted her over and laid down next to her as she curled around me, holding me. She turned onto her side and buried her face in my chest. The tears had stopped, but her body was tense. I leaned my head down and pressed a soft kiss to the top of her head. Instead of pulling back, I stayed there, my lips pressed against her hair.

Isabella's breathing got slower and deeper as she drifted off to sleep. I knew we needed to head down to dinner soon, but I couldn't bear to wake her up. Hearing Terry talk about what happened had almost made me shift, I could only imagine how she must have felt. So, I let her sleep for a while. She needed time to relax, and I needed to be there for her.

I shut my eyes and concentrated on her breathing. My wolf wanted to kill everyone who had ever hurt her, and it was killing me to not know who that was. For the moment, I concentrated on keeping her safe and happy. Once the files arrived from the council, we would go over every single note and paper until we got some answers. I wouldn't stop until we got to the bottom of this.

"Jaxon, is Bella ok?" Tristan mind-linked me.

"She's sleeping. But she will be fine," I replied.

"Oh good. You ok?" he asked.

"No, but I will be. Something is just not sitting right. I can't help but think that Cameron was right. That all of this is connected. The attack on Blackwood, the rogues, the attack on Isabella, all of it," I responded.

"I'm beginning to agree with you. We have never had a problem until Bella came," he began, stopping when I growled at him through our link.

"Let me finish," he pleaded. "I don't think that whoever is behind the rogues knows who she really is. If they did, they would have done something to get her by now. But I do think that they are somehow being drawn to her without knowing why. That rogue that attacked her could've really hurt her but didn't. Under questioning, he admitted that he didn't know why he took her just that something made him choose her. We need to find out if Terry's pack has had trouble with rogues lately."

"I will talk to him after dinner. We'll be down soon. Isabella is waking up," I replied before cutting him off.

I felt Isabella begin to stir in my arms. I pulled back slightly to see her face, causing her to groan. I smiled, knowing that she didn't like me pulling away, it was quite the ego boost. She opened her eyes and looked up at me.

"Were you watching me sleep?" she yawned.

"Maybe," I smirked.

"Creepy," she sang, giggling softly.

"You like it," I murmured, leaning down to capture her lips with mine. She responded instantly, pulling me closer and parting her lips, allowing me to deepen the kiss. Our lips and tongues moved in sync with each other. I couldn't seem to get enough of her. When she moaned softly, I almost lost it. I pulled back, resting my forehead against hers, fighting to contain my wolf.

"Everything alright?" she asked breathlessly with a knowing smirk.

"Yeah, just trying to contain my wolf. He is very eager to make you his." I replied, panting.

"Oh, I get it." She giggled, pecking my lips before trying to pull away. I growled low causing her to freeze.

"If you get up, he will chase you. If he chases you, he will catch you, and when he catches you, he will mark you and mate you, whether you are ready or not. So please, don't move. I can't bear to do that to you," I begged her.

Isabella relaxed and stayed still next to me. She kept one hand on my chest and the other on my back. She slowly began to move her hand on my back, lightly rubbing circles to soothe me and my wolf. It helped. Once I was sure he wasn't going to gain control, I pulled back and smiled at her.

"Sorry. He's just really impatient. He finally has his mate with him and not marking you and mating you is driving him crazy," I confessed.

"It's alright. Trust me, I would like nothing more than to bear your mark and fully mate with you. I hate waiting and patience is not a virtue of mine. We will have answers soon. I know it. Once we do, we won't have to wait any longer," she reassured me. "For now though, we need to get up and change, or we will be late to dinner."

We both got up off the bed and headed for our closets to change. I kept my jeans on and just swapped my wrinkled shirt for a new one. I headed into the bathroom to brush my teeth and tame my hair, then returned to the bedroom to wait on my mate.

I didn't have to wait long. Isabella quickly changed from her dressier outfit into some jeans and a sweater. I was beginning to think I might have to burn every pair of those jeans she owns, her ass looked way too good in them. I couldn't help but be mesmerized by the sight. I finally noticed that she wasn't moving and looked up at her face. Judging by the smirk, I was totally busted. I just grinned, not

aahamed at all. She shook her head at me and went into the bathroom
to fix her hair and brush her teeth.

She stepped up close to me and wrapped her arms around me,
holding me close. I leaned against her, resting my head on hers and
relaxed.

After a couple of minutes, I stepped back, turned around, and
squatted down slightly.

"What are you doing?" she asked me slightly confused.

"Waiting for you to hop on so I can carry you to the elevators.
Unless you want to walk?" I explained.

"Hell no!" she shouted, jumping on my back. I grabbed her legs as
they wrapped around my waist, chuckling.

I headed for the elevator with her on my back. We got in and
waited as it headed down, only to have it stop on the floor below us.
The doors opened to reveal our parents and Terry and Karen. They all
stood there staring at us before my dad cracked up laughing, the rest
of them quickly joining him.

"Son, you are whipped already," he laughed.

"Shut up," I mumbled.

"It's ok, baby. You aren't whipped. Besides, I like riding you," She
whispered in my ear so only I can hear her. My growl told her that I
got the double meaning, loud and clear as she threw her head back
and laughed out loud.

"Not cool, mate. Not cool." I grumbled, shifting uncomfortably.
Everyone else looked at me wondering what I meant. Not wanting my
dad to make a comment that would embarrass us further, I decided to
let them know that we want to make our announcement at dinner.
But first, I had to make sure she was still good with this plan.

The elevator finally reached the bottom floor, and we all stepped
out and headed to the dining room. I fell to the back and stopped,
letting everyone pass us and leaving just the two of us in the hallway.
Glancing over my shoulder at her, I asked her if she was still ok with
me announcing that she was my mate to the pack at dinner.

"Of course," she replied. I could feel her tense up even as she was agreeing with me. I decided to do something about that and get back at her for that little comment in the elevator.

Before she could react, I let go of her legs and pulled her around until she was in front of me. I backed her up against the wall, my hands cupping her ass as I held her in place. I nuzzled her neck causing her to squirm and rub against me.

"That wasn't very nice, sweetheart," I whispered against her neck, causing her to shiver.

"I don't know about nice, but it sure was amusing," she giggled.

"Let's see how funny it was." I began to kiss her softly on the cheek, making my way towards her lips. I stopped at the corner of her mouth and then moved to the other side of her face, only to do the same thing. When I got close to her lips again, she tried to turn her head to force me to kiss her, but I grinned and moved down to her jaw. I began to slowly kiss up and down her jaw, causing a low moan to escape her.

"Shhh," I whispered softly. "Wouldn't want anyone to hear you."

She groaned and I chuckled as I continued my assault of her jaw and neck. She grabbed my hair, pulling harshly and making my head snap back. She kissed my neck, shifted her hips forward, grinding right where I fucking needed her. I couldn't contain the loud moan that escaped my lips.

"Two can play that game, my love," she whispered against my throat.

Before I could react, she swiftly arched her back forcing us both away from the wall. I stumbled slightly which loosened my grip on her, allowing her to escape my grip. She quickly slipped out from between the wall and me and headed for the dining room.

"I told you two could play that game," she called back to me over her shoulder, laughing. I could hear Tristan asking where I was when she walked in.

"Oh, he will be in shortly. He had something come up that he needs to take care of first," she said with a laugh.

CHAPTER TWENTY-TWO

Jaxon

I walked into the dining room and gave Isabella a playful glare which caused her to giggle. My pack members looked at me, some with delight and some with confusion. Time to clear a few things up.

"Can I have everyone's attention please?" I called out, waiting for everyone to quiet down. I nodded at Tristan who grinned and opened up a pack wide link for those who weren't present. Once they were quiet, I continued. "I have a small announcement I'd like to make. I know that I introduced Isabella to everyone at dinner the other night and thanked them for making her feel so welcome. I have a reason for being so thankful. I am happy to announce that Isabella Greyson is my mate."

The silence was almost deafening. The roar that followed it definitely was. There was cheering and clapping and more than a few tears. It seemed like everyone there wanted to shake our hands or give us hugs. Isabella's relief was more than evident on her face and in her posture. She'd turned from nervous to proud, which in turn, filled me with pride.

The rest of dinner went smoothly. We chatted with our parents and ate. Karen and Donna both joked that they were going to be sneaking our cook back with them when they left. I had to admit, she was amazing.

After dinner, we all headed upstairs to the third floor. Isabella and I led our parents and guests to the game room. Terry kept saying that he was going to add one of these to his pack house, while Karen kept shaking her head and mumbling what I am pretty sure were curses.

Isabella went to sit on one of the sectionals with the ladies to chat while the men and I gathered around the small bar. My dad and I began fixing drinks for everyone. My dad took care of the drinks for the guys while I fixed margaritas for the ladies. Once I had them ready, I put them on a tray and carried them over. I set them down on the table and kissed Isabella before heading back over to the bar. As I was walking away, I heard her Aunt Karen whisper, "That one's a keeper, Bella!" I couldn't help but grin.

We all hung out in the game room talking, laughing, and drinking for a couple of hours.

When I noticed Bella start to yawn, I said good night to the guys and walked over to where she was sitting. Without saying a word, I reached down and picked her up before sitting down with her in my lap. She snuggled into my chest and sighed, clearly comfortable. I knew I needed to talk to Terry about the rogues, but that would have to wait.

"I'm so happy that you two found each other," her mom said quietly. "We were so worried after everything that happened back home."

Karen sighed before speaking, "I hope you don't hold anything against us for what happened between Bella and Chad."

"Not at all," I replied honestly. "You and Terry seem like great people. It's obvious that you care a great deal for Isabella, and she cares for you. Your son made his choices. He is the one that has to live with his decisions. If you don't mind me asking, what happened to him?"

Karen glanced over at her mate before answering. "He's gone...

well, Terry banished him, sort of. After Bella left and Chad woke up, he went crazy. Demanding to know where she was, demanding that Terry reinstate him. He even attacked Andrea, his newly marked mate. That didn't work out so well since he could feel everything she did. Terry had him locked up so he wouldn't hurt anyone else. He made some calls and found a pack in England that would take him in. Even had an elder come and dissolve the bond between Chad and Andrea. Apparently, the pack in England is very traditional, following the 'old rules'. Meaning he would be doing nothing but hard labor and training until he could prove himself worthy. He's still over there doing hard labor and living in their dungeons. He refuses to admit that he made a mistake and refuses to learn from his mistakes. I love my son dearly, but I do not love his choices or behavior."

"I'm sorry that you had to go through this. Even more sorry that Isabella did. But I am glad that he's gone. I'll be honest with you, if he ever comes near her, I'll kill him. I won't even stop to think about it. I know that's not what you want to hear, but it's the truth and I wanted you to hear it from me," I stated.

"You're right, it's not what I want to hear, but I do appreciate your honesty. We will do everything we can to keep him away. The odds of him leaving the pack in England are very slim, but if he does, we'll let you know," she replied, wiping a tear away.

"I'm so sorry, Aunt Karen," Isabella whispered. "I never meant for any of this to happen."

"Oh sweetie, it's not your fault. What you went through was terrible and it was no one's fault but Chad's. Terry and I did our best to stop it, but it wasn't enough. The Goddess picks our mates for a reason. Why she did this, we may never know. But it isn't our place to question it, it's our place to trust her and her wisdom. I may not like what has happened, but it has led you to your rightful mate. Your true mate. Like I said, I love my son dearly, but I'm so thankful that he was not your mate," she admitted.

We all sat quietly after she finished speaking. I felt terrible for Terry and Karen, knowing that there was nothing they could've done to prevent this. I wondered if their son lost his mind when he found out that Isabella was his mate, but he was not hers? Would that have been like your mate dying? Some wolves went insane when they lost their mate. Isabella said that Chad was never very nice to her but finding out that he was not her mate could have pushed him over the edge. It made me feel slightly sorry for him. Not sorry enough to not kill him if he came near her, but still.

I noticed Isabella trying to hide a yawn and chuckled. "I think it's time we get you to bed, sweetheart. Those yawns are getting pretty big," I teased her.

"Oh hush," she grumbled, before yawning again. I laughed and squeezed her side making her jump and smack my chest.

"I am going to get this one to bed before she starts snoring. Don't want to scare anyone," I laughed. "We'll see everyone in the morning."

"I do not snore!" she protested.

"Yes, you do!" her parents and I answered at the same time, causing everyone to laugh.

"Thanks for the support," she muttered to her parents. "Oh, I won't see you guys until tomorrow afternoon. I have work."

"Not this week you don't," I countered. "I already spoke with your boss, and she gave you the week off to spend with our guests."

"You did? Thank you!" she gushed. "Then I will see you guys in the morning. Goodnight. Love you guys."

Everyone said good night as we headed out the door to the elevator. Once we got to our room, we headed to our separate ways to change and get ready for bed. After changing, I crawled into bed to wait for her. When she came out of the bathroom, I pulled up the corner of the covers and she climbed over me and snuggled up next to me, sighing contentedly.

"Comfy?" I teased.

"Very." She sighed. "Thank you for bringing my family here. I really missed them."

"No need to thank me. It's my job to keep you happy," I replied, kissing the top of her head. "Now get some sleep. You've had a long day." She tilted her head back to look at me and smiled. I leaned down and kissed her gently. She snuggled closer to me and laid her head on my chest, quickly falling asleep. I grinned down at her and closed my eyes, feeling content and complete.

CHAPTER TWENTY-THREE

Isabella

Waking up in Jaxon's arms was like nothing else. Opening my eyes, I saw that he was still asleep. I took the time to really look at him. The way his long eyelashes framed his eyes. Most women would be jealous of those lashes. His straight nose and chiseled cheekbones were perfect. His jawline, drool worthy. His hair was all mussed up from sleep. His lips were slightly puckered making it look like he was pouting. I couldn't resist leaning forward and pressing a light kiss to them.

"Feel free to wake me up like that every morning, sweetheart," he murmured, startling me.

"I didn't know you were awake," I said, kissing him again. "So, what's on the agenda for today?"

"Haven't really planned anything. I was thinking about going for a run, maybe seeing if the guys wanted to go. You want to go for a run with us?" he asked.

"Yeah, sounds great," I replied. "I'm going to get dressed. Will you have Cameron clear an area for us to run in so no one else sees me?"

"Yeah, I'll take care of it. Hurry up," he said, swatting my butt as I get out of bed, causing me to yelp. I turned around to glare at him only to have him laugh at me. I needed to work on my mean face.

After we both got ready and met everyone for breakfast, we all headed out in a couple of the big jeeps they have. Cameron had managed to rearrange the patrols so they avoided the area we would be running in. My dad was super excited that we were finally going for a run together after so long.

Once we got to the spot, we all got out of the jeeps and headed into the woods. We walked for about half a mile before Jaxon told us we had arrived. The guys all headed behind the trees to strip and shift. I watched the tree that Jaxon disappeared behind. I had yet to see his wolf and I was curious, to say the least. When he walked out from behind the tree, I caught my breath, completely in awe of his wolf. His wolf was gorgeous. And huge. The biggest wolf I had ever seen. Blackwood wolves were known for being the biggest wolves and he was bigger than me. He walked towards me as I drank in every detail about him. He still had the same blue eyes, just slightly brighter and his fur was the same auburn color as his hair. The combination was striking.

"You, my dear mate, are incredible. I've never seen a red wolf before. Absolutely gorgeous," I whispered, running my fingers through his fur. He practically purred when I leaned against his side and ran both hands down his back. We were oblivious to everyone and everything around us until one of the others huffed at us, causing Jaxon to growl and me to laugh.

I stepped away from Jaxon and shifted into my wolf again. Jaxon and I were definitely the biggest wolves there. Robert was close, but still smaller than me. Together, my midnight blue wolf and Jaxon's red wolf made quite the sight.

Robert let out a quick bark and motioned his head to the north. We all gave a small bark of acknowledgement and off we went. It had been months since my wolf had been for a run and she was in heaven. The wind in my fur, the trees and ground flying by, I gave myself completely over to her control. I pushed myself faster and faster, only paying attention to the euphoric feeling. I slowed down when Terry managed to break through and tell me that I needed to stop and wait for everyone else. I slowed down and skidded to a stop and looked around. Jaxon skidded to a stop beside me a few seconds later, panting and shaking his head at me. It took another minute for everyone else to catch up. Guess I was running a little fast. Oops.

We spent the rest of the day running, only stopping for a few breaks and lunch. By late afternoon, we were all worn out and Jaxon led us back so we could all shift and they could get dressed. Once everyone was changed back, we headed for the jeeps and back to the pack house to shower and change before dinner.

After dinner, I asked my mom, Karen, and Kathleen if they wanted to spend some time with me. They did, and we all headed up to the game room together. We were quickly joined by Evie, Kayleigh, and Jade. Taking advantage of our girls only time, Kayleigh and I made a few pitchers of margaritas while Evie and Jade went down to the kitchen to scrounge up some treats. It didn't take them long to come back, loaded down with all the things we needed for ice cream sundaes. Cookie sure knew how to spoil us.

We gorged ourselves on ice cream, talking about anything and everything, before hitting the booze. Evie, Jade, Kayleigh, and I made it our mission to get the other three drunk which was not an easy task. It only took us six bottles of tequila, the big bottles, but we managed it. I laughed so hard tears were running down my face as my mom and Karen stumbled out of the room singing loudly and off tune. Kathleen was only slightly less drunk and shook her head at the two of them before following them down the hall. Kayleigh and Jade took pity on them and headed out after them to make sure they all made it to the correct rooms.

"I had so much fun tonight," I sighed, leaning my head on Evie's shoulder.

"Me too. Your mom is hilarious," she giggled.

"She has her moments."

"So, how are you with all of this craziness?"

"What do you mean?" I glanced up at her.

"So much has happened lately, at least it seems that way. The party, that rogue, meeting my brother and finding out he's your mate. I know he can be a bit of a bossybutt, and we haven't really had much of a chance to talk," she shrugged, making my head bounce.

"Aww, boo boo. You missed me?" I teased. She reached down and pinched my leg. "Ow. Turd. Seriously though, I'm good. He's not as bossy as you think, at least not to me. I mean, about some stuff he is but I think that's just because he wants me to be safe."

"Is that why you have a team of guards following you everywhere?"

"Noticed that, huh? Yeah, he can be a bit overzealous with his protection at times."

"Understatement of the year." She giggled. "I just want you guys to be happy."

"We are. Very much."

"Good. Now get the hell off me, I'm tired and want to go to bed." She laughed as she shoved me across the couch.

I called her a bitch and threw a pillow at her as she cackled like a damn witch. She might be a jackass, but she's the best friend a girl could ask for.

CHAPTER TWENTY-FOUR

Jaxon

The next morning, I slipped out of bed without waking Isabella and headed to take a shower. After, I walked out of the bathroom to my closet to get dressed, only to be stopped by the sight of my mate stretching in bed.

"Not cool, Jaxon. First, I have to go to sleep without you and now I have to wake up without you. Not liking this one bit," she grumbled.

"I'm sorry, sweetheart. Won't happen again," I apologized.

"Not good enough. Need kisses. Now," she demanded.

"You don't have to tell me twice." I chuckled and walked over to the bed, never once taking my eyes off of her. I knelt down on the bed next to her and leaned over to press a light kiss on her lips. Before I could pull away, she slid her hands into my hair and pulled me closer to her, deepening the kiss. What started as an innocent good morning kiss, soon turned into a full blown make out session. I needed to put a stop to this before it was too late, but the amazing sounds coming from her were making that impossible.

Just as I was reaching my point of no return, Isabella pulled back, breaking the kiss. I couldn't help but groan. Judging by her giggle and the position we were currently in, me pinning her to the bed, she could feel exactly why I didn't want to stop. I closed my eyes to try and control my wolf. When I did, Isabella took advantage of the situation and rolled us both over. She was now straddling me, causing me to moan out loud when she shifted her weight.

"That's what you get for not being here this morning." She smirked before jumping off the bed and running into the bathroom. She shut the door behind her and locked it.

"I hope you know that lock wouldn't do a damn thing to stop me if I wanted in there!" I yelled. Her response was very loud laughter. *That woman will be the death of me. Damn, I needed a cold shower.*

After dressing, we both went downstairs for breakfast. The menu was pancakes and there was no way we were missing that. Our cooks had yet to make anything bad, but the pancakes were my favorite, besides the chocolate cake. My dad said it was wrong to use an Alpha command to get cake for breakfast. One time, when I was little, he tried, and my mom let him have it. Crazy old man.

Isabella and I were just finishing up breakfast when my dad walked in with Terry.

"Jaxon, Isabella. The packages are here," my dad said softly, making sure no one else could hear us.

"Finally," I muttered. "Would you mind taking them up to my office? We'll be up there in a few minutes. Have Tristan, Cameron, and James join us too, please."

"You got it son," he replied, before walking out of the dining room.

I glanced over at my mate to see that she had gone slightly pale, and her hands were starting to shake. I reached over and pulled her chair closer, taking her hands in mine.

"This is a good thing, sweetheart. I know it's probably going to hurt but remember we're finally going to get some answers." I reminded her.

"I know," she whispered. "I'm just scared."

"I've got you." I whispered back. "Always."

I knew she was nervous about what we might find out, but I also knew that we needed to know what we were up against. There had to be something in there about who attacked her pack and what would happen once we mated.

We were the last ones to get to my office. As soon as we walked in, James and Terry walked over and gave Isabella hugs knowing that she would need them today. I walked over to where my dad was standing, and we began to open the boxes. As we did, we began assigning the different types of files to people. We gave the financial records to Tristan and Cameron. Terry and my father were to go over the council's files on the attack. James would be going over the rest of the council logs for the pack. Isabella and I would be looking over the rest of the files regarding the history of the pack. I was hoping that we would be able to find some information about marking and mating so we could get to it. Not only was I anxious to make her mine but my wolf was getting harder and harder to control.

Before I could get too lost in my thoughts about what I would do to my mate, I could hear Terry try to have a hushed conversation with my dad.

"Robert, you getting the feeling that something isn't right with these files? Or is it just me?" Terry asked.

"Not just you. Something just isn't adding up, or something is missing. Your pack was the first on the scene after the attack, did you guys see any of these marks that are described in here?" my dad asked.

"No. We didn't see any defining marks on any of the buildings or trees. No marks, no smells, no nothing. It was like ghosts came in, killed everyone, and left without a trace."

"Then why do these reports go into great detail about marks and scents? It's like they are trying to point fingers at someone without naming names," my dad said, seeming confused.

"Have you seen any names in the reports? I have yet to see a single name of who wrote the reports or even who from the council investigated."

"What are you talking about? Let me see," I interjected. My dad held out the file unfazed that I was listening. I looked over the report he was reading and didn't understand it either. Nothing made sense.

"Well, either you've been lying to everyone, Terry, or someone completely falsified these reports." That earned me the growl I knew my comment deserved.

"You know damn good and well I'm telling the truth."

"I know. Something isn't adding up. We need someone that we can trust from the council to come look at this."

"I know just the man," Terry smirked.

"You're sure he can be trusted?" I asked.

"Positive," Terry assured me.

Before I could ask him who it was, Tristan spoke up needing clarification on something. I got back to work, focusing on what needed to be done. The hours passed quickly as my frustration grew. More and more I became convinced that the attack reports weren't the only ones that had been falsified.

"Jaxon, I think we may have found something." Tristan announced. Everyone immediately stopped what they were doing and looked over at him and Cameron.

"What is it?" I asked.

"Blackwood lists several attempted business deals with another pack. These deals are not listed in the council's records. It was a pack attempting to buy land from Blackwood. Even though the deals were not approved and finalized, Blackwood turned them down each time, they still should have been in the council's files," he replied.

"Who is the pack, Tristan?" I practically growled.

"Red Moon."

We all knew Red Moon. They were the scum of the shifter world. Violent, greedy, always in trouble with the council. They had gotten even worse since Blackwood was attacked.

"Their Beta was there the day of Bella's party," Terry said quietly.

"What?" Robert asked, clearly shocked.

"He showed up unannounced and uninvited. Claimed he didn't know they were having a party that day, but we all knew he was lying. Karen and I got there the night before the party. We all got up early the morning of the party, and Kane, the Beta of Red Moon, showed up before we had even finished breakfast demanding a meeting with

Michael. I asked Michael if he wanted me to join them, but he declined. I waited in the hallway outside his office while they spoke, thankful that Michael left the door open. Kane demanded that Michael agree to the land purchase and Michael refused as he always did. Kane then said that they figured he would say that and had a proposition for him. Red Moon's Alpha, Jarek, wanted Isabella, Alexandra to them, to mate with his son Jagger and unite the packs. Kane was furious when Michael began to laugh at him. Michael naturally refused. Said he would never take away his daughter's right to her true mate. Kane stormed out screaming that this was not the end, and that Red Moon would get what they wanted. Michael just laughed at him and told him good luck. I asked him about it, and he just laughed it off and said that Red Moon must be drinking tainted water. He wasn't concerned at all. Michael's Beta wasn't so sure. He wanted Michael to double the patrols for the party that night. Michael refused saying that no one was stupid enough to attack him on the night of his child's birthday. He had already upped the patrols and didn't see the need to up them again. At that point, Elizabeth came in demanding we come help set up and everything was forgotten," Terry revealed.

We all sat there stunned for a few minutes without speaking. The more I thought about it, the more convinced I became that Red Moon had attacked Blackwood. My hands began to shake as I fought off to control my anger and my wolf. Isabella reached out and took my hand in hers, tugging until I looked at her. I took a deep breath, drawing in her scent and my temper cooled.

"Terry, why didn't you tell us before?" Robert asked.

"Honestly, it just didn't cross my mind. Until Tristan said Red Moon, I had forgotten all about him showing up that day. We have never had any major problems with Red Moon. They are not too far away from us, in fact now they are the closest pack to us. Alpha Jarek even offered help after the attack on Blackwood. It was turned down by the council, obviously. They would never ask for the help of one of the most troublesome packs," he explained.

"Well, it's pretty obvious to me who attacked Blackwood," Tristan stated.

"Maybe so, but we have no concrete proof," Dad replied.

"Then we find it," I commanded.

Dad turned to Terry. "Can you call your contact with the council? Today?"

"Of course."

"Terry, would he be able to get Red Moon's files without anyone else knowing? I know Robert has a contact in the council, but I think if we can have another there it would be even better. Especially if they didn't know about each other," Tristan suggested.

"Yeah, I think he can do that. He's always helped me out in the past and been very discreet about it. I'll call him now," Terry said.

"Go call him. You can use my phone if you'd like. In the meantime, I would like the rest of us to focus on something else. Isabella and I aren't even halfway through our research of Blackwood's history. We could use some help. James, have you found anything unusual in the files you have been looking through?" I asked.

"Nothing. I'm about three quarters of the way finished, and everything looks normal. No big gaps in the files, nothing missing, just nothing. That in itself is almost strange. There should be at least a couple of minor discrepancies," he reported.

"That is strange. I want you to keep going through them with a fine-tooth comb. Cameron, you help him out. We'll all work for another hour and then break for dinner. After dinner, I want everyone back in here working again. I want some answers tonight!" I commanded.

Everyone replied, "yes, Alpha."

Terry hung up the phone after calling his council contact.

"He'll be here first thing in the morning and he's bringing Red Moon's files with him," Terry said.

"Thank you, Terry." I sighed.

We all worked until it was time to head down to dinner. Once we got there, we saw that Karen, Donna, and Kathleen were not happy with us.

"Jaxon, why are you keeping everyone locked up in your office?" Mom demanded.

"Honey, Jaxon has a very good reason for keeping us so busy," Dad tried to soothe her.

"And what would that be?" she asked angrily.

"Why don't you ladies join us in Jaxon's office after dinner and we will fill you in on everything?" Dad coaxed.

"Fine. But this better be good. I haven't been able to spend any time at all with my son's mate. I am not happy about this," she grumbled. Dad kissed her and she relaxed somewhat.

Dinner was excellent as always. Homemade lasagna, garlic bread, salad, and my favorite chocolate cake for dessert. After we finished stuffing ourselves, we all headed back up to my office. When we walked through the door and the ladies caught a glimpse of all the paperwork scattered everywhere, they came to a halt.

"What is all of this, Jaxon?" Mom asked.

"The council's files on the Blackwood Pack," I answered.

"Blackwood? Why are you looking into the Blackwood Pack? They were wiped out years ago. Why dig up the past?" she asked quietly.

"Because not all of them are dead," Terry responded, causing them to gasp.

"Terry, why would you say that? You saw what happened there! You helped investigate the attack. You yourself said they were all dead!" Donna asked, glancing around the room.

"You know why, Mom," Isabella spoke up.

CHAPTER TWENTY-FIVE

Isabella

"What are you talking about, honey?" my mom asked.

"It's okay, Mom. They all know. With Jaxon being my mate, they kind of have to."

"Are you sure?" she asked Terry. He nodded his head.

"Terry didn't find me on the side of the road in Louisiana. He found me at Blackwood. I'm Alexandra Isabella Blackwood, daughter of Michael and Elizabeth Blackwood. I'm the only surviving member of the Blackwood Pack," I announced.

Kathleen handled the news far better than everyone else. She was clearly shocked. Karen and my mom teared up, but Kathleen just stared at me.

"Show her, sweetheart," Jaxon whispered to me. I shifted into my wolf and slowly trotted over to where they were standing. My mom ran her fingers through the fur on my head and smiled. Kathleen sat down on the couch—hard—like her legs gave out.

"You ok, Kathleen?" Terry asked.

"I'm fine. Just a bit of a shock. I never thought I would see a blue wolf again. You are magnificent. It's incredible really, but I think we need to hear the whole story," she replied.

"Agreed, but now is not the time." Robert answered her. "We are going through the council's files, trying to find out what will happen when Jaxon marks Isabella and they mate. If he wasn't an Alpha with his own pack, this wouldn't be an issue. Since he is, we need to know what will happen. Will he become a Blackwood? In the past, that is how it worked, regardless of which mate was Blackwood. Not that Jaxon doesn't want to become a Blackwood, but we need to keep Isabella's existence a secret. Jaxon changing into a midnight blue, Blackwood wolf is going to let the cat of the bag with a quickness."

"Well, then why are we standing around talking? Let's get to work!" Kathleen commanded.

"Yes, ma'am!" we all responded.

We all worked until eleven o'clock when Robert announced that we should all head to bed and get some rest and start up again in the morning after meeting with Terry's council contact.

Standing up and stretching, I listened to Jaxon argue with his father about whether or not to tell the council elder who I really was. No one could agree on this. Jaxon absolutely refused to tell him.

"The council can't be trusted!" Jaxon insisted.

"Jaxon, we are currently the enforcers for the council! How can you say that?" Robert countered.

"Because I see firsthand what goes on with council business. Tell me, after looking at all of this, that the council doesn't know who attacked Blackwood. It's bullshit. We all know it!"

"Without concrete evidence they can't do shit. You know that as well as I do."

"We're still not telling them who she is!" Jaxon snapped.

"Why don't we wait until tomorrow to figure this out, sleep on it?" Terry suggested.

"It won't make any difference. I don't give a damn if he is your friend, my friend, or the Moon Goddess reincarnated! We are not telling him who my mate is until he proves that he can be trusted!" Jaxon roared.

"Son, calm down. I know you're upset, and you have every right to be. If you want us to keep this from him, then we will. However, if he knew Michael and Elizabeth, he might recognize her if he sees her," Robert cautioned.

"That's true. As the council's enforcers, Blackwood worked very closely with the council elders," Terry added.

"Then we won't let him see me," I decided. "I'll stay away from the pack house tomorrow. I need to go to the school and get some work done anyway."

"I don't..." Jaxon began.

"I'll take my guards with me. You can add even more if you want. I won't even complain or be difficult about it," I interrupted him.

"Fine. But I'm adding more guards. Take the usual eight and four more," he demanded.

"Yes, dear," I teased him.

He glared back at me, clearly not amused. I walked over and wrapped my arms around his waist and laid my head on his chest. He immediately began to relax and hugged me back.

"Sorry," he whispered. "I don't mean to be an ass. I just don't like you being out of my sight right now. Especially with what we have found out so far."

"It's ok. I get it," I reassured him. "Now let's go to bed. I need to cuddle and make out with my mate."

Jaxon growled softly before picking me up and throwing me over his shoulder, causing me to squeal and everyone else to laugh.

"Night, everyone. We'll see you all at breakfast. Tristan, make sure you take care of the guards for tomorrow. I want Grant and Thomas's team to take lead," Jaxon ordered on his way out the door.

"Yes, Alpha," Tristan responded.

Jaxon carried me to the elevator and refused to let me down until we got to our room. Once inside, he walked over and tossed me gently onto the bed, quickly climbing up and laying down on top of me.

"Ugh, Jaxon you're heavy!" I groaned.

"You like it," he chuckled.

"You're kidding me, right? Get off, fatass!" I joked.

"Nope. I'm quite comfortable," he chuckled, laying so that all of his weight was on me. Turned out my mate was fucking heavy. When he heard me cough, he rolled off to the side and grinned at me. I rolled my eyes before letting them roam down his body, pausing on the growing bulge in his jeans. *Damn.*

"See something you like?" he smirked.

Ugh. I can't believe Jaxon caught me staring. In my defense, that bulge in his pants was rather sizable. I didn't know whether to feel intimidated or impressed. A little bit of both I guessed.

"Maybe. More like thinking it sucks to be you right now," I shot back.

"You have no idea," he groaned. "It's shower time. Cold shower time."

I watched Jaxon roll off the bed and head to the bathroom, my wolf growling in my head. She was pissed at me. She wanted to have a chat and it wasn't really up to me whether or not that was happening. One of the perks of the inner wolf was that you could talk to each other, but it wasn't always when you wanted to. And it was usually emotionally driven.

"Damn right I'm pissed. I want my mate!" she retorted and growled at me.

"I know you do. You think I don't? But until we know what will happen when we mate, we need to be careful."

"He will be ours and we will be his. Nothing else to know, stupid human."

"Watch it, bitch. There's more to the story and you know it. Someone killed our pack in case you forgot. We're trying to keep a low profile until we figure out who. So, unless you know exactly what will happen when he marks me and we mate, keep your whining and complaining to a minimum."

"Bitch? That's original. Let's call the female wolf a bitch. Seriously? That's the best you could do? Damn, Bella. You suck at this insulting thing," she laughed.

"Oh, shut up. Seriously though, do you have any idea what will happen?" I asked her.

"Not really. Something is telling me that he will become like us but that

he will keep his Alpha title and claim to his pack. The pack won't change with him. That happens later. I think. I think there is some kind of ceremony you have to do to keep your claim as Alpha of Blackwood. It's to prevent the Blackwood line from dying out completely," she responded.

"Any idea where we can find out about this ceremony?"

"Our pack house. There's a book of our history. It's in there."

"So, we have to go back to Blackwood?"

"Yes."

"How do you know all this?"

"Not sure, I just know it."

'Then why haven't you told me before now?'

"I didn't know that I knew it until now. I know that doesn't make sense but it's true. It's like it's in my DNA and I can only know things at the right time."

"Ok. I know you wouldn't hide things from me. Pretty sure you want to mate with him more than I do, and that's saying something."

"Damn right it is!"

"Isabella?" Jaxon stood in front of me with a worried look on his face. "You ok, sweetheart? I've been calling your name for five minutes."

"Sorry, baby. I was having a little chat with my wolf," I reassured him.

"She have anything interesting to say?"

"Actually yes. There's a ceremony we need to perform before we mate. It allows you to keep your Alpha title and claim to your pack and it allows me to keep my claim as Alpha of Blackwood. It will change your wolf to have some of the same qualities as mine," I told him.

"Wow. How does she know about this? And what do we have to do for this ceremony? Is there documentation of it?"

"She just knows. She said the information comes to her when we need it. We have to find a book on the history of Blackwood. The book is in my pack house. In Blackwood." I informed him.

"So, we have to go back to Blackwood?"

"Yes."

"Holy shit. Well, I guess we will tell everyone in the morning before breakfast. We will set up a trip there as soon as the council rep leaves. We just need to make sure that no one knows we are going there," he said.

"Hopefully, he leaves soon."

"If not, we'll leave my dad and Terry here to keep him busy and we'll go. In fact, we might just do that anyway. He gets here tomorrow morning. We can leave the next morning and be back that night. The sooner, the better," he decided.

I was excited and nervous about the thought of returning to my old home. I couldn't help but wonder what we would find there. Sensing my nervousness, Jaxon climbed into bed next to me and pulled me into his arms. The next morning, Jaxon and I got up early to get ready for breakfast. He let everyone know that we needed to meet in his office before breakfast to discuss something. I knew I would be heading to the school, so I made sure to dress nice. After fixing my hair and makeup, we headed down to Jaxon's office.

CHAPTER TWENTY-SIX

Jaxon

Isabella and I arrived at my office before everyone else. We decided to take a look at some of the remaining files and see if any of them mentioned the book her wolf told her about. So far, we weren't having any luck. By the time everyone else has joined us, we finished the rest of the files with no mention of the book.

"Isabella and I had a talk last night and we have come to a decision. We are going to mate today. We don't want to wait," I announced.

"What?" Terry roared. "You can't do that! You have no idea what will happen!"

"Jaxon!" Isabella snapped at me. *Uh oh.* Maybe I should've clued her in on my little prank first.

"Yes, dear?" I mumbled.

"That is not what we talked about!" She growled at me. *Damn that's hot.*

"Sorry, sweetheart. Just thought I'd make sure everyone was awake." I smirked at her. She closed her eyes and appeared to be counting under her breath. Yep, definitely should've clued her in. I walked over to where she was standing and attempted to pull her to me, only to get an elbow to the ribs. I grunted in pain, and she laughed at me.

"You deserved that, and you know it!" she laughed.

"Yes, I did. Sorry everyone. Just wanted to lighten the mood a little."

"Next time you want to lighten the mood, try chocolate," my mom replied while glaring at me.

"Anyway, what was this conversation you guys had?" my dad asked.

I glanced at Isabella and nodded for her to tell everyone.

"I know this is going to sound a bit strange, but just hear me out. I had a talk with my wolf last night. She has never been one for long conversations, so this took me by surprise. She had some enlightening information to share. There's a book that tells of the history of the Blackwood Pack. In this book, there are details of a ceremony to join two mates. This ceremony only applies when one mate is an Alpha of another pack. Jaxon and I need to perform this ceremony before he marks me. The book is in the Blackwood pack house," she explained.

"How does she know for sure?" my mom asked.

"I really don't know. I asked her how she knew, and she got offended and said she just does, that it's part of her makeup to know these things," Isabella answered.

"Well, when are we going to Blackwood?" Terry asked.

"Isabella and I are going tomorrow morning. Before you all start complaining or protesting, I need you all here to keep the council rep busy and to help out with the pack. We will take the lead warrior and all of Isabella's guards with us," I told them.

"Well, I suggest we all head down to breakfast and eat before the rep arrives," my dad replied, seeming to keep in his arguments.

We all headed down to the dining room to eat. Isabella finished before the rest of us and decided to head over to the school to get some work done before the kids arrived for the day. Thomas and Grant both nodded in my direction before following her out. The rest of us quickly finished up and went back to my office to clean up the Blackwood files while we waited for the council rep to arrive.

We were all sitting around chatting when Tristan was informed of the reps arrival. He and Terry headed downstairs to greet him and bring him upstairs.

"Jaxon, why don't you and Isabella leave for your trip tonight? You can search the pack house in the morning and come back tomorrow evening after you find the book," my father suggested.

"Good idea. I'll have the plane prepped and ready to go. We'll leave after dinner," I agreed.

We both fell silent as Tristan and Terry walked in with Terry's friend from the council.

"Gentlemen, this is my friend Nikolas. He's the head of the council," Terry said.

Holy shit. The council head. Had Terry lost his freaking mind?

"Before you say anything, I trust this man with my life. With my mate's life. He is my uncle," Terry explained.

"Thanks for the heads up, Terry," my dad grumbled. Nikolas and Terry both laughed.

"I do apologize for my nephew. He loves doing this to people." Nikolas chuckled. "Now gentlemen, I brought all of the information regarding the Red Moon Pack as requested. I do have to get back to the council as soon as possible to avoid any inquiries as to where I've been, so let's get started."

This was going to be a long day. I just hoped that we would have the answers we needed by the end of it.

A couple of hours after lunch, Terry and Nikolas hit paydirt.

"I have something!" Nikolas shouted. "Red Moon made a formal request to have the council intervene and force a mating between their Alpha's son and the daughter of Blackwood's Alpha. The council denied the request, of course. I remember my father speaking of this. He laughed at the thought of them even filing a request to force this."

"I think we have something over here as well," my father added. "The reports of the failed transactions between Blackwood and Red Moon. These go back years, Terry. Red Moon made more than a dozen attempts to buy land or companies from Blackwood every year, going back almost fifteen years before the attack on Blackwood."

Nikolas seemed to realize what my father was saying. The rest of us sat there quietly while the council head put two and two together.

"You all think Red Moon attacked Blackwood. Don't you?" he asked.

"Yes," Terry answered him.

"Why now? Why are you investigating this after all these years, Terry?" Nikolas questioned him.

"It's not after all these years, Nikolas. I've never stopped looking for the murderers who killed my best friends. And I never will," Terry responded.

"I understand, nephew. I will help as much as I can. Am I safe in assuming you have Blackwood's files here as well?" he quietly asked.

"Yes, we have them." I answered.

"Then perhaps we should pull them out and start comparing the files side by side. We will need every bit of proof we can find to restart the investigation and lodge a formal complaint against Red Moon. They, unfortunately, have supporters in the council," he stated.

"Then let's get started," my father said.

CHAPTER TWENTY-SEVEN

Isabella

I stayed late at the school after all the kids left to work on lesson plans and catch up on grading papers. I only missed a few days of work, but I had really missed my class. They were some great kids. I finished up the last of the papers and made sure everything was ready for the substitute. As I was looking over my notes, Grant's phone rang. I'd managed to pretty much tune out my guards for the majority of the day. They stayed in the background and didn't interfere with anything.

"Luna, that was Alpha Jaxon. We can head back as soon as you are ready," Grant said.

"Thank you, Grant. I'll be done in just a moment."

"I'll let Thomas and the others know."

While Grant went to speak to Thomas and the other guards, I finished gathering my papers and leaving instructions for the substitute. Luckily, it would be the same sub that taught my students earlier in the week. She really had a handle on things and was good with the kids.

"Ready, Luna?" Thomas asked me.

"Yes, I'm ready." I grabbed my bags and headed towards the door. Thomas insisted on taking my bags for me. Knowing that arguing would get me nowhere, I thanked him, and we headed for the car. It was a short, twenty-minute walk from the pack house to the school, but Jaxon insisted we take the car. The only reason I agreed to his request was because I got to drive my car. I hadn't driven my baby in way too long. Too bad the drive was only five minutes. *Oh well, it was still a drive.*

Once we got back to the pack house, I parked the car near the garage, and we all headed around back to go inside. Grant made sure the coast was clear before Thomas and I went in. We headed straight for the elevator and made it upstairs without running into anyone. I took my bags from Thomas once we reached the bedroom door and thanked him and Grant again. They both just nodded their heads and took up their posts in the hallway.

I opened the door to the room and saw Jaxon standing by the window looking out. I slipped off my shoes and set my bags down by the door, shutting it softly. Jaxon grinned when our eyes met. I quickly ran over and jumped into his open arms.

"I missed you," I whispered, my face buried in his neck.

"I missed you, too," he replied. My stomach decided that now would be the perfect time to imitate a dying animal.

"Hungry much, sweetheart?" he laughed.

"Shut up. And yes, starving. I ate lunch on the run today trying to catch up on all my work," I grumbled.

"Then let's feed you. We're going to have a busy night." he winked at me, which made me blush. "Not like that, perv. You've got a dirty mind, sweetheart. I like it."

"Stop teasing me, Jaxon," I groaned, hiding my bright red face from him.

"Sorry, sweetheart. You just make it too easy sometimes. Now let's get some food in that belly of yours. We can talk while we eat."

I sat down at the small table Jaxon had set up with our dinner. He went to tell Grant and Thomas to go eat while I filled both of our plates. When he got back, we both started eating while he filled me in on what they found out.

"So, what did you find out today?" I asked.

"Have you ever met Terry's contact with the council?"

"No, Terry always made sure to keep me hidden. I look a lot like my mother, so he knew that they'd instantly know who I was."

"So, you didn't know that his contact was his uncle?"

I couldn't help but laugh. "No, I didn't but it doesn't surprise me. Terry loves doing shit like that."

"Have you ever heard of the Red Moon Pack?" he replied.

"Not much. I know that Terry doesn't like their Alpha. Well, I guess he would be the old Alpha. His son took over as Alpha a few years ago. Other than that, nothing."

"Well, Terry isn't the only one who didn't like their old Alpha. The son doesn't seem much better. We went through their files today and there are quite a few records indicating that they were trying to buy land from your father. He refused every request and that's not all. We found a formal request to the council to force a mating between the son of Red Moon's Alpha and the daughter of Blackwood's Alpha," Jaxon paused.

"Wait, what? They wanted to force me to mate with him? Why?" I asked, bewildered.

"We aren't really sure. We can only guess at this point. Best guess, Red Moon wanted in Blackwood and your father wouldn't let them. Blackwood served the council as warriors and council enforcers. Red Moon were criminals, still are. Our only other guess at this point, perhaps Red Moon's Alpha thought that if he mated his son to you, any pups you had would be stronger because of your bloodline. Either way, your father and the council denied the request. Terry also told us that Red Moon's Beta was at Blackwood the day of your birthday party. He met with your father to try and buy land and your father turned him down again. He was angry when he left and when Terry questioned your father, he just laughed and said they were always angry. Terry didn't think anything else of it."

"You think they attacked my pack that night, don't you?" I whispered.

"Yes, I do. We're trying to get as much proof as we can so the council can start a formal inquiry. That's what everyone else will be working on tomorrow. You and I have other plans."

"Oh really?"

"We're leaving tonight for Blackwood. I spoke with my father earlier and we both agree that it would be best for us to leave tonight and search for the book first thing in the morning. Once we find what we are looking for, we can head back here, hopefully tomorrow evening. You ok with that?" he asked.

"Of course. The sooner we find that book, the better," I agreed.

"Good. We can pack as soon as you are finished eating," he told me.

"I'm finished. Let's get started," I said, standing up from the table.

"My bag is already packed. Once you're ready, I'll let the guards know and we can head for the airport." he chuckled.

"Ok, give me a few minutes to get packed. What about our dinner?"

"I'll ask Evie to have someone take care of it. Go pack."

While Jaxon took care of asking Evie to clear up our dinner, I grabbed a duffel bag and shoved a couple of changes of clothes in there before changing into some leggings and a t-shirt, grabbing a sweatshirt just in case. A quick trip to the bathroom to grab what I needed, and I was done.

"All done, sweetheart?" At my nod, he grabbed my bag and headed for the door. "Let's go."

We made it downstairs and out to the garage without being seen by anyone, which was, quite frankly, a miracle. Grant and Thomas were waiting there with the other warriors for us to load up into three SUVs and leave for the airport. We arrived with no troubles and immediately boarded the plane and took off for Texas.

I must have fallen asleep because the next thing I knew, I heard "Sweetheart, wake up. We're about to land."

"Ugh. Five more minutes."

"You said that fifteen minutes ago, love. Time to wake up."

"Fine, but you're carrying me," I groaned.

"Always, sweetheart. Always," Jaxon chuckled.

I sat up and stretched, feeling sleepy and a bit sore from sleeping on the plane. It's a nice jet, but I would much rather sleep in a bed than on a plane seat.

The landing was smooth and as promised and there were three SUVs awaiting our arrival. We loaded up and headed for the hotel. Everyone was pretty quiet during the drive, probably because it was almost three in the morning thanks to the time difference.

Thomas went in the hotel to check us in while we waited in the cars. He came back out a few minutes later with a smile on his face and key cards in hand. Thank the Goddess.

"I want everyone to meet here at the cars at eight tomorrow morning, sharp," Jaxon ordered.

"Yes, Alpha," they all responded.

"Come on, sweetheart. Let's go get some sleep," Jaxon said, wrapping an arm around my waist.

"Sounds great to me," I agreed.

We walked inside, took the stairs up to the second floor, and quickly found our room. Jaxon and I both brushed our teeth, changed our clothes, and fell into bed. A quick kiss goodnight and we were both out.

CHAPTER TWENTY-EIGHT

Tristan

With Jaxon and Isabella gone, the rest of us were still going through the council's files, checking, and rechecking everything. Terry's uncle had extended his stay here to help us find every scrap of evidence to build a case against Red Moon. He wanted to be able to present the case to the council when he returned in the hope that we could use the element of surprise in our favor. If Red Moon didn't know what we were up to, we stood a better chance of them not getting their supporters together in time to fight the case. So far, we had managed to find dozens of inconsistencies in Red Moon's records. We compiled a list of all of them, but it still wasn't enough. I couldn't help but think that we were missing something. Something obvious. We knew that Red Moon had supporters on the council, but what if they had someone working on the inside? That would definitely explain the missing records.

"Nikolas, I know the council seats are passed down through families, but what is the process for everyone else who works for the council? How do they get their jobs?" I asked.

"Pretty much your standard interview process," he began to explain. "Minus the application part. Most of the council workers are recommended by someone either on the council or who already works for the council. Once we receive a recommendation, we do a thorough background check. We speak to their Alpha, Beta, parents, family, friends, anyone who might have any sort of knowledge about the individual. Why do you ask? Thinking of joining us?"

"No, not at all." I laughed. "No offense. I was just looking over everything we have so far, and I feel like we are missing something. Something obvious. I don't want to make accusations, but I am beginning to think that Red Moon has someone on the inside working for the council. Not necessarily an elder, but someone who would have access to the files. That seems to be the only logical explanation for the missing records."

"I hadn't thought of that until now, but it is definitely something that I will look into. After seeing just how many records are missing or just wrong, it is obvious that someone has tampered with them. Perhaps it is time to rethink our hiring practices and reevaluate the ones who are currently working for us," he responded, a serious expression on his face.

"Nikolas, is it true that you have the power to Alpha command anyone? Including rogues?" Cameron asked.

"Yes, that is true. Why do you ask?" Nikolas replied. Everyone in the room stopped what they were doing to see where Cameron was going with this. I had a pretty good idea.

"Cameron, he doesn't know who Jaxon's mate is. We can't tell him without Jaxon's permission," I mindlinked him.

"I'm not going to tell him who she is. I just think that maybe he can get some answers out of the rogue that Jaxon couldn't."

"And what if the rogue knows who she really is? If he tells Nikolas, we are going to be in deep shit!"

"I don't think the rogue knows who she really is. He's doing someone else's dirty work. You never tell the grunts the important stuff, only just enough so they know what to do."

"Fine, but if this goes bad, I am throwing you under the bus."

. . .

Cameron started laughing out loud at my last comment. Nikolas looked at us, clearly amused, while everyone else was staring at us like we were crazy.

"Finished your discussion?" Nikolas chuckled.

"Yes, we have. Cameron, this is your show," I said. Cameron muttered something that sounds like chicken under his breath. I glared at him and flipped him off, causing Kathleen to smack me in the back of the head and Robert to laugh.

"Anyway, we have a rogue in our cells. Been there for a few days now. Caught him attacking a female on our territory. We think he was here for a reason and that it wasn't just random. Jaxon cannot Alpha command him because he's a rogue. This particular rogue has so far been immune to our interrogation techniques. Perhaps you would be willing to give it a go?" Cameron explained.

"I'd be happy to. Any particular reason why you think this was something more than just a random attack?" Nikolas asked.

"We've had trouble with rogues for the last couple of months. Until this attack, they had stayed just off territory, only venturing on like they were testing our patrols. Because of who they attacked and where they attacked her, we were thinking there must be something else going on."

"If I may, who is the female that was attacked?"

"Evie's best friend," Cameron answered smoothly.

"Well, then let's get some answers," Nikolas replied, as he headed for the door.

Robert, Nikolas, Terry, and I followed Cameron over to the building that housed the cells. It was a short fifteen-minute walk from the pack house. We kept it close but not too close. There was a large fence around the building with razor wire on top and four guards at the gate with another ten guards patrolling the perimeter.

"Quite the setup you have here," Nikolas commented.

"We sometimes take in prisoners from other packs," Robert explained. "We need the extra security."

We followed Cameron through the gates and up to the door. He swiped his card in the reader and entered his code on the keypad. Once that was done, there was a buzz and the door opened. Robert pointed out the different security features in place around the building. There were cameras all throughout the interior of the building and on the exterior. Those were monitored twenty-four hours a day from a separate location. Each door into the building required an ID card as well as a pin number. These were also required to access the elevators.

We walked inside and headed for the elevators at the end of the hallway. The building looked like a one story from the outside but was really four stories. We were currently on the ground floor, G. The other three floors, B1, B2, and B3, were all below ground. B3 was the lowest floor. We were heading down to the floor below us, B1.

When the elevator doors opened, there was a guard there waiting for us. He escorted us to a waiting room while the rogue was moved to an interrogation room. Once he was moved, the guard returned to take us to him.

"Will you be needing additional guards, Beta?" he asked.

"No, that won't be necessary. I'm pretty sure we can handle it. Thank you," I replied. He nodded his head and walked back to his post.

I swiped my card and entered my pin number to unlock the door. I stepped aside to allow the others to enter. The rogue was sitting in a chair that was bolted to the floor and had silver handcuffs on his wrists and ankles. He sat silently, smirking at us. I closed the door and got right to it.

"Do you know who this is?" I asked the rogue, gesturing towards Nikolas. As I thought, the rogue just smirked and didn't say a word.

"Let me tell you, then. This man is an elder and he's here to make you talk." I smirked right back. "Nikolas, he's all yours."

Nikolas chuckled and stepped forward. He stared at the rogue for a few minutes, not saying a word, not even moving a muscle. Just staring at him. This went on for about five minutes before he smiled and spoke.

"Tell me your name, rogue," he commanded. The rogue's eyes got wide as saucers, and you could see him gritting his teeth trying not to answer.

"Steven," he grunted.

"Very good, Steven. Tell me how you became a rogue."

"I attacked my Beta's mate."

"What was the name of your pack?" he commanded again.

"Fire Stone."

"Ah, Canadian. Very good. I have been to Fire Stone Pack several times. Met the Beta's mate. Lauren is her name. Beautiful woman. Kind. I guess you are the one who left the scars on her face. Perhaps after I get the answers I am after, we can do them a favor and return you to them. I am sure Beta Markus would love to have you back." Nikolas chuckled.

Steven started shaking his head. He knew how much pain he would suffer at Beta Markus' hands for harming his mate.

"Now then, tell me why you came here to this pack," Nikolas commanded.

"I was ordered to," Steven bit out.

"By whom?" Nikolas asked.

"I can't. Pl-please don't m-make me tell you," he begged.

"Tell me now!" Nikolas commanded him.

"R-r-red M-m-m-moon. Th-the Al-Alpha there i-is h-hiring rogues to come here." he stammered.

"Why?"

"I don't know. I swear. He only told us that he needed people to keep an eye on the pack here. Said you might have something he wants."

"What? What is it he wants?" Nikolas commanded him.

"I don't know. I swear."

"How many rogues are there? How many did he hire?"

"There were ten in our group. I don't know for sure how many groups total, but I do know there are at least six groups. Ten each per group."

"Who do you report to?" Nikolas asked.

"One of the rogues in my group. Says his name is Mills. No clue if that is really his name."

"Who does he report to?"

"Red Moon's Beta."

"How long have you been here?"

"Since July. The others have been here longer, but I don't know how long," Steven answered.

"Nikolas, can we speak to you in the hallway?" I asked. He nodded his head and we all stepped out, leaving the rogue in the chair.

"What are we going to do?" I asked.

"What do you mean?" Nikolas replied.

"This is clearly a sign of war. They are spying on our pack." Cameron growled.

"No, they are looking for something. You cannot attack them, not yet. We need to find out why they have rogues watching your pack." Nikolas stated, trying to keep the peace. "Do you have anything else you want me to ask him?"

"Yeah, ask why he attacked our L– pack-member," Cameron demanded, stumbling over his words, and almost outing our Luna.

"I will. Anything else?" Nikolas calmly asked.

"That's it for now. Are you going to tell Fire Stone that he is here?" I asked.

"Eventually, yes. I think it would be best for us all if I wait to do so. Red Moon will know that Jaxon cannot use his Alpha command on a rogue and that this rogue will not give up anything for fear they will kill him. We do not want to give anything away just yet. This will definitely add to the case against Red Moon, though," Nikolas stated.

I saw Robert and Terry exchange looks before Robert spoke up. "Why would this add to the case against Red Moon? I thought that case would be solely about Blackwood."

"It was up until now. Now though, I think we need to build a case with anything and everything we can get. Whatever it takes to bring them down," Nikolas explained.

"Then let's find out why he attacked that female and get back to the pack house," Robert said, heading back to the door. I opened the door and we all stepped in again. The rogue was sitting there with his head hanging down, not even bothering to look up at us.

"Steven, I have one last question for you. Why did you attack that female?" Nikolas commanded him.

"I don't know. I was chosen to go that night because I am one of the younger wolves and I don't have as many scars as the others. I wasn't planning on doing anything but sit in a dark corner and watch everyone. I was near the hallway that led to the bathrooms. When I saw her coming towards me, something came over me. It was like I couldn't control myself. Like something else was controlling me."

"Have you ever felt like that before?" Nikolas commanded him.

Steven hung his head and sighed before answering. "Yes. When I attacked Lauren," he whispered.

We all looked at each other confused. What did he mean he couldn't control himself? Was he drugged? Was he commanded?

"Steven, did someone command you to attack these women?" Nikolas commanded.

"I-I don't know. I don't remember anyone commanding me to attack them. I swear I am not a violent person. Lauren was my best friend growing up. I was happy for her when she found out that Markus was her mate. Markus and I became friends. Good friends. I would never do anything to hurt them. I don't know what happened. I don't remember attacking her. I don't remember attacking this other girl, either," he confessed.

"One last question, Steven. Do you have a mate?" Nikolas commanded.

"Yes."

"Where is she?"

"She's at Red Moon. They said she could stay there until this job was done. That she would be safe there."

"What is her name?"

"Dani."

"Thank you, Steven. You have been most helpful," Nikolas told him. He just sat there with his head down and didn't say a word as we walked out of the room again. I mind-linked the guard and told him that we were finished. He showed up a minute later to escort us back to the elevator. I told him to make sure that the prisoner was taken back to his cell.

We all left the building and walked back to the pack house in silence. No one said a word until we were back in Jaxon's office and the door was shut.

"Now that you have your answers gentleman, I have a few questions of my own," Nikolas said.

"I'm sure you do, Nikolas. We will answer them the best we can, but please understand that there may be some questions that are better left for my son to answer," Robert told him.

"I understand and I will respect that. First, who is the female that was attacked?" Nikolas asked.

"That would be one of the questions better left for our Alpha to answer," I told him.

"Very well then. I think that perhaps all of my questions should wait until Jaxon returns," Nikolas sighed.

"That might be for the best," Robert said. "I am sorry, Nikolas. We don't mean to be rude, especially after all of your help, but Jaxon is the Alpha now. We must respect his wishes."

"You are not being rude. Far from it. I understand the need to protect and respect your Alpha. My questions can wait," Nikolas assured us.

"I think that we have all had a long day. What do you say we grab some dinner and take the rest of the night off?" I asked everyone.

They all quickly agreed, and we headed down to the dining room. I considered calling Jaxon and letting him know what we had found out today, but I didn't want to interrupt their trip. For now, I was going to enjoy the cook's food and then go to bed early.

CHAPTER TWENTY-NINE

Isabella

The next morning came way too damn early. We dressed, packed our bags, and headed out to breakfast. We all finished eating fairly quickly and headed out after paying the bill and leaving a large tip for the waitress. We got into the SUV's and headed out. Jaxon said it was about an hour drive to the Blackwood Pack house. We didn't tell the others where we were going, just that we were heading to the house of a pack that no longer existed. Well, Jaxon told them there was a threat to their Luna and we were going to search for clues. Needless to say, they were extra observant and on edge.

After an hour of driving, we turned off the highway onto a private road. We drove for about a mile before pulling up to a large house. It was much smaller than Jaxon's pack house, but still huge. It seemed to be in really good condition considering it had been empty for almost sixteen years.

"Thomas, Grant, I want you to split up into three teams and search the house and surrounding lands. I want to know if anyone is here or has been recently. One team inside, the other two outside. Thomas, I want your team outside," Jaxon ordered.

"Yes, Alpha," they replied.

Jaxon and I waited by the car while the guards completed their initial search. I couldn't help but stare at the building I once lived in. It was a farmhouse style, white siding, large wraparound porch, wide picture windows, beautiful flower beds and gardens, even a cute gazebo off to the side. I could just picture my parents sitting on the porch talking with the other pack members while little kids played in the yard.

"All clear, Alpha," Thomas reported back.

Jaxon nodded his head at Thomas and took my hand. We walked up the porch to the front door. Jaxon took a step back and let me open the front door. I took a deep breath, wrapped my hand around the door handle, opened the door and paused for a moment before stepping inside. The dark hardwood floors gleamed as if they had just been cleaned. Looking around, I noticed that there wasn't a speck of dust to be seen anywhere. I sniffed the air to see if I could catch a scent, but there was nothing fresh, other than the guards we brought with us. There was a faint hint of humans, but it was at least a week old. The furniture was covered in sheets to protect it. I could see the outlines of a couch and a couple of armchairs, as well as a coffee table.

Walking further into the house, I lost myself completely in my memories, smiling as I recalled the fun times I had here as a child. So far, I had managed to avoid any of the bad memories, there would be time for those later. I made my way through the living room, the dining room, and the kitchen. I decided to hold off on going into my father's office for now. Instead, I walked upstairs to the bedrooms. I headed for my mom and dad's room first. Again, the furniture was covered in sheets to protect it. I sat down on the edge of their bed and picked up a picture from the nightstand. I felt the bed dip beside me as Jaxon sat down.

"My parents on their wedding day," I whispered. "I always loved this picture as a child."

"You look just like your mother," he whispered back, kissing my cheek softly. "You ok?"

"Yeah, I think I am. I wasn't sure how I was going to feel coming back here after everything that happened. But I'm ok. I would like to know who is taking care of the place, though," I replied.

"Terry hired a human couple from down the road. He can't do much anymore because of a bad back and she has never had a job outside the home. Times were getting rough, and money was tight for them. Terry hired them to come in once a week. She cleans the house, and he mows the yard. Terry even bought him a riding mower so he wouldn't have to push one. One of their grandkids comes over once a month to weed the flower beds and do some of the bigger jobs," Jaxon told me.

"Remind me to thank him when we get back," I murmured, leaning my head against Jaxon's shoulder.

"Will do, sweetheart. Is there anything here that you want to take back with us? Pictures, furniture, anything?" he asked.

"Yes. I'd like to take all of the pictures back with us, my mom's jewelry, and anything else I can think of later," I replied.

"I'll have Grant and his team come through in a bit and start gathering the pictures for us. Where's your mom's jewelry?"

"In the safe in the closet."

"Do you know the code?"

"Yeah. It's my birthday," I chuckled.

"Go grab that stuff and I'll meet you downstairs. I'm sure you need some time to look around on your own," he responded.

"Thank you, Jaxon."

"My pleasure, sweetheart. I'll be in the living room if you need me."

After Jaxon left, I walked into my parent's closet and opened the safe in the back wall. I grabbed one of the small cases on the floor and carefully filled it with my mom's jewelry. Just as I went to close the safe door, I noticed a piece of paper sticking out of the corner. I carefully pried the corner back and saw that it was a false wall in the safe. Behind it, there were several large envelopes and a small yellow envelope with what felt like a key in it. I grabbed them all and placed them in the case with the jewelry.

I walked out into the hallway and down to another door. Setting the case down, I took a deep breath, grasped the handle, and opened the door. It looked exactly as I remembered it. Even with the bed covered, I knew nothing had changed about the room. Pale pink walls with silver stripes, light gray carpet, white furniture, and hot pink and silver bedding. It still had the posters of unicorns on the wall and a stuffed unicorn on the bed.

It took me a few moments to gather myself together before I could go into my childhood bedroom. I couldn't help but think about what my life would've been like if my parents and pack hadn't been killed that night. I'm so grateful for everything Terry, Karen, and my adoptive parents have done for me, but it doesn't take away from the pain and heartache of losing my family.

I sat down on the bed and let the tears fall. The silent tears soon turned into heart-wrenching sobs as the pain took over. It was seconds later that I felt arms wrap around me.

CHAPTER THIRTY

Isabella

Jaxon held me until my tears dried up. I kept my head tucked under his chin until I was ready to talk. Jaxon seemed to sense that I wasn't ready yet and just held me, not saying a word.

"Thank you," I whispered.

"For what?"

"Being here for me. I didn't think I would react this way. It just brings back so many memories."

"This is not the time to reminisce, Bella," my wolf broke through my thoughts. "We need to find that book. Now."

"We're looking for it," I tried to tell her. She had been quite anxious all day.

"Look faster. I have a bad feeling."

"About what?" I asked.

"Not sure. Just a bad feeling. Now get to looking. It's here somewhere. I can practically feel it," she demanded.

· · ·

I didn't bother to respond to her. Instead, I turned to Jaxon and told him what she said. He quickly linked with his warriors to tell them to be extra cautious.

"Do you want anything from the house, other than the pictures? To take back with us?" he asked on our way downstairs.

"Yeah, I would. A few things from my dad's office, some books and a carved wolf if it's still there."

"Anything else?"

"There's a few things in my room but I can grab those before we leave."

"I'll tell Grant to come in and start grabbing the pictures."

Jaxon let Grant know what to do as we headed downstairs to my dad's office. While Jaxon began searching the shelves, I turned to the desk. I looked through all the drawers, making sure to check for false bottoms. Finding nothing, I moved on to search underneath the desk and then moved to search the cabinet behind the desk. Again, nothing. Ugh! Where could this damn book be?

Jaxon's search of the shelves turned up nothing. We were both beginning to feel very frustrated. I walked over to where Jaxon was standing, only to trip over the edge of the rug, causing it to flip up. Luckily Jaxon caught me before I hit the floor.

"Stupid rug!" I growled.

"I think there is something under the rug," Jaxon mumbled, grasping the edge of the rug, and throwing it back.

Sure enough, there was a small section of the floor that looked different from the rest of the flooring and had a small handle. We looked at each other, before looking back down at the floor. Jaxon reached out and grasped the handle and gave it a pull. The floor section came up like a trap door. Underneath was another small safe. Unlike the one in my parents' closet, this one required a key instead of a code.

"We need a key for this one," Jaxon stated.

"I think I have it. There was a small envelope with what felt like a key inside in the safe upstairs. It's in the case in the living room." I told him, already heading for the door to go get it.

I quickly grabbed the case and brought it with me into the office. Jaxon had managed to get the safe out of the floor and placed it on my father's desk, shoving everything else to the side. I opened the case and searched through the envelopes to find the one with the key. Once I had it, I opened it and dumped the key out into my hand. My hands had started to shake, so I handed the key to Jaxon for him to try.

Jaxon took the key from me and hesitated only slightly before trying it in the lock. He twisted the key to the right and we both held our breath waiting to see if it would work. The resulting click made us both gasp. It worked. It actually worked. Jaxon quickly opened the safe and inside was what we were looking for. The history of Black-wood. I was stunned.

Before I could say or do anything, the look on Jaxon's face changed from one of shock to one of anger.

"We have visitors," he growled. "Not friendly ones either."

"What do we do?" I asked.

"Thomas says they are about thirty minutes out. I want to be out of here in fifteen. Go through the house quickly and see if there's anything else you would like to take with you. I'll send in the rest of Grant's team to help you. I've pulled Thomas and his team back to the house so we can leave as soon as possible. Everything will be fine, but I'm not taking chances," he stated.

"Alright. I'll head upstairs first. There are only a couple of things I want from up there," I replied.

Jaxon went outside to gather the rest of Grant's team while I quickly ran up the stairs. Grant and the other two men had already gathered the pictures up here. I ran to my parents' room first and went straight to their closet. In the back on my mom's side was a long white garment bag. When I saw it earlier, I knew that it must be her wedding dress. I grabbed it and stepped back into their room to take a look around. Not seeing anything else, I left the room and headed down the hall to my old room. I knew there were a few things in there that I wanted.

As I got to my door, Grant came running back up the stairs.

"Need any help, Luna?" he asked.

"Yes, please. Take this dress for me. Careful please, it was my mother's. I'm just doing to grab a couple things from my room, and I'll be right down," I told him. He took the dress and headed back down the stairs with it.

I went in my room and grabbed a small jewelry box off the top of my dresser. I then went to the bed and dropped down to look underneath it. Sure enough, there was my old shoe box full of treasures. I grabbed it and the stuffed unicorn off my bed. Once I had these things, I left my room and ran back down the stairs.

I looked around the living room and pointed out a few pieces that I would like to take with me before heading back to my father's office. There I took several books from the shelf that I could vaguely remember my father reading to me, and a small carved wolf my great-grandfather had carved as a small boy. I took one last look around the room before heading back to the living room.

Jaxon came back in the front door as I was walking back into the living room.

"Everything else is already loaded up. Do you have everything you want?" he asked me.

"Everything that I can think of. You have the safe and the case?" I responded.

"Yes, I have them both. If that's everything, we need to leave," he stated.

"Alright, let's go," I took one last look around me before walking out the front doors. Jaxon quickly ushered me into the waiting SUV. As soon as we were in and the door shut, we took off down the driveway.

"Who's coming, Jaxon?" I asked him.

"I don't know. Thomas didn't wait around to get a look, but the feel from them was not good," he replied.

"The feel? I don't understand."

"Thomas and Grant are special wolves. You know they're warriors, but what makes them special is that they can sense another wolf's intentions. They have to be in wolf form to sense this, but it's highly accurate and apparently far-reaching," Jaxon explained.

"Thomas and Grant have to be in wolf form or the other wolves do?"

"Thomas and Grant," he clarified.

"Wow. That's impressive."

"Thank you," Grant replied from the driver's seat.

"Where are we going? Back to the hotel?" I asked.

"No, we are going straight to the airport. All of our bags were already in the cars. No need to go back to the hotel. I want to take off as soon as we get there," Jaxon replied.

"I've already contacted the pilot. He is prepping the plane as we speak. He said it would be ready before we got there," Thomas assured him.

"Good. Now drive faster, Grant," Jaxon demanded. I knew he was tense. I scooted closer to him and wrapped my arms around his waist. He immediately did the same and leaned down to bury his face in my hair. I could feel him taking deep breaths, inhaling my scent, and calming both himself and his wolf. The tension slowly began to leave his body.

"Better?" I smiled at him.

"Better. My wolf is on edge," he murmured, his face still buried in my hair.

"It's alright. We'll be on the plane and on our way back home before you know it," I assured him.

"I love you," he whispered softly.

"I love you too," I whispered back.

CHAPTER THIRTY-ONE

Jaxon

As Grant drove us to the airport, I mind-linked Thomas to get more details about what he saw.

"Thomas, tell me exactly what you sensed and saw," I demanded.

"Yes, Alpha. A group of wolves coming in fast. At least a dozen, maybe more. It was hard to get a fix on their exact number because of the distance. I saw red all around them. Not sure what they wanted, but whatever it was, it wasn't good," he replied.

"Any idea who they were?" I asked.

"Can't say for certain."

"But you have an idea, don't you?"

"Yes, Alpha. Pretty sure it was Red Moon's Beta. I've seen him before and one wolf gave off the same feeling he did," Thomas confessed.

"Red Moon's Beta? Fuck! This isn't good," I replied.

"Is there something we need to know, Alpha?" he asked.

"No, not yet. I will tell you when the time comes," I replied.

"Yes, Alpha."

"Grant, how much longer?" I asked.

"Five minutes, Alpha," he replied. Damn, he must've really stepped on the gas.

"Alpha, looks like we have company," Thomas spoke up.

I turned and looked at the side mirror. Three black cars were gaining on us fast.

"Grant, I have an idea who that may be. Step on it, now! Do not let them catch us!" I yelled.

"Already on it, Alpha," he replied as I felt the SUV lurch forward.

Watching the mirror, I saw with satisfaction that the cars were falling back. Without looking away, I reached to the side and made sure that Isabella's seatbelt was on and tight. I felt her grab onto my arm. I turned towards her and wrapped my arms around her, holding her tight to me.

"It's alright, sweetheart. They won't catch us," I whispered.

"Who is it, Jaxon? You know, don't you?" she asked quietly.

"I do know who it is. We will talk about it later," I replied. I felt her nod her head.

"We're here, Alpha," Grant stated.

As soon as the SUVs came to a stop, everyone jumped out and grabbed our bags and everything we took from Blackwood's pack house. I could see someone come out of the main building at the airport to yell at us for parking on the tarmac. I ignored him, knowing we would be in the air before he even reached us. Less than a minute after stopping the vehicles, we were all loaded up in the plane and shutting the doors. Isabella sat in her seat with the case in her lap and the safe between her feet. I sat down next to her and fastened both our lap-belts.

"Take off now!" I roared.

"Yes, Alpha," the pilot responded. I immediately felt the plane begin to move to the runway to take off. A moment later, we were in the air, and I felt everyone relax. I took off my lap-belt and motioned for Isabella to follow me to the back of the plane. She kept the case with her, and I picked up the safe to carry with me.

"Everyone, headphones on and music turned up. Now," I commanded. They didn't bother replying as they quickly moved to obey my order.

I led her to a small bedroom. I closed the door behind us and set the safe down on the floor. Isabella set the case down beside it.

"Jaxon, you're scaring me. What is going on? Who was that back there?" she whispered.

"Shh, sweetheart. Come here," I murmured, pulling her to me. "I'm sorry. I didn't mean to scare you." I held her in my arms until I felt her trembling stop. I felt bad for scaring her, but I would rather her be scared and safe than hurt.

"Let's sit down and I will answer your other questions. Okay?" I asked. She nodded her head and we both sat down on the bed facing each other.

"Who was back there and why we had to leave so quickly have the same answer. Red Moon." Isabella gasped at my reply. I hurried to continue before she could ask anything else.

"Thomas sensed there were at least a dozen wolves heading towards the pack house and they were not planning on being our welcoming party. He also sensed that one of the wolves could be Red Moon's Beta. We don't know for certain as he has only sensed their Beta one other time, but he is pretty sure that is who it was. If so, it only makes sense that the other wolves would be pack warriors," I told her.

She took a moment to think things over before replying. I didn't rush her. When she finally said something, I couldn't help but laugh.

"Well, shit, that's not good," she replied. I chuckled and shook my head at her.

"No, not good at all. The last thing we need is them finding us there or worse, figuring out who you are."

"I'm so thankful we had Thomas and Grant with us. It could've been much worse if they weren't there," she sighed.

"Very true," I replied. "Do you want to open the safe and look at the book now or do you want to wait until we get back?"

"As much as I want to know right now, I think it might be better for us to wait. If my wolf finds out what we need to do for you to mark me so we can mate, she will probably take over completely and perform the ceremony right here on the plane," she giggled.

"Waiting it is. Now, here is the more serious question. Do you want to go back out there and sit with everyone, or do you want to stay here and make out with me?"

She answered by pulling me toward her and capturing my lips with hers.

CHAPTER THIRTY-TWO

Isabella

Once we arrived back at the pack house, Jaxon mind-linked Tristan and told him that we found the book we were looking for and about the unexpected visitors we managed to avoid. As much as I wanted to see everyone, I needed some down time with Jaxon. He let Tristan know that we would meet with everyone in the morning in his office. On our way up to our room, Jaxon told me that he mind-linked his mom and asked her to have someone send dinner up for us. I thanked him and walked into the room behind him. We were both exhausted after the quick trip and from all of the stress and excitement. We set our bags down by the door and placed the case and safe on our bed.

"I'm going to grab a quick shower before dinner comes," Jaxon said with a smirk. "Want to join me?"

"Go!" I laughed because as much as we both would love that, we knew it wasn't something we could do without taking it too far.

While Jaxon was taking a shower, I decided to open the case I had packed and take a look at my mom's jewelry and the papers I found. First though, I grabbed an empty jewelry rack from my closet so I could lay everything on there and separate it and make sure nothing was damaged.

I set the jewelry rack and the case on the bed. Opening the case, I took the papers out and placed them on top of Jaxon's nightstand to look through later. I began to take the jewelry out piece by piece to carefully look them over.

I was surprised that everything was still in really good condition. Several pieces were in need of a good cleaning, but nothing was broken. When Terry told me that there was a safe in the closet and that my mother's jewelry was still in there, I was shocked to say the least. He told me that he had left everything in there so that I could go back and get it one day myself. He didn't feel right taking it out of there. After having wolves follow and try to catch us, I am so thankful that nothing has happened to the house over the years. It was a huge risk for Terry to leave everything there. One I was thankful had paid off. Once I had all of the jewelry transferred to the jewelry rack, I placed it back in my closet. As I was walking back to the bed, someone knocked on the door. I headed over and opened the door to see Jaxon's mom, Kathleen, with our dinner.

"How was your trip, dear? "she asked.

"Eventful." I laughed.

"Did you find what you were looking for?" she questioned me.

"We did. We plan on looking through it after we eat so hopefully, we'll have some answers tonight," I told her.

Before I had a chance to say anything, Jaxon walked out of the bathroom. "Hey, Mom. Thanks for bringing up dinner."

"Absolutely. I know you two must be hungry and tired, so I'll leave you two to eat and relax. If you need anything else just let me know. I'm glad you are back safe," she said before hugging us both and leaving.

As Jaxon and I sat down to eat dinner he asked, "Did you get a chance to look at the papers from the safe yet?"

"No, not yet. I just went through the jewelry and made sure everything was ok."

"Was it?"

"Yes, surprisingly. I can't believe that it was still in there and that it is in such good condition. A few pieces need to be cleaned, but that's it," I remarked.

"That is surprising. I'm just glad that we were able to get everything you wanted. I wish we hadn't been rushed at the end." he said.

"Me too. What do you plan on doing about it?" I asked.

"Not sure yet. I want to meet with everyone tomorrow morning and go over what happened and get their opinions," he stated. He gestured to my empty plate. "You finished?"

"All done. Want to get started on that book?"

"Hell yes!"

Jaxon and I pulled out the *Blackwood Pack History* and sat down on the bed to start reading. It almost seemed like a fairytale. Apparently, there used to be a wolf shifter king and queen. The wolf shifter king decided that he needed a special class of warriors to protect his kingdom and his mate. He decided to watch the current warriors train to see who was the best. The king chose the best warrior he could, which turned out to be my great, great, times however many greats, grandfather, Titus Blackwood.

The book described Titus Blackwood as a beast of a man. Standing almost seven feet tall in wolf form, he was the largest wolf the king had ever seen, even compared to the royal wolves, who were supposed to be the largest. He was a broad man with jet black hair and bright green eyes. He was stronger and faster than the other wolves. When he fought, he fought with such a passion and rage it was almost beautiful.

The wolf shifter king chose Titus to start a pack of warriors and be its Alpha. The wolf shifter queen decided that Titus needed a mate. Warriors at that time did not have mates as they were considered a distraction from their job. The queen decided to help Titus choose his mate. She chose her most loyal handmaiden, Rebecca. Rebecca's family had served the royal family for over ten generations and were known for their loyalty above all else. The king and queen both agreed that with Titus' strength and Rebecca's loyalty, their offspring would be the perfect warriors. Before the two could mate, the king had his personal sorcerer cast a spell to strengthen the bond between Titus and Rebecca and to also change the color of their wolves to signify that they were the elite warriors.

"Whoa. Did you know that there was a king and queen?" I asked Jaxon.

"No. I wonder what happened to the royals," he said.

"I don't know. I hope the book tells, though."

Titus and Rebecca became the Alpha and Luna of the Blackwood Pack. They worked together and chose people they thought were both strong and loyal to join their pack and become elite warriors. Together they had two children, a son and a daughter. The son found his mate in the pack and the daughter found her mate in the royal family, the third son of the king and queen. The young prince joined the Blackwood Pack to be with his mate, thus beginning the tradition of mates of females joining the pack rather than the females leaving.

We read several more chapters, but it never told us what happened to the king and queen of the wolf shifters. Jaxon and I were both kind of disappointed but made mental notes to ask his father and Terry if they knew anything.

We'd read about half of the book and were both so tired and ready to go to bed when we finally came across the chapter we were looking for. It was simply titled "Ceremonies".

"You know, after all this, I kind of expected a grander title," Jaxon joked.

"I know, right. Something long and complex, not 'Ceremonies'." I laughed.

"Well, hopefully these ceremonies are as simple as the title, and we can get to the good stuff." He waggled his eyebrows suggestively. I laughed and smacked him on the arm, not admitting that I was hoping for the same thing.

Jaxon and I began reading through the chapter to find the ceremony we were looking for. My wolf was excited and smug at the same time. She couldn't help saying I told you so over and over again in my head. We found the ceremonies for rogues, for families, even a ceremony to leave the pack before we finally found the one, we were looking for. The Ceremony for Alpha Mates. This ceremony was specifically for the Alpha of Blackwood and their Alpha mate, allowing the Alpha mate to keep his pack until he chose to join it with Blackwood.

"If the Alpha of Blackwood finds their mate outside the pack and that mate is already an Alpha of another pack, a special joining ceremony must be performed. It must be held under a full moon, outside, under the stars. The pair must each cut their own palm, press the bleeding palms together and recite the following pledges. Once the pledges are made, the Alpha mates will be joined as one and can then mark and mate with one another. Once the ceremony to join the two Alphas is completed, both Alphas will feel a strong burning sensation throughout their entire body. This is the bonding of the wolves and the beginning of the changing of the mate's wolf to become a Blackwood. The color of the mate's wolf will not change until the ceremony to join the packs is completed. It is possible that both Alpha's will lose consciousness. This could last anywhere from a couple of minutes to a couple of days. Once they regain consciousness, they will then be able to mark and mate. There is a separate ceremony to join the two packs and that must be conducted after the mating bond is completed."

Once I finished reading, Jaxon and I both sat there in silence. We finally knew what we had to do to be able to mate. I looked over at Jaxon and could see that he was thinking hard. Curiosity got the best of me after a few minutes, and I asked him what he was thinking about.

"What are you thinking?" I asked quietly.

"I was talking to my dad and Tristan and making arrangements for them to watch over the pack in case I'm unconscious for a long period of time," he replied.

"Oh. Okay. It looked like you were having a debate with yourself," I chuckled.

"Nope. Just a debate with them. You do realize that the next full moon is tomorrow night, don't you?" he asked.

"Oh wow, I didn't. That's actually great news. At least we don't have to wait another month," I laughed.

"I don't think I could wait another month," he chuckled. "Tristan will watch over the pack until I can take over again. We can do the ceremony tomorrow night. I was thinking that we could have my dad and Terry watch over us while we perform the ceremony. That way they can bring us back to the pack house if we don't wake up right away. Is that alright with you?"

"That's fine with me. Although, my parents are not going to be happy about not being there," I replied.

"Ok, so maybe we have your parents, my parents, Terry, and Karen. Everyone else stays here in the pack house. Sound good?" he asked.

"Yeah, that sounds great," I agreed. "Just think, this time tomorrow we will be joined, and we can finally mark each other and complete the mating bond."

"I can hardly wait, sweetheart," he replied. "Once we wake up, I want us to go somewhere, just the two of us. I want to make everything special."

"Where do you want to go?" I asked.

"It's a surprise," he replied.

"Good thing I love surprises," I giggled.

"Good thing, indeed. Now, let's get some sleep. Tomorrow is going to be a very busy day."

I set the book on my nightstand, making sure to mark the page. I then crawled under the covers and snuggled up to my mate. He wrapped his arms around me and held me close as I laid my head on his chest, listening to his heartbeat. I slowly began to relax and close my eyes.

"I love you, Jaxon," I whispered quietly.

"I love you, sweetheart. Sleep well," he murmured, kissing my head softly. I couldn't wait for the next day.

CHAPTER THIRTY-THREE

Tristan

Jaxon and Isabella returned from their trip last night. After Jaxon told me all about Red Moon's Beta showing up at Blackwood, I decided that it might be best to wait until morning to tell him what the rogue said. I was afraid Jaxon would lose it, kill the rogue, and go hunt down the others.

I told Robert that I would speak to Jaxon this morning and fill him in on everything. I mind-linked him and asked him to meet me in his office before breakfast so we could talk. I waited for about ten minutes before he finally walked in.

"What's going on, Tristan?" he asked immediately.

"We found out some new information yesterday. We wanted to tell you last night but decided that it might be best if we waited and gave you some time to cool down," I started.

"I get the feeling that I'm about to be really pissed off," he sighed.

"That might be an understatement. I had a theory yesterday that I ran past Nikolas. He agrees with me and is going to start investigating. I think that Red Moon has someone on the inside at the council.

That is the only logical explanation for the records being so different." I told him.

"Okay, sounds logical to me. This isn't what's going to piss me off, is it?" he stated.

"No. Cameron had a theory that the rogue that attacked Bella was working for someone. We know that you can't use your Alpha command on him because he's a rogue and Council elders are not subject to that rule, so we asked Nikolas to use his Alpha command on the rogue in the cells. He's part of a group of rogues staking out our territory. There are at least six groups, each with about ten rogues," I hesitated before I continued, "They were hired by Red Moon."

"What?" he asked quietly. *Oh shit.* Quiet was not a good thing.

"Nikolas doesn't know who your mate is or that she was the one attacked. We told him that the female that was attacked was Evie's best friend. He does not know about Bella. The rogue doesn't know who she is either," I quickly spit out.

Everything was quiet for a few minutes while Jaxon stood there breathing hard and shaking. I didn't say a word. I knew he was on the verge of shifting. If his wolf took over completely, things were going to get ugly.

The next thing I knew, the door flew open, and Bella came rushing in. She ran up to Jaxon and wrapped her arms around him. She held him tight, rubbing her hands up and down his back and whispered to him. It must have worked because he stopped shaking and wrapped his arms around her, pulling her tightly to him.

"What on earth did you say to him, Tristan?" she demanded.

Jaxon answered her before I could speak. "The rogue that attacked you in the club, was hired by Red Moon. There are at least sixty of them spying on our pack."

Bella was stunned. She stood there for a minute, not saying anything. Then she quietly asked, "It's my fault, isn't it?"

"What? No, not at all!" Jaxon exclaimed.

"Bella, that rogue didn't even know who you were. This is not your fault. He was there that night because our pack was there. Nikolas commanded him to tell us why he attacked you, he doesn't remember attacking you. He has no clue why he did it. Nikolas believes that someone commanded him to attack you. Whether you were chosen at random or not, we won't know until we find out who commanded him. Either way, this is not your fault," I explained.

"Does Nikolas have any idea who could have commanded him?" Jaxon asked.

"No. Only an elder has the power to command rogues. The thought of an elder aiding rogues and commanding them to attack innocent people... I just can't imagine it," I admitted. "Nikolas said he would do whatever he can to find out who did this. I know we have been keeping him in the dark about a lot of things, but I think maybe it's time to tell him who Bella is."

"I think you might be right. However, this is something we need to talk about first," Jaxon sighed.

"I understand. I'll leave you two alone," I smiled softly at Bella.

"No, stay Tristan. You're my Beta and I trust your opinion," Jaxon told me.

"What are you thinking?" Bella whispered.

"I'm thinking that we need a vacation," he laughed. "How do you feel about Nikolas knowing who you really are?"

"Well, if it was anyone else, I would say no way in hell. However, this is Terry's uncle we're talking about. I trust Terry with my life. He saved my life. If he trusts Nikolas, so do I," she told him.

"Tristan, what are your thoughts on this?"

"I think Bella's right. Nikolas is probably one of the most honest men I've ever met. He knew Michael and Elizabeth, worked with them some. He took their deaths hard. All of the council did. Plus, he agrees with us about Red Moon being the ones who attacked Blackwood."

"Then I guess we need to have a meeting with everyone so we can tell Nikolas and make sure that we all know all of the information and are all on the same page." Jaxon sighed.

"Sounds good to me. But first, let's go eat breakfast. I'm starving," she said.

We left Jaxon's office and headed down to the dining room for breakfast. Because of our chat, almost everyone else had already finished and left.

"Tristan, after you finish breakfast, please let everyone in our little group know that we would like to meet with them in Jaxon's office at nine-thirty. Please inform Nikolas that we would like for him to join us at ten," Bella requested.

"I'll make sure they are all there," I replied.

"Thank you. I think we should let everyone else know what we are planning on doing, that way if anyone has any objections, we can hear them out," Jaxon said.

"Sounds good. I'll go track everyone down now. See you in a bit."

CHAPTER THIRTY-FOUR

Jaxon

Isabella and I headed up to my office to wait on everyone. Instead of doing something productive, we curled up on the couch and got comfortable. We didn't have to wait long before everyone else showed up. Isabella and I stood up and greeted them as they walked in. I walked around and took a seat behind my desk and waited as my mate pulled a chair over to sit next to me.

"Thanks for meeting with us. I know we've been crazy busy lately, but I wanted to go over a few things with everyone," I began. "I spoke with Tristan this morning and he filled me in on everything that happened yesterday with Nikolas and the rogue. Isabella, Tristan, and I talked it over, and we think it's time to tell Nikolas who she is, not just my mate, but a Blackwood as well. However, we wanted to hear from you all first."

Everyone was quiet for a few moments, obviously thinking over what I had just said. I pulled Isabella closer to me, resting my head on her shoulder. She leaned back against me, completely at ease.

"Well, I for one think it's a great idea. Nikolas is a good man, who has proven himself and his loyalty since he arrived. I have no problem with him knowing," my father broke the silence. Everyone else nodded their heads in agreement.

"I agree. I know I am slightly biased because he is my uncle, but Bella has always come first for me. Her father was my best friend, and she is like a daughter to me. I would never do anything to put her life in danger. I think Nikolas can help us with everything that is happening. Especially when it comes to Red Moon," Terry agreed.

"Any objections?" I asked. When no one spoke up, I continued. "Good, because Nikolas is meeting us here in a few minutes. Now, does anyone have any ideas on how to handle the rogues we have watching our pack?"

We spent the next ten minutes discussing the rogues and what we should do. We couldn't agree on a plan. Some wanted to attack the rogues and kill them all—that would be Cameron and me. Some wanted to capture them—Terry and my dad. Some thought we should leave them alone for now and not give away any hints that we knew what was going on—all of the women. Nikolas knocked on the door interrupting our discussion. Tristan opened the door letting him in.

"Thank you for joining us, Nikolas," I greeted him.

"Of course, Jaxon. I understand Tristan filled you in on what happened yesterday?" he replied.

"Yes, he did. Thank you for your help. I'd like for you to meet someone," I said, standing up and gesturing for Isabella to join me. We walked around my desk and stood next to Terry and my father.

"Nikolas, this is the woman who was attacked by the rogue in the cells. Her name is Isabella Greyson, and she is my mate," I explained.

"It is a pleasure to meet you, Ms. Greyson. I have had the pleasure of meeting your parents several times, but never you," he said, shaking Isabella's hand. He stared at her, his brow creased, as if trying to solve a puzzle.

"It's a pleasure to meet you as well, Nikolas," Isabella replied.

"We have another confession for you, Nikolas. Once you hear this, I think you will understand our need for secrecy. Isabella, would you like to tell him?" I asked.

"Actually Jaxon, I was thinking I should handle this one," Terry broke in. Isabella nodded her head and motioned for Terry to continue.

"Uncle, remember when you called me to investigate the attack on Blackwood?" he nodded his head, waiting for me to continue. "I told you that we didn't find any survivors. I lied. I found a survivor, Bella. Karen, James, and Donna were the only ones I told. Karen because I couldn't lie to my mate and James and Donna because they adopted her. The council never knew anything because I told them that everyone at Blackwood died. No one made the connection. Isabella is the daughter of Michael and Elizabeth Blackwood and the Alpha of the Blackwood Pack," Terry finished.

Nikolas sat in silence, a stunned look on his face. We all sat and waited to see what his reaction would be once the shock wore off. After a couple of minutes, a look of wonder and excitement crossed his face, causing him to break out in a huge grin.

"Blackwood. All these years we have been without our warriors. We thought you were all dead. It's amazing. I can hardly believe it! May I see your wolf, dear?" Nikolas responded at last. Isabella giggled and nodded her head. She stepped away from me to an open space in the room and quickly shifted into her wolf.

Nikolas sat down in the chair next to him, shaking his head and grinning. Isabella shifted back and walked back over to me. Nikolas grinned even bigger.

"May I ask a rather personal question?"

"I have a feeling I know what you are going to ask, but by all means ask away." I shrugged.

"Why have you not completed the mating bond?" Nikolas inquired.

"Because I am Alpha of this pack and Isabella is Alpha of Blackwood. We needed to be certain what would happen once we did. It would be rather obvious if my wolf was suddenly the rather distinctive Blackwood midnight blue, don't you think?" I answered.

"Yes, of course. I didn't think of that. Do you have any idea what will happen?" he asked.

"We do now. We did some research and managed to find some

information on the subject," I answered truthfully, without telling him about the book. I didn't want anyone else knowing about it just yet. Especially since we hadn't read the entire thing.

"I am shocked. In a good way, of course. And I can assure you both, everyone here, that you have my support, my trust, my loyalty, and my silence. What I have learned here today shall never pass my lips without your permission," he vowed.

"Thank you, Nikolas. Isabella and I both appreciate it. Now, I think we should all have the rest of the day off. We've been running ourselves ragged these last few days. We can pick back up tomorrow. Agreed?" I asked.

"Agreed," they all replied.

CHAPTER THIRTY-FIVE

Jagger

"Kade, do you have the reports from the rogue teams?" I asked.

"Yes, Alpha. I have them right here," he responded, picking up a file from his desk. He walked across the hall to my office and handed it to me.

"Have you gone over them yet?"

"I have. Only a few things to report. There was a visitor to the pack, but they haven't been able to determine who he is. He hasn't been spotted outside since he arrived. The rogues asked for permission to cross the borders to determine who he is, I told them no. I believe it is Elder Nikolas from the council. He left the council on the same day the visitor arrived. Plus, his nephew is there, Alpha Terry," Kade replied.

"Makes sense. What do we know about Elder Nikolas?"

"He is the head of the council. Very strict. Not one to break rules. Our man in the council says he is untouchable. His family has always been the head of the council."

"Find out if he took anything with him to Dark Sky. Files, reports, anything. How often are the rogues checking in?"

"Will do. Once a week. Why?" he asked.

"Have they said anything else?"

"Only that one rogue is missing. Went to the Halloween party that Dark Sky threw and never came back," he reported.

"And you didn't think that was important enough to tell me right away?" I growled. I was surrounded by idiots.

"Rogues go missing all the time. They're rogues," he shrugged.

"Don't you think that they could have captured him? Did that cross your tiny little mind? Who was the rogue?"

"I didn't think of that. Steven, from Fire Stone," he said.

"He's the one that attacked the Beta's mate, right?"

"Yeah. Still doesn't know he was commanded," he chuckled.

"Commanded? By who?"

"My secret weapon," he smirked.

"And that would be?" I asked, growing more and more frustrated with my Beta.

"My brother. A council elder," he revealed.

CHAPTER THIRTY-SIX

Jaxon

I asked my dad and Terry to stay back while everyone else headed out for the day. It was time to tell them that we are going to perform the ceremony that night during the full moon.

As soon as everyone left, I closed the door and locked it so we wouldn't be interrupted. This was not a conversation I wanted everyone knowing about.

"What's going on, Jaxon?" Terry asked.

"You know the full moon is tonight?" I asked. They both nodded their heads and waited for me to continue.

"Isabella and I are going to perform the bonding ceremony tonight during the full moon. We would like for you two to join us and keep watch over us as we will probably lose consciousness and we aren't sure how long we will be out. Isabella and I talked about having mom and her parents join us as well, but I don't think that's such a good idea now. I plan on speaking to Tristan later and having him take over in my place until it's over," I explained.

Terry and my dad both looked back and forth from us to each other several times, almost like they were shocked by what I'd said. Not sure why. They knew that we had found the book and the ceremony. I guess the timing was pretty quick, but it's just the way it worked out with the full moon being tonight.

"What do you need us to do, son?" my dad asked.

"We're going to a clearing in the woods tonight around eleven. I'm going to change the patrol routes to keep everyone away. I want the patrols tripled to make sure that the rogues don't get anywhere near us while we're doing this. The last thing we need is Red Moon finding out who Isabella is. I need you guys to keep watch over us while we do the ceremony. It should only take a few minutes. We know that we will lose consciousness, the book tells us that much. It doesn't say how long we will be out. If we are out for more than five minutes, I need you to bring us back to the pack house. I'll have the pack doctor on standby. He won't know what's going on, just that he might be needed. If we have to go there, you tell him that he is to monitor us and nothing else until we wake up. I don't want anything interfering with the ceremony. I don't want anyone else knowing what we're doing tonight. Just you two and Tristan. No need for everyone else to worry. Any questions?" I asked them.

"No, I think that just about covers it. You're going to talk to Tristan after lunch?" my dad asked. I nodded. "I would like to make one suggestion. Perhaps you would consider having Grant and Thomas with us while we watch over you. Just in case. I know the rogues haven't gotten through our patrol lines, but with the patrols upped tonight, they're going to know that something is happening. They'll want to find out what that something is. I know Terry and I can handle ourselves, but we have no idea how many rogues could try to cross. Grant and Thomas are our best warriors, next to Calum but I don't think you want to have him involved. Too many questions will be asked if you bring the head warrior in at this point. However, having Grant and Thomas there as a precaution is a good idea."

"I think that would be a good idea as well," Isabella spoke up.

"Fine, we'll include them as well. I'll have them sit in on my meeting with Tristan. Anything else?" I asked.

"No, I think we're all pretty clear on what's happening," Terry stated.

"Good, let's go eat some lunch then," I said.

After lunch, I asked Tristan to get Grant and Thomas and meet me in my office.

Tristan informed me that Grant and Thomas were on the training grounds and would meet us in my office in a few minutes, so we went upstairs to wait for them. When they arrived, I greeted them and got ready to tell the story again. "Thanks for meeting with us. You guys are going to hear some things in the next few minutes that cannot be repeated to anyone outside this office, understood?" I asked.

"Yes, Alpha," they both replied.

"First, I want to thank you both for watching out for Isabella. She is my mate and your Luna, and you both have done an excellent job of keeping her safe. We both appreciate that," I began. They both started to say something, but I cut them off.

I held my hand up. "Let me finish first. Isabella is special. Not just because she is my mate and your Luna. Isabella is the last of the Black-wood Warriors. To be more specific, she is the daughter of the last Blackwood Alpha and Luna, which makes her Blackwood's Alpha. We all know what happened to Blackwood. The council doesn't even know that she survived. Terry found her and lied to everyone to protect her. We have been doing some research lately and believe that Red Moon is responsible for the attack on her pack. That makes their presence at the Blackwood pack house even more suspect. The reason we went to Blackwood was to search the pack house for a book. This book contains the history of Blackwood and the ceremony necessary for Isabella and I to be able to mate without me losing my pack and causing all of you to become rogues. We found the book and the cere-mony and will be performing the ceremony tonight on the full moon. We need for you to help watch over Isabella and I while we do this. The ceremony will cause us to lose consciousness. We aren't sure for how long, but my father and Terry will both be there with you. Any questions?"

Grant and Thomas both stood there with their mouths open in shock. It was really quite funny. I couldn't help but chuckle at their expressions. Thomas recovered before Grant did.

"Holy shit! Are you serious?" he exclaimed.

I looked over at Isabella and nodded to her. She grinned and then shifted into her midnight blue wolf. Grant stumbled backwards until he fell into a chair. Hard. Isabella's wolf made a snorting noise that sounded like she was laughing. It caused the rest of us to crack up laughing as well, Grant included. She then shifted back and walked over, taking a seat.

"Dude. That is the coolest thing I have ever seen!" Grant shouted, before turning red and staring at the floor in embarrassment. We all chuckled again. "Sorry, Luna," he mumbled.

"It's ok, Grant. Please, call me Isabella or Bella," she giggled.

"No can do, Luna. It is against warrior's code to call our Alpha or Luna by their first name," Grant explained. Isabella just sighed and nodded.

"Now, Tristan. I am going to need you to watch over the pack for me. Like I explained before, Isabella and I will lose consciousness. While I'm out, I need for you to take over Alpha duties and keep the pack together. We don't know if the pack will be able to feel anything during or after the ceremony, but I suspect they will. I need you to be here to keep them calm if that happens. Also, I want you to up the patrols starting now. I want to triple the number we have out there now. We'll be doing the ceremony tonight sometime before midnight at the small clearing in the woods near the pack house. I want everyone to stay away from there. Patrol needs to be extra vigilant tonight in case the rogues try to cross the border. There is a good chance that they will once they see we have upped the patrols. They'll know that something is going on and will want to find out what it is. That cannot happen. Grant and Thomas will be there with my dad and Terry in case anything happens. Understood?" I asked.

"Understood, Alpha. I'll take care of the patrols right away. Anything else?" Tristan asked.

"No that's it. We don't want everyone worrying tonight. If there is nothing else, Isabella and I are going to go rest before tonight. Mind-link me if you need anything," I replied.

"Yes, Alpha."

CHAPTER THIRTY-SEVEN

Isabella

After lunch, Jaxon and I went upstairs to rest for a while before the ceremony. We knew that it would take a lot out of us, but we didn't know how much, and we didn't really know what to expect. I was slightly nervous about the fact that we would be unconscious. More so that Jaxon would be unconscious than me. He was Alpha to a pack. A large pack that would definitely miss their Alpha if he was gone for an extended period of time.

"What are you thinking about?" Jaxon asked me.

"The ceremony. Wondering how long we will be out and if your pack will feel anything," I admitted.

"Stop worrying. Everything will be fine. If they do feel anything, Tristan can handle it," he told me, pulling me closer to him. "Now, let's get some rest. After dinner we can hang out with our families and friends."

Knowing he was right, I snuggled up closer to him and closed my eyes. I felt my body relax and the tension leave just from being close to him. I couldn't wait until we were able to complete our bond. Soon, all coherent thought left my mind, and I embraced the slumber that was calling to me.

I could feel Jaxon's fingers trail up and down my arm. I kept my eyes closed and my breath even. I just enjoyed having my mate close to me with no interruptions.

"I know you're awake, sweetheart," he whispered, kissing me softly.

I opened my eyes, looked up at him, and smiled. He was gorgeous. Absolutely breathtaking. I couldn't believe how lucky I was to have him.

Jaxon and I laid there for a few more minutes, just enjoying each other's company. After a while though, we had to get up to join everyone for dinner. We made it downstairs just as everyone was entering the dining room.

After dinner, we all headed up to the game rooms. My parents and Jaxon's parents were playing cards with Terry and Karen. Cameron and Kayleigh were having a rowdy game of air hockey. Tristan and Evie were sitting next to the fireplace.

As I watched everyone interact, I couldn't help but feel happy. My friends and family all in one place. Everyone I loved. I was so blessed.

After a few hours, my parents headed off to bed. Karen followed soon after, as well as Evie, Cameron, and Kayleigh. Kathleen finally headed up to bed around ten-thirty. That just left Robert, Terry, Jaxon, Tristan, and me.

We decided to head downstairs to wait for Grant and Thomas. Once we arrived at the living room, we sat on the couches and made small talk until they got there.

After the two warriors showed up, Jaxon and I left them for a few minutes to go change and grab the book as well as some flashlights and a knife. After changing, we headed back downstairs to meet up with the others.

Tristan stood up as we walked into the room. "You guys should probably head out. I am going to wait here in case anyone comes downstairs. The doctor is waiting in the medical center. Anything else?" he asked nervously.

"No, Tristan. Don't worry so much. Everything will be fine," I assured him with a smile.

Jaxon spoke to Tristan for a few minutes and then we all headed out to the clearing. It was only a ten-minute walk from the pack house. When we arrived, the full moon was high in the sky.

"Ok, Grant and Thomas, I want each of you to patrol the perimeter of the clearing in wolf form. Dad and Terry, you two stay just outside of the clearing until the ceremony is over. Do not enter the clearing for at least five minutes after we have lost consciousness. Everyone clear?" Jaxon ordered.

"Yes, Alpha," Grant and Thomas responded.

Jaxon turned to me and held out his hand. "It's time, sweetheart," he grinned. I smiled and took it as we walked into the clearing. We set the book and flashlights down in the center when we arrived.

"You ready?" I asked quietly.

"I have never been more ready, sweetheart," he replied.

The full moon was high in the sky, providing plenty of light especially with our enhanced vision. I looked up at Jaxon and saw that he was smiling down at me. I couldn't help but grin back, I was excited, and the anticipation was overwhelming. We were finally going to do this. The ceremony, marking, mating. It was finally happening. I just hoped that we won't be unconscious for very long.

"Let's do this," I grinned at him.

Jaxon and I knelt on the ground next to the book. I opened it to the correct page and placed it between us. Jaxon picked up the knife and held his hand out, waiting. He looked at me and I nodded my head for him to begin. He pressed the knife across his right palm and quickly swiped it across, cutting the skin. As the blood in Jaxon's hand began to well up, I took the knife from him and quickly cut my left palm. I knew it would hurt so I made sure to keep my face from showing my pain. Once our palms were cut, we pressed them together and Jaxon began speaking.

"I, Alpha Jaxon Oliver Daniels, pledge myself to my pack, Dark

Sky, and to Blackwood as the mate to Alpha Alexandra Isabella Blackwood Greyson. I pledge to protect my packs and my mate and to honor them before all others. I pledge to give my pack-members the choice to join Blackwood freely or to leave to another pack when the time comes. I pledge to help them find another pack if they so choose. I promise to be strong and loyal and defend those who need defending. I promise to be just, honorable, and worthy of the Blackwood name," Jaxon proclaimed.

"I, Alpha Alexandra Isabella Blackwood Greyson, of Blackwood Pack, pledge to protect my mate, Alpha Jaxon Oliver Daniels, and his pack, Dark Sky. I promise to let them join Blackwood or help them find a new pack. I promise to be strong, loyal, just, honorable, and worthy of the Blackwood name," I read aloud.

As soon as I finished speaking, I began to feel a burning sensation in my hand. My first instinct was to jerk my hand back, but I couldn't, it was like our hands were fused together. I looked up at Jaxon's face and saw him grimace. I knew that he was feeling the same burning sensation I was, only stronger. The burning soon spread up my arm and throughout my entire body. I could feel Jaxon shaking and hear his grunts of pain, but I couldn't respond to him. The fire soon erupted in my body causing me to scream out. Jaxon growled loudly when I screamed, but his growls soon turned into a scream of his own.

Soon after, I could feel that the fire began to die down in my body. My screaming stopped and I was able to focus on Jaxon. He was still upright on his knees, but only because our hands were still joined. I was panting, completely exhausted, when the final flames licked through my body catching me off guard. I threw my head back and screamed louder than before. I'm not sure how long the pain lasted but it felt like hours. I lost consciousness before it ended, my final thoughts centered on my mate.

CHAPTER THIRTY-EIGHT

Terry

Once Jaxon and Bella stepped into the clearing, the moon seemed to glow even brighter and the silence surrounding us was unnerving. Robert and I watched them walk to the center of the clearing and kneel down. I briefly saw Bella nod her head at Jaxon. A moment later, I could smell the faint tinge of blood in the air. They had begun the ceremony.

Robert and I watched Bella and Jaxon as the spoke, but their words were too soft for us to hear. I took the time to look at our surroundings, not wanting to lower my guard. Thomas and Grant were two of their best warriors, but I still wasn't taking chances. Sensing Robert stiffen beside me, I quickly returned my attention to the couple in the clearing. Just as I did, Bella screamed out in pain. I went to take a step forward, but Robert grabbed my arm, stopping me in place. Then, I heard Jaxon grunt in pain.

Bella's screams got louder and were quickly followed with Jaxon's. It took everything we had to not enter that clearing. It felt like their screams lasted for hours, but it was only a few minutes. Bella finally stopped screaming and continued to kneel in front of Jaxon, panting. I heard Robert breathe a sigh of relief which didn't last long because only a minute later, Bella threw her head back and screamed even louder than before. Jaxon roared so loudly it shook the ground and caused nearby trees to lose branches.

Suddenly, their screams stopped. We watched them both collapse on the ground. I went to step forward again and Robert grabbed my arm. I looked at him and he shook his head at me.

"Remember what they said. We have to wait at least five minutes before we can enter the clearing," he reminded me.

"Fuck! This is going to be the longest five minutes ever." I grimaced. Robert nodded in agreement.

"Grant and Thomas are making a couple more passes and then heading here. It should be time to go in once they get here," Robert told me. I nodded, not bothering to reply as my attention was focused on Bella and Jaxon.

Robert and I stood there in silence, watching Bella and Jaxon for any sign of movement. By the time the five minutes passed, Grant and Thomas had arrived. We all stepped into the clearing together, not sure what to expect. As soon as we did, the power emanating from the center was overwhelming. As Alphas, Robert and I were able to continue without much trouble. Grant and Thomas however, stumbled and fell to their knees. After a minute, they were able to shake it off and stand up and continue.

Once we reached them, I immediately began to check Bella's vitals as Robert rushed to do the same to Jaxon. Assured that they were both okay, I gently picked Bella up and Thomas helped Robert pick up Jaxon and get him situated over his shoulder. We began to walk back towards the house, Thomas and Grant back in their wolf forms in case we came across any trouble.

Upon reaching the house, Tristan threw open the doors and came rushing out. "Are they ok?" he quickly asked, looking them both over.

"They're fine, Tristan. Just unconscious. Is the pack doctor here?" I asked him.

"Yes, he is in the medical wing waiting for us. Everyone else is in bed or has orders to stay off this floor," he assured me.

"Please place Alpha Jaxon here and Luna Isabella on the bed next to his," Dr. Phillips stated. He didn't bother saying anything else as he began to check their vitals for himself. Once he was finished, he turned to us and motioned for us to sit.

"I'm not sure what is going on or what caused this, but I can tell you that their vitals are good. They seem to just be asleep, almost like a coma. I'll hold off on administering IV fluids until morning. Hopefully they will both wake up and we won't have to do anything. There's nothing else I can do tonight, so I'll leave them with you. Call me if there is any change, otherwise I'll see you in the morning," he told us. I nodded at him and thanked him for helping us. Once he was out the door, I turned and looked at Tristan.

"I told him only what Jaxon wanted me to. That they might come in unconscious and that he was to make sure their vitals were ok and leave it at that, only administering fluids if it became necessary," Tristan explained.

"Ok good. I think that we should take shifts keeping an eye on them. I want one of us with them at all times. Grant and Thomas, you two head to bed and get some sleep. Terry and I will take first watch. Tristan, you take over at six o'clock tomorrow morning. Grant, I want you here to relieve Tristan at noon. Thomas, if necessary, you will take over from Grant at six tomorrow evening. We will keep taking six hour shifts as long as we need to. We tell no one that they are in here. Not even her parents. If they ask, we tell them that Jaxon and Isabella needed a break and decided to head to one of the cabins we have on the property. Nothing else. Understood?" Robert ordered.

Everyone nodded. Tristan, Grant, and Thomas all headed out to get some sleep. After they left, Robert told me he was going to head over to the kitchen and grab us some food and drinks.

When he returned from the kitchen, I was in the same spot, sitting next to Bella, holding her hand. He handed me a sandwich and a water bottle and then sat down in the chair next to me. We both ate our food in silence. After we ate, I grabbed the remote for the TV. I turned it on and found a movie about werewolves playing. I stopped on it and looked over at Robert. He looked up at the tv, turned his head to look at me, and we both cracked up laughing. I finally found something promising on the Discovery channel, Alaska: The Last Frontier. We settled back in our chairs and divided our attention between the show and Jaxon and Bella.

CHAPTER THIRTY-NINE

Tristan

It had been two days since Jaxon and Bella completed their bonding ceremony. Two very long days. They were both still unconscious in the medical wing while the pack thought that they were taking a short break at one of our cabins. That's also what we told the rest of our small group, but they were starting to ask questions.

It was my turn standing watch over Jaxon and Bella, I had just relieved Terry and Robert. I decided to take care of some of the pack paperwork while I was there. I pulled out the files and set everything up on the small table we had brought in. I opened the first file and sighed. I really didn't want to do paperwork, but it had to be done.

An hour later and I was still on the first page. My mind was not on the task at hand. I groaned and stood up, stretching my back. I couldn't sleep at night, my mind wouldn't focus on anything. Well, that wasn't true. It would focus, but only on one thing. Or rather, one person. Evie.

Looking back and Jaxon and Bella, I couldn't help but be a little jealous of what they had. Even knowing the hell that Bella went through in her old pack from that little fuckhead. I wanted what they had. I wanted to have a mate of my own. That one person meant for just me.

Sighing, I ran my hands down my face scrubbing at my eyes. Feeling this way was stupid. I didn't have a mate. I knew that. I could still remember the pain of that moment, the moment I lost her, like it was yesterday. There were times that I wondered what had happened. Did she give up and find someone else? Did she die? And the biggest one of all, why me?

Of course, all these thoughts did was bring me right back to my thoughts of Evie. The one who wouldn't leave my mind. I saw her the morning after the ceremony. She asked me where Bella was, and I told her the cabin story. She just nodded her head and walked away. I hadn't seen her since. I wanted to ask Robert about her, but I didn't want him to become suspicious.

Not that there is anything to be suspicious of. Fuck. Who was I kidding? No one, not even me. My wolf was even calling me an idiot. He thought Evie was our second chance mate. I wasn't so sure. Robert had told me that finding a second chance mate was rare. He said that when you found them, it might not be obvious at first that they are your second chance mate. I'd known Evie my whole life. I just didn't think it was possible.

"That's because you're an idiot," my wolf huffed at me.

"I am not an idiot. What makes you so damn sure that she is our second chance mate?" I grumbled.

"Because I'm not an idiot," he replied.

"Then prove it. Tell me how you know she is our second chance mate. And why now? We have known her our whole life. We lost our mate only a few months after we came of age, it's been years. Why now?" I asked.

"I can't tell you how I know. You have to figure it out on your own. Just give it time. Give her time. She has only known that her mate is gone for a few days, she needs more time," he explained.

"Do you know when she lost her first mate?" I asked him.
"Yes, but I can't tell you. That's something she needs to tell you herself."
"Fine. But I am talking to Robert about this again."
"Be my guest," he replied before shutting me out.

Ever since Robert told me about mates and second chance mates, I'd been waiting for mine. Robert was the one to fill me in on mates since my own parents weren't around. He told me what mates were, how to know when you find your mate, everything. He explained it all and stayed with me when I went to him after feeling the pain of losing my first mate.

I snapped my head at the sound of someone groaning. Checking Jaxon first, I saw that he was still unconscious. I looked over at Bella and noticed that she was moving her head and her eyes were rolling under her eyelids. I quickly mind-linked Robert and told him that she was waking up. I then mind-linked the pack doctor to come, just in case.

Walking over to Bella's side of the bed, I gently took her hand in mine.

"Bella, it's me Tristan. Can you open your eyes for me?" I whispered, not wanting to talk too loudly and startle her. She just groaned again and squeezed my hand. "It's ok, take your time. Jaxon is here beside you. He is still unconscious, but he is fine," I assured her.

After a few long minutes, Bella finally managed to open her eyes and look up at me. I smiled down at her and squeezed her hand.

"It's nice to have you back, Bella," I smiled.

"Th-thanks Tristan," she whispered, trying to clear her throat.

"Hold on, let me get you some water," I gently laid her hand back on the bed and hurried off to get her a drink. Once I got back with the glass, I helped her sit up a bit and take a sip. She quickly drained the glass and asked for another. When I got back with the second glass, Robert and Terry were just walking in the door.

"How are you feeling, Isabella?" Robert asked.

"Like I got hit by a bus. How's Jaxon?" she asked, her voice shaking.

"He's ok. He is still unconscious. The doctor says his vitals look good, he started an IV for him, so he doesn't get dehydrated. We're just waiting for him to wake up," I assured her.

"How long have we been out?" she asked quietly.

"Two days. Two very long days." Terry answered.

CHAPTER FORTY

Isabella

Two days. Wow, I wasn't expecting that. I really thought that we would be out for a few hours at most. My wolf just snorted. It's not like I had anything to go off of. The book didn't exactly give us a specific timeline. I turned my head and looked over at my mate. So close, yet still out of reach. Time to fix that. I tried sitting up on my own, but I wasn't strong enough yet.

"Easy, Bella. You've been out of it for two days, and that's after your body went through some intense pain. Your energy is drained. You need to rest," Terry cautioned me as he helped me sit up.

"I need my mate," I snapped. I immediately felt bad for being rude to Terry. It wasn't his fault, I was just sore, tired, hungry, and grumpy and I really just wanted Jaxon to wake up.

"I'm sorry, Terry. I don't mean to bark at you. I just really need Jaxon right now. Please," I apologized.

"It's ok, Bella. I'll help you," he said. "Tristan, would you ask someone to bring up some food for her? I'm sure she's hungry."

"I'll go downstairs and get it. Any requests?" he asked me.

"No, just food. Thank you, Tristan," I replied. He nodded at me and left the room.

"Isabella, do you want to take a shower first? Your clothes are in the bathroom here," Robert asked.

"Actually, yes. I would love a shower. I'm just worried about standing for that long," I admitted.

"No worries there. This is the medical wing. We have seats in the showers for those who can't stand for very long." Robert chuckled.

"Oh, thank goodness." I laughed.

"Come on, I'll carry you in and help get the water started for you," Terry said. He gently lifted me off the bed and carried me in the bathroom, setting me on the counter. Robert walked in after us and turned the water on for me, adjusting the temperature. While he was doing that, Terry set up a small chair next to the shower stall and set out two towels for me.

"Water is ready. Take your time. If you need anything, just let us know. The doctor's office is just a couple of doors down and he has a couple of females that help him out in the clinic. We can get one of them here to help you. Males too but I doubt you or Jaxon would appreciate that," Robert told me. Terry and I both chuckled.

"Thank you both. I should be fine," I smiled. Terry picked me up off the counter and set me on the chair so I wouldn't have to walk so far. I thanked them both and they nodded before walking out the door and giving me some privacy.

I sat in the chair and pulled off my socks and my shirt before standing up. Once I got my balance, I quickly pulled off the rest of my clothes off and stepped into the shower. The hot water cascading down my body brought me instant relief. I could feel the soreness and tiredness being washed away. I tilted my head back and let the water flow over my head. I held onto the handle on the wall and closed my eyes, relishing the heat as it soothed my aching muscles.

Knowing that my newfound strength wouldn't last long, I quickly washed my body. As I rinsed the soap off, I began to feel weak again. I sat down on the seat before I fell. Once I was sure that I wasn't going to pass out, I grabbed the shampoo and lathered up my hair, scrubbing my scalp and working the suds down to the tips. I rinsed the shampoo and repeated the process with the conditioner. I tilted my head back again and began to rinse the conditioner out. I took my time, not wanting to have greasy hair.

After getting dressed, I went back out into the medical room. Robert and Terry were sitting in the chairs next to Jaxon's bed. I walked over and climbed up on the bed next to him. The two men just watched as I laid my head on his chest, closed my eyes, and breathed his scent in. Knowing he would be okay calmed my wolf down and me as well. I hated that I was unconscious for so long, but I hated even more that he was still unconscious.

I looked up when someone knocked on the door. Robert stood up and opened it, letting Tristan in the room. He had a tray of food that smelled heavenly.

"Hope you like chicken and dumplings, Bella. I have a big bowl for you, a salad, roll, cheesecake, a glass of water, and because I'm so awesome I also brought you a Dr. Pepper." Tristan grinned.

"You *are* awesome, Tristan. Now give me my food before I chew your arm off!" I laughed.

I could tell that they were all relieved that I was awake, but we were all still worried about Jaxon. Tristan set the tray on the bed in front of me and I immediately dug in. I couldn't help the moan that slipped out. I was so hungry I didn't do anything more than glare at the guys when they laughed at me.

"I really need to hug this cook of yours. She's amazing." I groaned, leaning back on the pillows, and rubbing my full belly.

"She'd love to hear that. She's been with us since before I was born," Robert chuckled.

"How old is she?" I asked.

"I think she just turned ninety-seven, so she's definitely no spring chicken. Still looks like she is in her fifties, though. Not sure how she manages it. I know we live longer than normal humans, but she's something special," He replied. I was shocked. Even Terry looked surprised.

"That's incredible. I'd love to meet her," Terry stated.

"I'm sure we can set something up," Robert grinned.

We sat there quietly for a little while, each wrapped in our own thoughts. I was kind of surprised when a yawn slipped out. You'd think after two days of sleeping, I wouldn't be tired.

"You should probably get some rest, Isabella," Robert said quietly.

"You'd think two days would be enough rest," I complained.

"Apparently not," Terry chuckled. "Get some rest. We'll be here when you wake up."

I nodded my head and laid down next to Jaxon, curling up as close as I could. Before long, my eyes closed, and I drifted off to sleep.

I wasn't sure how long I was out. I could barely remember falling asleep. I could feel someone brush the hair out of my face. Knowing Robert, Terry, and Tristan wouldn't touch me, especially not while I was sleeping, I had a small moment of panic. I snapped my eyes open and was overwhelmed with relief when I saw who was staring back at me.

"Hello, sweetheart. Sleep well?"

CHAPTER FORTY-ONE

Jaxon

"Jaxon," she murmured, throwing her arms around me. "I was so worried."

"Shh. It's alright, sweetheart. I'm fine."

"Are you? Was it awful? Do you regret it? I'm so sorry," she whimpered.

Pulling back, I placed a soft kiss on her lips to quiet her rambling. "I'm fine. It wasn't awful. Nothing that allows me to be with you could ever be awful, nor could I regret it. So, stop apologizing."

"I just feel so terrible that you were out so long. Your pack!" she gasped.

"Our pack, and they are fine. Tristan made sure everything was taken care of," I assured her.

"Speaking of that handsome devil," Tristan smirked, poking his head through the door, "I have food for you."

"Oh fuck off, you idiot," I chuckled.

I ate my food as quickly as possible, probably looking like a pig. It's amazing what two days of unconsciousness could do to a person. I was starving, my whole body ached, and all I wanted to do was hold Isabella and sleep for another two days.

Tristan whisked my tray away as soon as I was finished.

"Feel better?" Isabella asked.

"Much. Although I probably smell like the south end of a north bound rhino right now," I grimaced.

"Well, you definitely don't smell like roses."

"Thanks." I mock glared at her.

"We have a change of clothes for you in the bathroom if you want to shower. I can help you," my dad offered.

"I can do it."

"Don't be an idiot. You'll need the help." Isabella muttered a whisper. "Terry had to help me into the bathroom."

"You sure?" my dad asked. "I don't mind."

"On second thought, maybe I could use the help. I'm not feeling a hundred percent right now."

Dad helped me to the bathroom and got the shower going for me. After he stepped out, I stripped my clothes off and stood under the hot water until I felt my strength begin to wane. Sitting down on the chair, I washed my body and my hair, scrubbing away the last two days of filth. I rinsed off, got out of the shower, and dried off and dressed as quickly as I could manage. When I opened the door and leaned against the door jam, Dad rushed over to help me.

"You want to stay here or go upstairs?" he asked.

"Upstairs, but I think I need a few minutes first," I admitted.

"Let's get you back on the bed then. You can rest for a bit and then we will help you guys back upstairs," dad replied. "We'll go make sure there's no one around."

Once on the bed, I pulled Isabella close to me and breathed her in. It helped my wolf and I relax, something he hadn't done since we'd met our mate. The ceremony bonded us in a way that few would ever experience and, for now at least, that was enough for him.

"What are you thinking?" Isabella murmured, bringing me out of my thoughts.

"How relaxed my wolf is right now. He's been a pain in my ass since we met, always urging me to mark and mate you," I chuckled. "Right now, he's as content as can be. I think this ceremony made him realize that we aren't going to lose you if we don't mark you right freaking now."

She giggled. "My wolf is pretty content, too."

I loved the sound of that little laugh. Pulling her closer, I leaned down and placed a gentle kiss on her lips. Of course, that's never enough for us. Her hand snaked up and around, cupping the back of my neck to hold me in place. Our lips parted and at the first taste of her I groaned, deepening the kiss. My hand skimmed down her body, slipping under her shirt. Just as I did, the door opened, and Tristan walked in.

"Whoa! Holy shit! Wasn't expecting that," he shouted, turning around. Isabella tried to pull back, but I wouldn't let her. Instead, I grabbed her pillow and chucked it at him, nailing him in the back of the head.

He just laughed and left the room. "Let me know when you're ready."

I couldn't believe Tristan interrupted us. Talk about shitty timing. And then he just laughed about it. He knew what he had interrupted. He'd better be glad he was my Beta and best friend, otherwise I'd kick his ass.

"Sorry about that, Jaxon." Tristan mind-linked me.

"Shut up. I hate you," I growled back. He just laughed in my head.

"I don't blame you. But do you really want the first time to be in the medical wing?" he replied.

"Still mad. How is the pack?"

"Everything is good. The pack started to get antsy after the first day, they could feel that you were disconnected from us. I kept everyone together and assured them that you were fine and would be back soon. We stuck with the vacation story," he informed me.

"I knew I could trust you. Good job and thank you. Any more concerns or issues with the rogues?"

"You're welcome. We haven't had any more rogues cross the borders into our territory, but patrols have reported scenting them close to the borders in several spots to the north and east," he said.

"Ok, sounds like they are keeping their distance for now. That's good. We shouldn't let our guard down though. Speaking of vacation, I want to take Isabella away for a few days. I don't want to be interrupted again," I grumbled.

"I said sorry! Where do you want to go? Do you need me to set anything up?" he asked.

"We have the beach house on the Oregon coast, I think I will take her there. It's cold this time of year, but maybe we will get lucky and catch a storm coming in. I bet she would love that. Make sure our local person stops by tomorrow morning and cleans it up and stocks the fridge. I want candles, flowers, chocolate, the whole nine yards. I want everything to be perfect," I instructed him.

"Consider it done, your majesty. Anything else?" he chuckled.

"Still hating you, remember?" I growled. He just laughed.

I looked up to see my beautiful mate staring at me. I guess that conversation took longer than I thought.

"Everything alright, sweetheart?" I asked.

"Of course. Were you talking to Tristan?" she replied.

"Yes. Just checking up on the pack and making sure that everything went smoothly while we were unconscious," I told her.

"I think we should head up to our room now, before someone else walks in on us."

"Probably a good idea. I'll ask my dad to come help us."

I linked my dad and asked him and Terry to come help us upstairs. He told us they would be right there.

My dad made sure that no one was in the hallway before helping me up. Terry held the door open for us and we left the medical room and headed to the elevator. We managed to make it up to our room without anyone seeing us, which was a very good thing.

Once we were in our room, my dad helped me to the bed and then bid us goodnight and left. Too tired to do anything else, I asked Isabella to help me take my clothes off so we could go to bed. She pulled off my shirt and I laid back and lifted my hips so she could take my pajama pants off as well.

"Well, I never thought I would undress you the first time, just for you to pass out on me," she teased as I climbed under the covers and sighed in relief.

"Oh, hush you. Now get in here and cuddle me," I yawned.

She climbed under the covers and scooted up next to me so I could wrap my arms around her. She rested her head on chest and sighed contentedly.

CHAPTER FORTY-TWO

Jaxon

Waking up in my own bed next to Isabella was, by far, one of the great joys of my life. I didn't have to open my eyes to know that she was still asleep. Her head on my chest, an arm over my waist, and her legs tangled with mine. I could feel her breath blowing gently across my skin. Her heartbeat was slow and steady.

Opening my eyes, I look down at her beautiful face. Her long lashes brushing the tops of her cheeks. Her hair splayed out like a halo around her head. Her lips slightly parted, making me want to kiss them. The only thing that could ruin the moment was the little puddle of drool on my chest. I couldn't help but chuckle. The shaking of my chest caused her to stir in protest and groan.

"Staring isn't nice," she grumbled.

"Neither is drooling," I chuckled. She snapped her head up and looked at my chest in horror. Letting out a little shriek, she wiped at my chest with the sheet and then buried her head under the covers, but not before I saw her red cheeks. I threw my head back and laughed loudly at her actions.

"I didn't say I minded, sweetheart," I laughed.

"Shut up!" she whined, still hiding from me.

"Oh, come on. It's not that bad. Come out, I was only teasing." I chuckled again.

"No. I am never coming out. Go away and leave me here to hide," she whined.

Before I could say anything else, her stomach decided to make its presence known. We both started laughing.

"Go take a shower really quick. When you are done, I'll take one and then we can go get something to eat. Don't want that monster getting out!" I chuckled.

"Oh hush! Pick me out something to wear, please," she replied, rolling out of bed, and heading for the shower.

I got up and walked into Isabella's closet to find her something to wear. Knowing she would probably still have sore muscles, because I sure as hell did, I picked out what I hoped would be comfortable for her. Once I finished with the outfit, I decided to be extra helpful and pick out her undergarments as well. I found the drawer with her panties and almost decided to go join my little mate in the shower. Some of them were sexy as hell. I finally decided on a pair of black and gray lace ones. I looked in her bra drawer and managed to find a matching one. Looked like my shower was going to be a cold one.

As soon as Isabella came out of the bathroom, I hurried in to take my shower, asking her to choose some clothes for me. I took the quickest shower possible. After drying off, I went back to the room and dressed as Isabella went to do her hair and makeup before heading downstairs.

As we got closer to the dining room, I could feel Isabella's nervousness. I stopped and pulled her to me, assuring her that everything would be fine.

We walked through the door, and everyone immediately stopped talking and turned to stare at us. Even I began to get nervous at the attention.

"Nice to have you back Alpha, Luna."

This sentiment was repeated in different forms many times over.

"Thank you, everyone. It's good to be back. I know this trip was unexpected, but it was necessary. Isabella and I went to negotiate with another pack. I know you were told that we were gone on a personal trip, but that is not the case. We simply didn't want anyone to worry about what was going on. The trip went great, everything was a success. I want to thank Tristan for stepping up and handling things while we were gone. He did a great job. Now that I have talked longer than I intended, please get back to whatever you were doing," I announced.

Everyone smiled and you could tell that they were relieved that nothing was wrong. I didn't tell them the truth, but it wasn't necessarily a lie either. Technically Isabella was from another pack. After finishing our breakfast, we headed upstairs to my office to meet with Tristan, Cameron, our parents, Terry, and Karen.

Isabella and I got to my office before everyone else. I decided to take advantage of the privacy and let her in on a little secret. I sat down in my chair and watched as she walked over to the window.

"Come here, sweetheart. I want to talk to you about something." I patted my lap for her to sit down. She walked over and sat down on my lap and wrapped her arms around my neck.

"I know that the pack thinks that we just left on a trip, but I think we should take a few days away for ourselves. What do you think?" I asked, rubbing my hand up and down her back.

"If you are sure that this is a good time, then of course I would love to. Where did you have in mind?" she replied, relaxing at my gentle caresses.

"That would be a surprise. We'll leave first thing in the morning and be gone for a few days." I chuckled at her pouty expression.

"A surprise? But how will I know what to pack?" she pouted.

"Don't worry about packing, I'll take care of everything." I assured her. Before she could respond, someone knocked on the door.

"Come in!" I shouted. The door opened and Tristan walked in, followed by our parents, Cameron, Terry, and Karen. Once they were all seated, I got right to it.

"I know that some of you are wondering why you're here. Isabella and I wanted to let you all know what is going on. She and I were not out of town on vacation or visiting another pack. On the full moon, we completed the Blackwood ceremony that would allow us to mark and mate. We spent a few nights unconscious, but we knew that would happen. We only told a few people so that everyone wouldn't worry. Isabella woke up yesterday afternoon, I woke up late last night. We're fine. No lasting side effects. Before I go on, does anyone have any questions for us?"

My mother stepped forward. "I don't really have a question, more of a statement. You do something like this again, put your life in danger and not tell us, I will kick your ass, Jaxon Oliver. Alpha or not, I am your mother. What if something had gone wrong? We wouldn't know anything, what to do, what to say. Nothing." The room went silent. "Now then, having said that and made my threats and promises, I am very happy for the both of you."

My mother was a small woman, only around five foot two, but they do say dynamite comes in small packages. That woman should have been a honey badger, small and dangerous. I couldn't help but duck my head and gulp when she made her threats, because I knew she meant them. Isabella giggled when she saw me looking sheepish and decided to help me out, I guess.

"We are sorry for not telling you, Kathleen. We didn't want everyone worrying. We told Robert, Terry, Tristan, and two of the warriors who were helping keep watch over us. We had a really good idea of what to expect thanks to the book and we made sure we took the appropriate precautions," Isabella stated.

My mother whipped her head around and glared at my father. "You knew?" she whispered quietly. My father gulped and nodded his head. "You knew and didn't tell me?"

"It wasn't his place to tell you, mom. It was our decision. If you notice, neither of Isabella's parents knew. We did what we thought was best. Now, if you're finished with your hissy fit, I'd like to continue." I reprimanded her. She bowed her head, realizing that her actions were becoming uncalled for, and it was time to remember that I'm the Alpha and move on.

"Now then, the pack believes that Isabella and I were visiting another pack in secret to form an alliance. We will continue to allow them to believe this. They don't need to know the truth right now. The time will come when our pack becomes the Blackwood pack–the book tells us this. When that time comes, they'll know the truth and will have to make the decision whether or not to stay. For right now, we will continue on as usual. Isabella and I are going to take a short vacation away from the pack for a few days. We're leaving first thing in the morning and will return in one week. Tristan will be in charge, with my father backing him up. Terry, I know that you, Karen, and Isabella's parents need to return to your pack soon. It isn't safe to leave your Gamma in charge for so long. It's probably for the best that you return tomorrow, I can have the plane ready for you. We will keep you up to date on anything that happens. When we decide to have the next ceremony from the book, we will let you all know so you can be here. For today, if you would like to spend time with Isabella before you go, I only ask that you stay in or close to the pack house. I'll be here in my office with Tristan and Cameron," I said.

"Thank you for your hospitality, Jaxon. We're happy for you and Bella. I'm sure that we'll see you at dinner tonight," Terry replied.

Isabella gave me a kiss and murmured a quiet thank you before heading out with Terry, Karen, and her parents to spend some time together. My mother and father left soon after, I am sure to have a "talk". Meaning she was going to yell at him, and he was going to kiss her to shut her up.

Tristan, Cameron, and I spent the rest of the day cooped up in my office. We went over everything that happened while I was out and what we could expect for the next week. The rogues had been quiet lately and we weren't sure if that was a good thing or not. We decided to keep the patrols the way they were just in case.

We finally took a break about an hour before dinner. I hurried up to our room and quickly packed bags for myself and Isabella for our little trip. Once the bags were packed, I set them by the door and decided to lay down for a little bit before dinner. I was still exhausted after the last few days.

I hadn't quite managed to fall asleep yet when Isabella walked in the room.

"Napping on the job, Jaxon?" she giggled, jumping up on the bed beside me.

"Trying to, sweetheart," I chuckled. "You have a good visit with your parents? They weren't too mad, were they?"

"It was a good visit. I feel bad for not spending more time with them while they were here. And no, they weren't mad at all. They completely understood the need for secrecy," she answered.

"I'm glad. I hate that they have to head back so soon, but hopefully they will all be able to come back when we finally join the packs. Who knows, maybe Terry will want to join his pack as well. Has he said what they plan on doing since he disowned his son?" I asked.

"I hope so, too. No, he hasn't. I didn't ask, either. Chad is still a sore subject for us. I can't even imagine what Terry must've gone through when he disowned him like that. I'm glad that Chad is overseas. I really hope that the pack there can help him get his head on straight. He has Terry and Karen's genes, so I know he could be a great Alpha. He just needs to grow up and realize that pack comes before all else. In his defense, only slightly, he did kind of get the raw end of the deal with me being his mate but him not being mine. I truly hope he finds his second chance mate. Karen told me that Andrea had their mating annulled by the council before he left," she replied quietly.

"This is why you will be a great Luna, your compassion for others, even those who have wronged you. You see the good in people, even when they might not see it themselves," I said, in awe.

"I won't be so naive as to say that everyone deserves a chance or a second chance, but if people are willing to work to make the changes that are needed in their lives, we should be willing to help them. Not everyone has been given the opportunities and advantages that we have. If I can help make things easier or better for someone, I believe that I have an obligation to do so. As long as they're willing to help themselves first." she stated emphatically. "Now, it's almost time for dinner so get your lazy butt up!" she laughed.

"Kiss first!" I demanded.

She laughed and leaned down to comply with my demand. Before I could wrap my arms around her though, she slipped away causing me to pout.

"You had your kiss, now get up," she giggled.

I grumbled and complained, much to her delight and eventually got out of bed. We headed downstairs and had a nice dinner with everyone before heading off to bed early. Isabella's parents were heading home early in the morning with Terry and Karen. We would be leaving shortly after for our time alone. Finally.

CHAPTER FORTY-THREE

Isabella

After having breakfast with our families and seeing my parents, Terry, and Karen off, we loaded our bags into the car and headed out. Jaxon warned me that the trip would take all day. As much I asked and begged him to tell me where we were going, the man wouldn't budge.

"Why don't you take a nap, sweetheart?" Jaxon asked, probably getting tired of my fidgeting. Car rides always made me fidgety if I'm not driving.

"I'm not tired, just a little bored," I admitted.

"Well, I have my camera in the small bag in the backseat if you want to take some pictures of the scenery," he tried again.

"Oh, that's a great idea, I love taking pictures," I gushed as he grinned at me.

I turned around and found the bag he was talking about. Digging through it, I found Jaxon's camera and pulled it out. Once I turned around, I fumbled with it until I got it set up the way I wanted, then snapped a quick picture of Jaxon, grinning as I did. He just laughed and shook his head. The drive really was beautiful. Mountains, forests, meadows, farmland, we even passed some waterfalls. I took too many pictures to count. I couldn't wait to upload them to the computer and see how they turned out.

About an hour later we came across a small town and decided to stop for a short break and stretch our legs. We walked around town, window shopping and just enjoying the chilly morning. I saw an antique store that looked promising and decided to drag Jaxon inside. We walked through the store, admiring some pieces, laughing at others, until we stumbled across a beautiful jewelry box. I looked at the tag and saw that it was handmade in France in 1892 from what looked like one solid piece of walnut. Absolutely amazing. And really expensive too.

Sighing, I walked away from the jewelry box and headed outside. Jaxon saw a cute little mom and pop diner that promised the best apple pie around, so of course we had to try it. We sat down at a table and placed our order when Jaxon jumped up.

"I left my wallet in the car. I'll be right back, sweetheart," he explained before rushing out the door.

He didn't even give me time to say anything. Silly man, I had my wallet. I sat there for a few minutes, admiring all of the unique decorations in the diner. Before I knew it, the waitress came back with two helpings of hot apple pie ala mode. As soon as she set the plates down, Jaxon walked through the door with a big grin on his face.

"Perfect timing, as always," he joked.

"Get your wallet?" I teased.

"Yes, I can't believe I left it in the car. Luckily it was in the console and not just sitting out for anyone to see," he groaned. "This pie looks and smells amazing."

"Yes, it does," I agreed.

I took my first bite and couldn't help the small moan that escaped. It was that good. Their sign did not lie. We quickly finished our pie and sat back with satisfied grins. So good.

"I'm going to assume by the empty plates and smiles, that you two enjoyed your pie?" Our waitress laughed.

"Oh yes, ma'am. It was delicious!" I exclaimed.

"Well, thank you. I'll be sure to let my mom know, she's the baker here. Her grandmother's recipe," she replied.

"Well, I hope that she's taught you how to make it so you can carry on the tradition when the time comes," Jaxon said.

"She has, no worries there. Can I get you anything else?"

"No thank you. I don't think anything could top that and we need to be back on the road," Jaxon replied.

"You guys have a great day and thanks for stopping in," she said.

"Isabella, wake up. We are here, sweetheart." I could feel Jaxon gently brushing the hair out of my face. I groaned and looked up at him, blinking my eyes to clear them. "Time to get up, sleepyhead. We're here."

"Already? It seems like we just left," I replied sarcastically, before yawning.

"Haha. Very funny. Now come on, let's get you inside. One of the ladies that manages the place left dinner for us. Afterwards, we can do whatever you want."

"Sounds good to me. I'm starving."

Jaxon grabbed the bags out of the trunk, and we went inside. I took a moment to look around as we walked inside. The house was beautiful. I could see touches of Jaxon in the design and Evie in the decorating. The entire place was rustic with little touches of modern throughout. Wide windows that opened up to the sea, antler lighting fixtures, and a massive stone fireplace similar to the one in the pack house. There were even small wooden carvings on the shelves.

"You designed this place, didn't you? And Evie decorated it."

"Sure did. Good eye, sweetheart," he replied, giving me a kiss on the side of the head. "My parents bought the land years ago but couldn't decide what to do with it, so it just sat here, unused. About five years ago I finally designed this house and had it built for them as an anniversary present. Evie decorated the inside. The only stipulation my parents made was that it be made available for everyone in the pack to use."

"I love it. I can't wait to see in the daylight."

"Plenty of time for that tomorrow. Let's go eat before the food gets cold."

After dinner, we showered and picked out movies before heading up to the bedroom. While I chose the movies, Jaxon made some popcorn and drinks. I had to have popcorn while watching movies. My first pick was Due Date. I loved this one. The part where Jamie Foxx is driving over the humps in the road with Zach Galifianakis in the bed of the truck is my favorite. Cracked me up every time!

We managed to make it to a third movie when I finally began to doze off. I heard Jaxon turn the tv off and move the popcorn bowl off the bed before pulling me close and relaxing.

CHAPTER FORTY-FOUR

Jagger

"Kade! Get in here!" I bellowed.

"Yes, Alpha?" Kade replied, walking into my office.

"Any news about Dark Sky? Is it true? Did their Alpha find his mate?" I demanded.

"Yes, I do have some news. Some interesting news. I just got off the phone with one of our rogues. He has managed to befriend one of the wolves in the pack. Alpha Jaxon has found his mate. She is Isabella Greyson, daughter of the Beta of Greystone Pack. Alpha Terry of Greystone is her godfather. The same Alpha Terry who found her as a small child. Around the same time that Blackwood was attacked and destroyed. Funny enough, she was the same age as the daughter of Blackwood's Alpha and Luna. Quite the coincidence, isn't it?" he grinned.

"Do not joke with me about this." I growled. "What makes you think that Isabella Greyson is the daughter of Blackwood's Alpha? Their daughter was killed along with everyone else that night. Don't be ridiculous!"

"It's not that far of a stretch. Especially when you consider that Alpha Terry, his mate, Beta James, his mate, Alpha Jaxon's parents, and Elder Nikolas were all there at the same time. People who were all very close to Blackwood's Alpha. And turns out they requested our pack records as well as Blackwood's pack records. I am telling you, that girl is a Blackwood." Kade insisted.

"Impossible," I muttered. "My father swore up and down that everyone was killed that night. He even killed the wolves that were responsible for the girl's death. She was supposed to be kept alive. She was promised to me."

Kade remained silent while I continued to mutter to myself. I found it hard to believe that Jaxon's mate could be a Blackwood. But Kade made a pretty convincing argument. Especially since we were pretty sure it was them at the Blackwood pack house a few weeks ago. Unfortunately, Kade and our fighters couldn't get close enough to verify who it was.

"Find me a picture of her! A clear picture! If she is a Blackwood, she'll look like one of them. Get it done now!" I ordered.

"Yes, Alpha," he replied, leaving my office.

If Isabella Greyson was Alexandra Blackwood, nothing could stop me from making her mine and finishing what my father started. It was a good thing I hadn't marked my mate. I knew the Moon Goddess made a mistake giving me that stupid girl as a mate. I hadn't rejected her yet, and I wouldn't until I got confirmation from Kade. Until then, I would continue to use her as I please. Not like she wasn't used to it.

"Carmen! My office. Now!" I mindlinked my mate.
    "Yes, Alpha."

Time to work off some frustrations.

CHAPTER FORTY-FIVE

Jaxon

I woke up early the next morning, my mate curled up next to me. I couldn't help but chuckle at her soft snores. She must've really been tired last night. Kissing her forehead softly, I eased out of bed without waking her. I headed downstairs to make breakfast, hoping I could finish it before she wakes up.

Isabella was still sleeping when I walked in. I set the tray of food down on the end of the bed before sitting down beside her. She must've felt the bed shift and she began to stir.

I brushed the hair out of her face, admiring her beauty. "Sweetheart, wake up," I whispered softly, kissing her plump lips. She smiled up at me before opening her eyes.

"You're up early," she yawned.

"Thought I would surprise you with breakfast in bed. You hungry?" I asked.

"Jax, this is delicious!" she groaned, barely pausing to tell me as she dug in.

"I'm glad you like it. Eat up, we have a busy day today."

Once we finished breakfast, Isabella offered to take everything downstairs and clean up while I showered. I didn't really want her to have to do anything, but she insisted.

After we had both showered, I decided to take Isabella on a tour of the area. Not that there was much to see other than the beach, just a few small towns. I figured we could go walk around for a while, have some lunch, maybe pick up some fresh seafood to cook for dinner.

We decided to head north towards the small town of Cannon Beach. It was only ten minutes from the house. We walked around the downtown area, checking out the local shops. After about an hour, we had seen pretty much everything, so we left and headed further north to Seaside.

Once we got to Seaside, we parked the car and decided to walk along the beach first. Due to the cold weather, the beach was deserted. I brought rain boots for both of us so we wouldn't have to get sand in our shoes. I also brought along a small bucket so we could collect shells.

We walked along the beach for a couple of hours, enjoying the sound of the waves and collecting shells. We even managed to find a sand dollar in one piece. Isabella was especially excited when we found a starfish that had been stranded on the sand. It was still alive, so we returned it to the water, feeling like heroes.

After filling the bucket with shells, I led Isabella back to the car to change our shoes and drop off the bucket. We then walked a couple of blocks over to the main street to look around. We passed by a small cafe that looked and smelled promising, so we stopped for lunch.

"I am starving!" Isabella exclaimed. "Who knew walking on sand would be such a good workout."

"Anyone who has ever been to the beach," I chuckled.

"Oh, shut up," she muttered, elbowing me in the ribs. I did tend to forget she wasn't from the area sometimes, so it was all new for her.

After lunch, we walked around some more, stopping in a few shops. We went into one of the numerous antique stores. I was hoping I could find something else that my little mate liked and buy it without her knowing again, maybe even something to go in the jewelry box.

We walked all around the store, which was much larger than we first thought. Isabella had fun trying on some old hats and clothes. I couldn't help but laugh along with her and take pictures. She even made me try on a top hat while she had on some big, feathery thing. It was hideous. Even the store owner couldn't help but laugh at us while she took our picture.

On our way out, I asked the owner if there was a seafood market nearby. While she was giving me directions, I noticed Isabella staring at something in a case. I walked over after getting the directions to see what it was. It was a beautiful, antique diamond ring. The owner noticed her interest and came over to take it out.

"Oh, that's okay. I was just looking," Isabella tried to stop her.

"There's no harm in taking a closer look, dear. Try it on," the owner insisted.

Isabella slipped the ring on her finger, and it fit perfectly. I heard the almost inaudible gasp from my mate. I knew then that this was her ring. Standing behind her, I looked up at the owner and we both shared a knowing look. She winked and nodded her head. I set the bag from another store down.

"It's beautiful," Isabella breathed. "Thank you for letting me try it on."

"My pleasure, dear. It really suits you," the owner smiled.

"We better get the seafood and head back before it gets too late," I said.

After bidding the owner goodbye, we headed out and down the street. Following the directions, we managed to find the seafood market. We went inside to see what they had available.

"Oh shit. I left your bag in the last store. Pick out something for dinner while I run get it before she closes," I handed some cash to Isabella and ran out the door before she could say anything.

I hurried back to the antique store as quickly as I could. The owner was still standing at the case where we left her.

"Long time no see," she laughed. "I take it you would like to buy the ring for your lady friend?"

"Yes, ma'am I would," I stated.

"Any questions about price?" she asked.

"Nope. She loves it and it fits her perfectly." I replied.

"Good man." she laughed. "Would you like for me to wrap it up for you?"

"No thank you. I bought a jewelry box in another town that she was looking at. She doesn't know about it either, so I'm going to use that," I told her.

"She sure is lucky to have you," she sighed.

"I'm the lucky one," I insisted.

After paying for the ring, I hid it in my pocket, grabbed the bag, and ran back to the seafood market. Luckily, Isabella was still waiting to check out as there had been a bit of a line.

"Got the bag. I swear I'd lose my head if it wasn't attached," I joked. "What did you decide on for dinner?"

"You're crazy." She laughed. "I got some fresh clams and some Dungeness crab. Never heard of it before, but the guy swears it's delicious. Even gave me a recipe to try."

"It is delicious, good choice. We had it every time we went to the coast as kids," I told her.

After paying for our food, we went back to the car and headed back to the beach house. We were lucky that the wind had died down enough for us to grill outside. I handled that while Isabella set the table, fixed drinks, and took care of the rest of the food. She found a nice bottle of Oregon pinot noir and opened it to let it breathe. Once the table was set, Isabella stepped outside to the deck to relax and wait for dinner to be ready. It was a very relaxed affair. We ate our fill, drank our fill, and laughed until it hurt. We took our time, talking about whatever came to mind, as long as it wasn't pack business. Afterward, I told her I had a surprise for her and asked her to wait in the living room for me to get it.

Rushing upstairs, I hurried to get everything ready. I put the ring in the jewelry box and wrapped it in paper I found in the hall closet.

Looking around the room, I wanted to do something special, but fuck if I knew what. I headed back out to the hall closet to see what else was in there. Candles, check. Fake rose petals? I guessed candles would have to do. I carried a few back in the room and looked for a lighter to light them. After scouring the room, cursing a lot, I determined that there wasn't one.

Pissed that this wasn't going to plan, I carried the candles back to the closet and threw them in. Just as I went to slam the door, I noticed a box filled with Halloween decorations. Digging through it I struck gold. Battery operated tealight candles! Romance saved! I hurried back to the room, turned the candles on, and placed them around the room. Romantic and safe. Finished with everything, I called Isabella upstairs.

CHAPTER FORTY-SIX

Isabella

"Sweetheart? Can you come upstairs please?" Jaxon called out.

"Coming," I replied, heading up to meet him.

When I walked in the room, I was shocked. There was Jaxon standing there holding a package. Glancing around, I saw the room was bathed in soft light from little flickering candles.

"Jaxon, what is all this?" I whispered, not trusting my voice to not crack.

"It's all for you, sweetheart. I wanted to show you how much you mean to me, how much I love you," he smiled. I wrapped my arms around his neck and pulled him closer to me. The kiss we shared was powerful. It was soft, sweet, and so full of emotion I almost cried.

"I love you, Jaxon. So much. I never thought that I would find you. Ever. I can't believe how lucky I am," I said.

"I'm the lucky one," he insisted. "Now, I have something for you. Open it," he insisted, handing me a package.

I slowly peeled away the wrapping paper to reveal the jewelry box from the antique store. Tears filled my eyes and I glanced up to see

Jaxon smiling softly at me, before continuing to unwrap it. Once it was open, I held it for a moment before setting it aside and jumping in his arms, sniffling.

"What's wrong? Do you not like it? I can find something else. Please don't cry?" Jaxon asked.

"You are so silly, Jaxon. I love it! These are happy tears." I cried, still sniffling.

"Oh. Thank fuck."

"I love it, Jaxon. But you shouldn't have. It's way too much money for a jewelry box," I chided him.

"You're worth more than any amount of money to me, sweetheart. This was nothing. Besides, I put a little something in there for you. I couldn't just give you an empty box. That would be rude," he said with a playful smirk.

I gave him an exasperated look before stepping back from his hold. He watched carefully as I picked the box back up. I looked up at him again before opening it. My hands started to shake, and my eyes began to water as a small gasp escaped. I plucked the ring from the jewelry box before carefully setting the jewelry box back on the bed. When I looked up at him again, I was shocked to find him kneeling in front of me.

Jaxon took the ring from my hand and gently pulled me closer to him. My heart began to race as he knelt before me. I knew what he was going to do but for some reason, I just couldn't comprehend it.

"Sweetheart, you mean the world to me. I had long since given up hope that I would find my mate, my love, my life. And then you stumbled in and turned my whole world upside down. I have loved every second of having you in my life and I will stop at nothing to make sure that you are the happiest woman in the world. I want you. Body, mind, and soul. I want to spend the rest of my life with you. Worshipping you, honoring you, treasuring you. Isabella, will you marry me?" he asked.

"Oh my gosh. Jaxon, I..."

I couldn't breathe. The words were trapped in my chest with the air. I wanted to say yes, I wanted to scream it from the rooftops so the whole world heard me. But I couldn't. It was like my entire body was frozen. I could see the panic in his eyes before he looked down. Shit.

"Yes," I finally managed to whisper.

His eyes shot back up to me to see if I really said yes. I was smiling, tears streaming down my face.

"What did you say?" he gasped.

"Yes. I said yes. I think, no I know, I really mean hell yes!" I squealed.

"Oh, thank fuck!" He groaned, before sliding the ring on my finger and pulling me down to him.

Jaxon kissed me like it was the last thing he would ever do. I didn't know how long we kissed. I didn't really care. All I cared about was that the man I love had asked me to marry him and was in my arms. Nothing else mattered at that point.

"I love you," I whispered over and over again, planting small kisses all over his face.

"I love you too, Isabella," he murmured.

He stood up, holding me in his arms, and walked towards the bed. I couldn't believe how lucky I was. He stopped as we reached the bed, setting me down on my feet, never taking his hands off of me. Leaning down, he softly kissed my cheeks, my nose, the side of my lips, everywhere but my lips. I finally had enough and roughly grabbed the sides of his face to kiss him like I wanted.

Reaching down, he grabbed my ass and lifted me up until I wrapped my legs around his waist. Two steps and he laid me back on the bed. He leaned down over me and kissed me, our tongues tangling together. He tasted like wine and chocolate. This kiss was like nothing else, like no other kiss we'd had before. It meant so much more.

Jaxon sat up and grabbed the bottom of my sweater, pulling it off and tossing it to the side. He reached behind his head with one hand and ripped his shirt off in one motion tossing it behind him. I reached up and pulled his mouth back to mine, needing that connection to him. I ran my hands down his shoulders to his back, loving the way the muscles rippled under my touch.

Jaxon couldn't seem to figure out where he wanted to touch me.

His hands buried themselves in my hair and tugged my head back as his lips trailed down to my neck. I moaned as his teeth grazed a sensitive spot. This just seemed to spur him on as he trailed a hand down my side to rest on my hip. As his tongue traced the cup of my bra, his hand reached for the button on my jeans. My body instantly tensed up and I froze. Sensing my discomfort, Jaxon paused.

"What's wrong?" he asked.

"Nothing."

"That was a lie. Try again," he demanded.

"I'm just, well, a little, I mean..." I stammered.

"Sweetheart, are you a virgin?"

I stared at his chest, unable to look him in the eye. Was I a virgin? Uh, yes. I'd only kissed one other guy in my life and that ended with him getting a black eye and a busted lip from Chad. Needless to say, sex was not an option with that jerk around.

"You've only kissed one other guy?"

I gasped and looked up in shock. "You said that out loud, sweetheart."

"Oh geez," I whispered. I squeezed my eyes shut and turned my head so he couldn't see me turn red. I was so embarrassed I wished the mattress would swallow me whole.

"Isabella, look at me please," Jaxon murmured, skimming his nose along my cheek.

I shook my head. Nope, I was going to lie here wishing I could turn invisible.

"Look at me or I'll put you over my knee and turn that pretty little ass as pink as your face." I opened my eyes and peered up at him. Not sure what I was expecting, but tenderness was not it. "Are you a virgin? Is that why you tensed up?"

I nodded my head. Jaxon leaned down and kissed me softly before pulling back.

"Sweetheart, as much as I want to be the typical Alpha male and strut around like a fucking peacock, I won't. I will tell you that anything that happens from this moment forward is up to you and at your pace. You run this show now, not me."

"How am I supposed to run a show I know nothing about?" I muttered.

"Oh trust me, you'll figure it out real quick." He smirked.

Before I could respond to that, Jaxon rolled over onto his back, taking me with him. I was now straddling his waist, looking down at him. My eyes grew wide as saucers. Jaxon chuckled and sat up, wrapping his arms around me. He scooted up the bed until he was leaned against the headboard. His hands slid up my back to tangle in my hair again, pulling my head towards him, stopping just short of his lips.

"Kiss me," he demanded.

I leaned in that last bit and pressed my lips to his. True to his word, he didn't rush me. He let me control the pace. Feeling somewhat emboldened, I parted my lips and traced his with my tongue gently urging them to part. When they did, I swept my tongue into his mouth and mimicked the movements he made before. He growled low in his chest and his grip tightened on my hair, his other hand slid up my side, stopping just as he reached the band of my bra. Knowing what he wanted, what I wanted as well, I reached behind me and unclasped my bra before sliding the straps down my arms.

As I tossed my bra aside Jaxon used his grip in my hair to pull my head back, breaking our kiss. I looked down at him and nodded at his unasked question. The corner of his mouth ticked up in a wicked little smirk. His hand curved upward around my breast, giving it a gentle squeeze causing my breath to catch in my throat. His tongue darted out to flick my nipple and every bit of breath left me in a loud gasp. He didn't stop. His lips parted and he pulled my nipple into his mouth, sucking hard. My back bowed as his teeth scraped against the sensitive skin.

"Jaxon, please," I groaned.

"Please what, sweetheart?" he said, nipping at my neck.

"I-I don't know, just I need something. More!" I cried out, my nails digging into his shoulders.

Jaxon turned us over and laid me on my back. His lips immediately met mine in a fierce, panty melting kiss that seared my lips and my soul. My hands gripped the sheets so hard I was surprised they didn't tear as he kissed his way down my body. He paused and looked up at me as he reached the waistband of my jeans.

"More?"

"More." I nodded at him to continue. He unbuttoned and unzipped them before pulling them off, taking my panties with them.

Jaxon laid down, his wide shoulders spreading my legs apart as he settled between them. I opened my mouth to ask him what he was doing, but all coherent thought left my brain as he sealed his mouth against me. All I could do was feel, and I felt everything. The way his tongue moved against me, the way his teeth nipped at me. When he added a finger, my body exploded. He slowed but didn't stop. I had barely regained my breath when he added a second finger, curling them both in a motion that had me screaming his name and seeing stars.

I felt him move then, groaning as his fingers left me and one hand trailed its way up my side. His lips closed over my nipple causing me to buck against him. His thumb circled my sensitive clit as the swollen head of his cock nudged my entrance. Before I could tense up, he pressed his thumb down and his hips surged forward. I screamed out as the pain sent me over the edge. He stilled, allowing me to adjust to the intrusion. He remained still until I rocked my hips against him.

His hips began to pull back and push forward slowly, gradually speeding up and I began to move with him. I wrapped my legs around his waist, and he growled, gripping my hips, and surging forward. I gasped his name, and all control was lost. His mouth came down on mine in a bruising kiss that spurred us both on.

As my release came crashing over me, I tore my mouth away from his. I could feel his growl before I heard it. Our mouths moved to those perfect spots as our wolves took control and teeth broke skin, each of us marking the other as our mate.

Warm. Safe. Comfortable. Completely satisfied. That is how I felt. Well, that and a little sore. I should add happy to that list. Yes, happy. Ecstatic. Thrilled. Over the freaking moon. Did I mention satisfied?

When I opened my eyes, I saw why I feel warm, safe, and comfortable. I was on my back and Jaxon was practically laying on top of me. His arms wrapped around my waist, his head nestled between my boobs, and his legs tangled with mine. Each time I tried to pull away, he groaned in his sleep and pulled me tighter. So much for surprising him with breakfast in bed. Oh well. That just meant more time cuddling. I closed my eyes and drifted off to sleep.

Feather-light touches against my cheek, against my lips down my neck. I slowly opened my eyes to see my mate, my oh-so-handsome mate, staring down at me. I couldn't help but smile.

"Morning, sweetheart. Sleep well?" he smiled.

"Morning, my love. Yes, I did. Pretty sure you did as well since you wouldn't let me get up earlier." I giggled.

"What do you mean?"

"I mean, every time I tried to get up, you pulled me closer and wouldn't let me. I felt like a teddy bear you were cuddling." I teased.

"I was comfy." He shrugged.

"It was cute, but now I need a shower," I told him, trying to get up and failing.

"A shower, you say? Don't mind if I do." Before I could react, Jaxon stood up out of bed, picked me up, threw me over his shoulder, and marched off to the bathroom, me laughing all the way.

CHAPTER FORTY-SEVEN

Jaxon

As soon as Isabella mentioned a shower, I got excited. No way was I letting her take one without me. I didn't even want to let her out of bed. Carrying her over my shoulder into the bathroom, I paused only to turn the water on. While waiting for it to heat up, Isabella begged me to let her down.

"Jaxon, please let me down! Please!"

"Nope. Don't want to."

"Please, Jaxon! I need to use the bathroom you caveman!"

"Oh, sorry, sweetheart!" I quickly set her down and laughed as she ran into the other part of the bathroom and slammed the door. Since the water was hot, I decided to go ahead and get in while I waited for her.

I stood there and let the water run down my shoulders and back, releasing any tension I had. The hot water was soothing. I closed my eyes and relaxed. Before too long, I felt two hands sneaking around my waist and a soft body press up against me. Without opening my eyes, I wrapped my arms around her and smiled.

Looking down, I saw my little mate staring up at me.

"Penny for your thoughts," I whispered.

"I love you." She smiled up at me.

Leaning down, I planted a soft kiss on her lips before replying, "I love you, too."

I reached around and grabbed the shower gel and poufy thing. I squeezed some gel onto it and worked it into a lather. Stepping back, I motioned for Isabella to turn around so I could wash her back. She did and moved her hair out of the way. I washed her back, shoulders, arms, butt, legs, butt again. Such a nice butt. And all mine. I couldn't resist giving her a quick swat to the butt causing her to squeal.

"Jaxon!"

"What? I like your butt," I mumbled, kissing her shoulder and neck. She moaned and leaned her head back to give me better access. Instead of continuing, I stepped back again and turned her around to wash her front, paying extra attention to her chest. I loved the sounds she made.

Once I finish washing her, I grabbed the shampoo and washed her hair for her. After rinsing it, I used the conditioner and then rinsed that as well. I went to grab my shower gel, but Isabella swatted my hand away.

"Turnabout is fair play, my love," she replied, grinning up at me.

She washed my back, shoulders, butt, and legs, paying extra attention to my butt like I did hers. She even swatted me on the ass before turning me around grinning. I couldn't help but smile back. Especially when she looked down and gasped at how hard I was. She began to wash my neck, shoulders, and chest making sure to take her time.

Once she washed my abs and hips, she skipped my groin and knelt down to wash my legs. She slowly made her way up my legs before finally getting to where I was dying to have her. I groaned when I felt her hand wrap around my hard cock and gently squeeze. My eyes rolled back, and my head fell back at the sensations. She began to slowly stroke her hand up and down my length, pausing to run her thumb over my swollen tip.

"Oh fuck. Shit that feels so good, sweetheart," I groaned. I felt myself begin to twitch and knew that I wasn't going to last much longer. "Faster!" I demanded gruffly.

Her strokes got faster and firmer, taking me closer and closer to the edge. I jumped as I felt her other hand reach down and cup my balls, gently squeezing and tugging on them.

"Oh, shit. I'm gonna come," I gasped. I moaned and jerked my hips forward before releasing all over her hands. I leaned back against the tile wall and panted, trying to gain control over my breathing.

Opening my eyes, I looked down and saw my little mate smiling back up at me. I grabbed her by the waist and picked her, spinning as I did to pin her to the wall. I kissed her hard, swallowing her gasp at my sudden movements. I kissed down her neck to where her mark was and gently bit and sucked on the sensitive skin. Her moans told me that she was enjoying every move I made.

Her legs wrapped around my waist, and she rolled her hips forward, brushing her wet core against my already hardening cock. I ground my hips back against her, relishing in the pants and moans coming from her. Not being able to wait any longer, I pulled back slightly and reached down to line myself up with her entrance before pushing forward and entering her fully in one hard thrust. I paused for a moment to allow her to get used to me.

"Jaxon, please move. I need you now," she panted, rolling her hips against me.

"As you wish, sweetheart."

I pulled out and pushed back in, making sure to keep my pace slow so I didn't hurt her. Last night was her first time and I knew she was sore. I kept the pace slow and gentle, kissing her softly as I thrust in and out of her. Her hands moved from my shoulders to tangle in my hair as her hips met my thrusts.

"Faster please, Jaxon. Stop torturing me!" she begged.

I gradually sped up my thrusts until I was pounding into her, the only sounds were our moans and grunts and our pelvises slapping together. I felt her walls begin to tighten, clenching around me. I grunted, trying to hold back my own release until she got hers first. Reaching between us, I found her clit and rubbed it fast and hard until she trembled and screamed out my name from the intensity of her orgasm. She clenched me so tight, I followed right after with my own, growling her name as I did.

We stood there for a few minutes, still connected, and panting. I leaned my forehead against hers before kissing her lips. That was amazing. I slowly pulled out of her and released her legs so she could stand up. I made sure to keep my hands on her waist just in case. I didn't want her to fall.

Once we caught our breath, we grinned at each other and quickly washed off since the water was beginning to cool down. Stepping out of the shower, we dried off and got dressed before heading down to get something to eat.

"How does a bacon, egg, and cheese sandwich sound?" Isabella asked, grabbing the ingredients.

"Sounds delicious. What do you need me to do?" I replied.

"Grab the bread out of the pantry and toast it please. Sourdough if you have it."

Isabella placed the skillets on the stove-top, before getting everything else ready. I was mesmerized as I watched her move around the kitchen like she belonged there. She fried the bacon, then the eggs in the same pan, sliced avocados, and when the toast was ready, she put mustard and cheese on it before adding the rest of the ingredients.

"Done." She smiled, handing me a plate.

"This looks so good," I said. I took a bite and moaned. "Tastes so good too."

"So, what do you want to do today?" she asked before taking a bite.

"I didn't make any concrete plans. I wasn't sure if you would feel up to going out today. We can go out or we can stay in. Completely up to you, sweetheart," I replied, finishing off my sandwich.

"Well, since it looks like a storm is coming in, why don't we stay in and have a lazy day?"

"Sounds good to me. One condition," I stated.

"Condition?"

"Yup. No pants for you." I smirked.

"Jaxon!" Isabella smacked me on the arm, causing me to crack up laughing. "Fine. If I can't wear pants, then neither can you!"

Challenge accepted, sweetheart. Judging by the shocked expression on her face, I guess she didn't expect me to stand up and strip my pants off in the kitchen, but that's exactly what I did. I looked over at her and raised an eyebrow.

"Fine." She stood up and took her pants off. I just grinned and picked them up, tossing them out of sight.

"Much better." I grinned. "Now, I think it's movie time."

We spent the rest of the morning and early afternoon cuddled up on the couch, watching movies and making out like teenagers. The storm that kept us in, finally rolled in around four in the afternoon. The waves were huge. The wind came in off the water and brought the rain with it. There was even some thunder and lightning, but Isabella said it was nothing like they had back in Texas.

Half an hour after the storm hit, the power went out. Luckily, the kitchen was equipped with a gas stove, so we would still be able to make dinner. I had brought some wood in earlier to start a fire for us. We ate dinner in front of the fire then headed upstairs to bed. With the power out, there was no way we could watch more movies, so we found other ways to entertain ourselves.

CHAPTER FORTY-EIGHT

Isabella

Jaxon and I headed back home after an eventful, yet relaxing, week at the coast. We were now fully mated and engaged. I couldn't wait to tell my family and the pack.

I spoke with Evie on the phone last night to see how everything was going. She said that everything was fine, but she sounded strange, nervous almost. Weird. I asked her about it, and she said it was nothing to worry about, that she would talk to me when we got back. Afterward, I asked Jaxon if Tristan had sounded funny on the phone.

"What do you mean?" he asked.

"I just talked to Evie and something's wrong. She sounded weird, almost like she was nervous or preoccupied."

"Now that you mention it, he did sound off. Kind of like he was preoccupied too."

I thought about what it could mean, but when my mate leaned over and kissed all thoughts went away.

Jaxon and I got up early so we could get on the road. That plan was derailed when I saw my gorgeous mate in the shower. I had to join him. We were finally on the road home, two hours later than planned.

"Do you want me to drive at all?" I asked.

"No, sweetheart. You just rest. I'm good." Luckily the traffic was really light, and we were making good time.

Shortly after a very quick lunch stop, my phone rang, startling us both.

"It's Terry." I told Jaxon, before answering the phone. "Hi, Terry. How is everything?"

"Everything is good here. How are you doing?" he replied.

"Good. Are my mom and dad there?"

"Sure are."

"Good, can you put me on speaker phone? I want to tell you guys something."

I looked over at Jaxon and smiled, mouthing that I was going to tell them about our engagement. Jaxon just nodded his head and smiled before turning back to the road.

"Bella, are you there? We're all here," my mom said, letting me know they could all hear me.

"I'm here. How are you guys? I miss you all!"

"We're good. How are you, honey? We miss you so much. What have you been up to?" my mom replied.

"I'm good, we're in the car and Jaxon is driving us back to Dark Sky. We just spent a week on the Oregon coast. It's so beautiful there. I absolutely love it. Are you guys planning on coming back up for Christmas?"

"We would love to come up for Christmas, if it's no trouble."

"Of course, it's no trouble. We would love to have you guys."

"Any chance you guys can come down for Spring Break? Give you some time to show Jaxon around the area," Dad suggested.

"Yeah, hopefully we can make it down in the spring. Depends on how busy we are. Planning a summer wedding on such short notice is going to be hectic."

As soon as I said that I pulled the phone away from my head and started counting.

"One, two, three, four, five." When I got to five, we heard screams and squeals coming from my phone. Jaxon and I both started laughing.

"Calm down, stop yelling and I will tell you everything!" I laughed. "Well, maybe not everything." I could hear Terry and my dad shouting threats and my mom and Karen giggling.

"So, here are the details I will give. Yes, we are fully mated now. Jaxon and I made a wonderful dinner and afterwards he proposed. It was amazing and I am extremely happy."

The rest of the conversation was focused on the wedding. Mom and Karen were ecstatic to say the least. Dad and Terry just sat back and let them go on, knowing they wouldn't be able to get a word in.

"Everything good with your family?" Jaxon asked as I hung up the phone.

"Yes. Mom and Aunt Karen are thrilled. I almost couldn't get off the phone with them. They wanted to plan the entire wedding right now." I laughed.

"Just wait until Evie hears. She's going to go nuts. I wish you luck, sweetheart," he chuckled.

"You mean you wish us luck! You are so not getting out of planning, Jaxon," I corrected him.

"Damn," he grimaced. I reached over and smacked him in the arm. "Ouch! I was kidding, sweetheart. No need to get violent."

"I mean it, Jax. I want you to help me plan the wedding. It isn't just about me, it's about us."

"Sweetheart, I will help you out every step of the way if that's what you want. Our wedding will be perfect. Even if it rains, the flowers are wrong, the cake falls down, and half the wedding party gets drunk before the ceremony. It will be perfect because I am marrying you," he promised.

"Oh, Jaxon. You sure know how to make a girl feel special," I sighed.

"Only you, sweetheart. Only you," he said, grabbing my hand and lifting it up to place a kiss on the back of it.

We drove in silence for a while, just listening to the radio and holding hands. It didn't take long for the drive to lull me to sleep. Before I could drop off, Jaxon nudged me.

"Sweetheart, there's a blanket in the backseat. Why don't you grab it, lay your seat back, and get some rest? I'll wake you up if I stop or when we get there."

"Are you sure? I hate to sleep while you are driving," I yawned.

"Yes, I'm sure, sleepyhead. Get some rest. We'll be home in a few hours anyway," he assured me.

"Ok, Jaxon. I love you."

"I love you too, sweetheart."

CHAPTER FORTY-NINE

Jaxon

Isabella slept the rest of the way home. Her soft little snores made me chuckle. That girl could sleep anywhere, I was sure of it. As we pulled through the gates, the guards nodded at my car, grinning when they saw Isabella asleep in the passenger seat.

Isabella groaned and rubbed her eyes when the car came to a stop in the garage. "Home already?" she yawned.

"Yeah, you managed to sleep through the boring parts," I teased.

"I think I could still sleep. I'm so tired."

"Well, why don't you head up to bed? I'm going to stop by the office and see Tristan really quick. I want him to fill me in on what's been going on while we were gone."

"I'll come with you. Maybe he knows why Evie has been weird."

I took Isabella's hand in mine, our bags in my other hand, as we made our way inside. I nodded to the few pack members we passed on our way to the elevators. It made me happy to see how they accepted my mate so readily.

Upstairs, I dropped our bags in front of my office before knocking on Tristan's door. It opened as I did. The sight in front of me had me losing all control.

"What the fucking hell is going on here?" I roared.

Evie and Tristan jumped apart. Why in the fuck was my best friend kissing my sister?

"Tristan, what in the hell are you doing?" I demanded, my eyes flickering back and forth between mine and my wolf's as he tried to take over.

"Jaxon, stop!" Evie yelled.

"Do not tell me what to do. Do not forget your place. You may be my sister, but I am Alpha, and you will respect me," my wolf commanded. I heard Isabella gasp behind me.

"Alpha, I can explain. Please just calm down and listen." Tristan stood, gently pushing Evie behind him.

"You have two seconds," I growled.

"She's my mate."

"Bullshit. You two have known each other for years. If you were mates, you would have known it way before now." I stepped forward.

"Jaxon, he's telling the truth," Evie cried, holding onto his arm.

"Shut up, Evie. This is between me and Tristan!" I yelled.

Tristan stepped forward, his eyes flashing and his skin rippling as his wolf fought to take over. Evie stepped forward, screaming for us both to stop.

"Stop this right now!" my father ordered. Tristan and I both pausing at his command. "What in the hell is wrong with you two?"

"This asshole was assaulting my sister!" I yelled, pointing at Tristan.

"I was not assaulting her! I was kissing her! Huge freaking difference, moron!" he yelled back.

I opened my mouth to yell at Tristan again but was again stopped by my dad. Only this time it was because he was laughing, not yelling.

"What the hell are you laughing at?" I demanded.

"You, Jaxon. I am laughing at you." My dad chuckled, walking over to sit down on the couch. My mom and Isabella stood by the door, watching everything. My mom was trying to hide her giggles, while Isabella was just staring at me.

"Didn't realize I was so funny, father," I growled.

"Don't growl at me. You may be Alpha, but I am still your father. Now sit down and shut up," my dad ordered. I growled at the command before sitting down in a chair. Isabella walked over to stand by me, but gasped when I jerked her down into my lap. I wrapped my arms around her and breathed in her scent, trying to calm down my wolf.

"Now that everyone has calmed down, maybe we can talk about this like adults," my dad snapped.

I looked over to see that Tristan had sat back down in his chair and Evie was sitting in his lap again. I started to say something, but my dad growled at me, and I stopped.

"Jaxon, there are some things that you don't know. Things that you haven't been told because frankly, they weren't any of your business. Before you get pissed at me, just listen. Tristan and Evie are mates. Second chance mates to be more specific. The reason it has taken so long for the bond to be made, is because Evie and her wolf did not know that they had lost their first mate until recently. We don't know who her mate was because they had never met. However, we do know that due to whatever circumstances, their bond was broken. He could have died, he could have mated with someone else, we don't know, and it really doesn't matter. After she found out that she lost her first mate, her wolf was able to take on a second chance mate. Tristan has known for years that his bond with his first mate was broken. You weren't told because mates are a very personal thing. Tristan came to me while I was still Alpha, and I helped him through it. Tristan was the one to explain everything to Evie and I confirmed what he told her. Their bond is very new and as such, Tristan is very protective of her. Be careful what you say and how you say it. I know that you might be upset because he is your friend and she is your sister, but you need to remember that we don't get to choose our mate. The Moon Goddess does," Robert explained.

I sat there for a few minutes, not speaking. I was pissed. At what, I wasn't sure anymore. Other than the fact that my best friend was kissing my sister. And they were mates, second chance mates. And he never fucking told me that he lost his first mate. What kind of friend am I that I didn't even notice when this happened?

"Jaxon, what's really bothering you?" Isabella asked through our link.

"She's my sister. My little sister." I growled.

"And? You knew she was going to get a mate sooner or later. Who better than Tristan? Someone you know and trust?" she asked.

"Doesn't change the fact that she is my sister. He is going to have sex with my sister!" I groaned.

Isabella laughed out loud, causing everyone in the room to turn and stare at us.

"Jaxon, get over it! After everything we just did this week, I don't think you have any right to judge someone else on their sex life." She giggled.

"That's different," I grumbled.

"How is it different? We are mates. So are they. Quit being a hypocrite, get over it, and congratulate your sister and best friend. You should be happy for them, not yelling at them," she chastised me.

I hung my head in shame. She was right, the way I acted was out of line. And now I had to apologize, something I never did. Ever.

"Tristan, Evie, I..." I began, only to stop.

"Jaxon, it's okay. You were only looking out for me," Evie jumped in, trying to let me off the hook.

"Yeah, that's true. But I was out of line. I shouldn't have yelled at you," I muttered.

"No, you shouldn't have, but we get it. It's all good man," Tristan assured me.

"It's not all good. I'm sorry. I shouldn't have yelled at you. Either of you. I really am happy for you both." Isabella kissed me on the cheek, letting me know that she was proud of me.

"All is forgiven," Tristan stated. "Now, I know it's late and you had some news for us, but perhaps we should save it for tomorrow."

"I don't think so," Evie disagreed. "Hold up that hand, missy."

Isabella laughed and held her hand up for everyone to see. Evie jumped up from Tristan's lap squealing. My parents cheered and I just sat back and laughed.

Everyone congratulated us on our engagement. Mom and Evie wanted all the details. Isabella promised she would tell them everything, tomorrow. It was late and we all needed to get some sleep.

After we all said our good nights, we headed off to bed. Isabella and I showered together before bed. I wished that we weren't so tired from travelling all day, because my mate was fine as hell.

CHAPTER FIFTY

Isabella

"Time to wake up, sweetheart." Jaxon whispered, kissing me softly. I groaned and rolled over, pulling the covers up to hide my face. Jaxon chuckled.

"Come on. I want to show you something."

"It's too early, Jaxon," I grumbled.

"It's six thirty, sweetheart. Besides, weren't you planning on going back to school today?" he chuckled.

"Oh yeah. I forgot," I admitted. "What did you want to show me?"

"Get out of bed and come see."

I finally threw the covers off and climbed out of bed. Taking my hand, Jaxon led me over to the window and waited. I looked at him confused before turning to look out the window. An excited squeal erupted from me.

"Jaxon! It's snowing! It's really snowing!" I screamed.

"I know. It's why I got you up." He laughed.

"Can we go play in the snow? I want to build a snowman!" I cried.

"Calm down, Elsa. We can go play in the snow later. First, you need to shower and get dressed so we can go eat breakfast."

"Ok, fine. But I want a really big snowman," I pouted.

"Yes, dear."

I was so excited about the snow. I'd only seen snow once before and it was nothing like what I just saw. Where I grew up, snow wasn't really snow. Sure, we would get some big, fat flakes, but they never really stuck. It was more slush than anything. When I looked out the window to see the ground covered, I got so excited.

I hurried through my shower, washing my body and hair, and shaving as quickly as I could. Once finished, I dried off and got dressed before grabbing the blow dryer for my hair. After finishing up in the bathroom, I walked out and found Jaxon still standing by the window watching the snow fall.

"All done?" he asked.

"Yep. Let's go eat so we can play in the snow."

"Ok, Elsa. Come on then." He chuckled as I smacked him on the arm for calling me Elsa. Again. I could be an ice or snow queen if I wanted to.

The dining room was pretty much empty when we got downstairs. I guess everyone was still sleeping. We filled our plates and sat down to eat just as Tristan and Evie walked in. She rushed over to give me a hug while Tristan filled their plates.

Tristan and Jaxon began discussing pack business, causing Evie and I to roll our eyes at each other and giggle.

"So, what are your plans this morning?" Evie asked.

"I really want to go play in the snow, but I need to go over to the school for a while. I feel bad that I haven't gone in. I want to check on my class and talk to the principal and see what she wants me to do as far as coming back to work. What about you?" I replied.

"Nothing much really. I had planned on helping Tristan with his work, but it looks like he and Jaxon have a lot to discuss." She shrugged.

"Come with me over to the school. They might need some help with the Christmas program." I suggested.

"Ok, sure." she nodded.

We finished our breakfast, and all got up to leave. I told Evie I would meet her by the door after grabbing my jacket, boots, and gloves. She reminded me to get a scarf and hat too. I just laughed and said *yes mom* as she flipped me off. I gave Jaxon a quick kiss before heading upstairs to grab my things. Once I had it all, I hurried back down to meet Evie.

We headed out to the garage, followed by Grant and Thomas, which was a bit of a surprise.

"Let me guess, back on guard duty?" I asked.

"You got it, Luna." Grant grinned. "Just the school this morning?"

"Yeah, I don't plan on staying all day. Just need to check in with my class and talk to the principal."

They both nodded their heads before gesturing towards one of the four-wheel drive Jeeps. We all climbed in, and Grant drove us to the school. Luckily it was a short drive and the roads had already been cleared.

When we got to the school, I sent Evie off to talk to the music director about the Christmas program while I went to talk to principal. I found her in her office, and we had a good chat. She congratulated me on becoming Luna and on getting engaged. After discussing how busy the next few months were going to be, we decided that I would take a leave of absence for the rest of the school year. I would come back next school year as a full-time teacher again. In the meantime, I would come in and help out with classes whenever they needed me. With that decided, I asked her if my current substitute could stay on for the rest of the year. She'd done a fantastic job so far and I hated the thought that my students might have to have someone else. She assured me that she had no plans to find anyone else for my class.

Walking out of the principal's office after our talk, I felt relieved. I was worried that I would lose my job after missing so much work. Thankfully she's a member of the pack and understood. Grant and Thomas escorted me to my classroom where I chatted with my sub as the kids started to arrive. They were all so excited to see me and I was just as thrilled to see them. I stayed there until morning break, helping with projects and lesson plans. The substitute was excited that she would be finishing out the school year. I promised her that I would put in a recommendation that she be hired on as a full-time teacher the next year. She really had done a phenomenal job as my substitute.

After finishing up in the classroom, my guards and I headed to the auditorium to look for Evie. We found her in a pile of costumes and props. We helped her sort them out and bag up the costumes that needed some work. She was taking those home to finish them up for the music director. We grabbed those bags and left to head back to the pack house.

CHAPTER FIFTY-ONE

Jaxon

After Isabella and Evie left, Tristan and I headed up to my office. We needed to discuss everything that had been going on and see if we had any more leads.

"Have you heard from Nikolas?" I asked.

"No, I haven't. He should've called me now. Maybe your dad or Terry has heard from him," he replied.

"Call Terry and talk to him, but first, tell Cameron to come in here. I want his input on everything," I ordered.

"Yes, Alpha," he nodded, grabbing his phone. He linked Cameron and told him to meet us in my office as he dialed Terry's number.

I sat back in my chair and listened to Tristan's one-sided conversation. Cameron came in about halfway through and we talked about the patrols. He was confident that our borders were secure. I trusted him on this as he was probably more familiar with our land than even I was.

Tristan hung up the phone with a big grin on his face.

"Terry spoke to Nikolas this morning. Really good news. They've found even more incriminating evidence against Red Moon for the attack on Blackwood. Turns out a council rep went to Red Moon the night of the attack and was turned away by patrols. Not taking no for an answer, he slipped past their guards and made it to the pack house. It was empty. Quite suspicious, don't you think?" Tristan grinned.

"Did Nikolas say what they planned on doing?"

"He said that he's playing everything close to the chest for right now. He's still afraid that if we don't have enough evidence, we'll be laughed out of the council."

"How much more do we need? We have the council's files on Blackwood and Red Moon, we have Blackwood's pack records, and now this guy's report. That should be more than enough to at least open a case," Cameron complained.

"We need to make sure that we have enough for the council to go in and take over, not just open a case. They open a case and Red Moon will attack anyone that they think had a hand in it. Right now, that is us and Greystone. Greystone is right there close to them. We wouldn't be able to get there in time to help them and I won't leave Terry to fight this on his own," I stated.

Tristan and Cameron both nodded their heads in agreement. We sat there for a few minutes thinking quietly to ourselves. I finally broke the silence.

"Cam, any news on the rogues? Have there been more sightings? Do we know if they have added to their numbers?" I asked.

"There have been a number of sightings. They keep coming close to the border but stopping short of crossing it. From what we can tell, their numbers have almost doubled. But again, they aren't attacking or trespassing so we really can't do anything about it," he replied.

"I want pictures of Red Moon's top fighters and enforcers shown to all of our patrols. Don't say what pack they are from, just show them the pictures. Someone has got to be there keeping these rogues under control. There is no way they could stay this calm for this long," I ordered.

"I'll print out the pictures for you, Cam," Tristan offered.

"I'll make sure everyone sees them as soon as possible," Cam assured us.

After talking business for a few more hours, we finally broke for lunch. I called for my lunch to be brought up to me since Isabella wouldn't be back yet. Tristan decided to stay with me.

"So, when are you going to announce your engagement to the pack?" Tristan asked.

"I'm sure mom will want us to have a big party, same with Evie. Honestly, I couldn't care less. I'd be happy just sending out a link to everyone and telling them. But we both know I won't get my way." I laughed, Tristan joining me.

"Damn right you won't."

"I'll probably just let them handle it. They can get together with Isabella and work everything out."

"Sounds like a good idea to me. We have enough to worry about with the council and Red Moon," Tristan agreed.

"I know. Hopefully once Cameron gets those pictures out to the patrols, we'll hear something back. I really do think Red Moon has someone up here controlling the rogues. A Gamma or Head Warrior at the least."

"I think you're right. Rogues that fight and attack packs like this, they're not known for their patience. If we can hold off on the engagement party for at least a week, I think that would be best. I'd really like to have a better idea of what we are dealing with before news gets out about you and Bella," Tristan stated.

"I'll do my best to hold them off for now. So, what else do we need to go over?"

For the next two hours, Tristan and I made sure that all of the pack's finances were up to date, all paperwork was filed, and all of the complaints and issues from pack members were handled. Once we finished all that, we decided to call it a day.

Heading downstairs, we got out of the elevator just as Isabella was walking in the door with Evie, Grant, and Thomas.

"Grant, Thomas. You guys can have the rest of the day off. I'll call you if we need you," I instructed them.

"Yes, Alpha," they replied, before heading towards the kitchen.

"How was your day, sweetheart?" I asked, walking up to my mate and wrapping my arms around her waist.

"Good. I talked with the principal, and she agreed to put me on a leave of absence until the end of the school year in May. I told her that I would help out as much as I could in the meantime. Also, I'll be back as a full-time teacher next school year. That should give me enough time to plan our wedding and get a handle on any Luna duties that I have," she replied, snuggling up to me.

"Good. You hungry?"

"Yeah, we didn't have lunch," she replied.

"Well, let's go get you some food. Then we can talk about the engagement party that I'm sure my mom and sister will want us to have." I chuckled as she groaned.

"Don't even bother with that groan, missy. You two will be having an engagement party. A big one," Evie stated.

"Fine. But you're planning it," Isabella grumbled.

"We all knew that. Don't act like anything else was going to happen." Evie snorted. Tristan looked at me and rolled his eyes while grinning.

After they ate, Evie insisted that she and Isabella go and find my mom to discuss the party. I told her that I didn't care what they decided to do for it, they had full control of everything, with the exception of the date. I had final approval of the date. Evie grumbled a bit before realizing that I was not going to budge on this. She finally agreed and they left to go find my mom.

"Any plans right now?" Tristan asked.

"Nope. What are you thinking?" I replied.

"A run."

"Let's go!"

CHAPTER FIFTY-TWO

Isabella

Evie and I left the main pack house to go find her mom. She was all excited about planning mine and Jaxon's engagement party. Honestly, I would be fine with just announcing it at dinner, but apparently that was not good enough.

After a short walk, made just a little longer because of the snow, we finally made it to her parents' house. The walk in the snow reminded me that I still needed to have Jaxon come and play in the snow with me. He did promise.

Evie knocked on the door before just opening it and walking in. I wasn't sure why she even bothered knocking.

"Mom! Where are you?" she shouted.

"In the living room, dear. Come on in." Kathleen called back.

We walked into the living room to see Kathleen curled up in a chair near the fireplace with a book and a mug of tea. She smiled up at us as we came into the room. Evie and I both headed straight to the fireplace to sit in front of it and warm up.

"So, what brings you two lovely ladies here today?" Kathleen asked.

"We're here to plan Jaxon and Isabella's engagement party," Evie announced.

"And did you clear this with Jaxon first?" her mom chuckled.

"Yes, mother. We cleared it with Jaxon. He said we have full control over everything but the date. He gets to choose that." Evie rolled her eyes.

"Excellent. Isabella dear, what would you like to have at your engagement party? Any color schemes? Flowers, food?" Kathleen turned to me.

"I would be happy with a simple dinner, but we know Little Miss Party Planner over here would never let that happen. I'm good with anything really," I told her.

"Yeah, simple is not in my vocabulary." Evie smirked.

"Never has been," Kathleen muttered. "I have an idea. Since we are in December now, what if we plan a big Christmas party for the pack and announce it then?"

"That's a great idea, mom!" Evie squealed. "What do you think, Bella?"

"Yeah, that sounds great. We can decorate the pack house for Christmas a little early and that takes care of decorations. Then for food, maybe just do lots of finger foods, appetizers, things like that," I suggested.

The next couple of hours flew by as I listened to Evie and Kathleen plan out my engagement party. I occasionally added in my two cents, but mainly just sat back and laughed at how excited they were.

Tristan and Jaxon stopped by just as it was getting dark. Evie and Kathleen filled them in on the plans. Jaxon promised them that he would check his calendar and let them know when the best time was.

"Bella, aren't your parents planning on coming up for Christmas?" Tristan asked.

"Yeah, not sure what the dates are yet. Why?"

"I was just thinking, maybe they would like to be here for the party as well."

"That's a great idea, Tristan," Kathleen smiled. "We can push back the date of the party until they get here. You really should have your family here for this special time."

"That works," Evie agreed. "Plus, it will give us more time to get everything ready."

Tristan and Jaxon exchanged a smile after Kathleen and Evie agreed to push back the date of the party. Something was up with those two and I made a mental note to ask Jaxon about it later.

"Well, ladies. It's time we head back up to the pack house. It's getting dark out and much colder," Jaxon said.

"You still owe me a snowman, mister," I pointed at him.

"Yes, I do. And tomorrow, I, along with Tristan and Evie, will help you build as many snowmen as you want," he replied, smiling.

Evie and Tristan just laughed. We all bid Kathleen and Robert, who had just come in, goodbye before heading back home. The walk back went much faster with Jaxon and Tristan shifting into their wolves and making a new path for Evie and me. We just laughed at their childish antics, tumbling and rough housing in the snow like pups.

Once back at the pack house, we all went upstairs and changed before heading back downstairs for dinner. After talking it over with Jaxon, I decided to take my engagement ring off while around the rest of the pack. We didn't want to give anything away before the party. Sighing, I placed it back in my new jewelry box.

After dinner, Jaxon and I headed back up to our room to relax for the rest of the evening. I decided that a bubble bath was just what we needed. I walked into the bathroom, turned the faucet on, grabbed some bath salts and bubble bath, and added both to the rapidly rising water.

Turning the faucet off once the tub was filled, I called out to Jaxon to come join me before stripping out of my clothes and stepping into the hot, soothing water. Jaxon walked into the bathroom and smiled at me in the tub before quickly removing his clothes and joining me, sitting down across from me, and placing my feet in his lap.

"Did you have fun with my mom and sister?" he chuckled.

"Yes, I did actually. We–well they–got a lot of planning done," I told him.

"It sure sounded like it. Are you happy with everything?" he asked.

"Yeah, I am. I really like the idea of a Christmas party for the pack."

"Me too. We always try and do something like that each year, so this won't be too suspicious," he said.

"You and Tristan seemed especially happy about pushing the date back until my parents get here. Any reason why?" I asked, cocking my head to the side, and raising an eyebrow at him.

"Truthfully, yes. Cameron is showing pictures to the patrols of some of the top people from Red Moon. We're thinking that they have to have someone higher up here to help keep all of the rogues under control. We both agreed that we would like to have a better idea of who, and what, we are dealing with before we announce our engagement to everyone," he sighed.

"You think that they would attack us after word gets out about our engagement?" I asked, a little afraid of what his answer might be.

"I don't know. I don't think they know for certain who you are, but there are too many coincidences for us to take risks. They may or may not know it was us at the Blackwood pack house. If they do know it was us, then they could easily put two and two together. Especially if they have a picture of you. I won't risk you. Not even a little bit. If there's a chance that they know who you really are, then I will do everything I can to stay at least one step ahead of them until we can get rid of them for good." he assured me.

"I love you, Jaxon. I have no doubt in my mind that you will do everything you can to keep me safe. Just as I will do everything I can to keep you safe. All I ask is that you keep me in the loop. Don't shut me out or not tell me something because you don't want to worry me. I would rather be worried and prepared than blissfully ignorant and unprepared," I told him.

"I promise to keep you in the loop on everything. I love you, sweetheart. Now, let's enjoy this bath together, get all nice and clean, and then go to bed and do dirty things to each other," he winked at me.

"Sounds like a plan, Alpha," I purred, running my hands up his legs.

"Ok, bath time is over. We're clean enough." He growled, standing up and grabbing me before getting out of the tub. I just laughed and squealed as he threw me over his shoulder soaking wet from the tub and headed for our bed.

CHAPTER FIFTY-THREE

Isabella

The sunlight streaming in through the window finally forced me to get up. We forgot to close the damn curtains again last night. I couldn't stop the smile that lit up my face when I thought of how we spent our night. Soft kisses, loving caresses, and mind-blowing sex. Goddess I love that man.

Rolling over, I reached towards Jaxon's side of the bed only to come up empty-handed. Opening my eyes, I looked around the room. He wasn't there. I listened for any sounds from the bathroom, but there was nothing but silence.

"Jaxon?" I mindlinked him.
   "Yes, sweetheart?"
   "Where are you?" I asked.
   "In my office. I'll be up in a few minutes."

. . .

I decided to take a shower while I waited for him. I went into my closet and grabbed some thick leggings, a tank top, and a long sweater, along with my bra and panties. With all of my clothes in hand, I headed to the bathroom to shower.

When I finally finished up in the bathroom, I walked out into our room and saw Jaxon sitting on the bed waiting for me. I hurried over and climbed up in his lap, wrapped my arms around him, and snuggled up close.

"Morning, sweetheart. How did you sleep?" he asked, kissing the top of my head.

"Good. I didn't like waking up without you, though," I pouted.

"Sorry. I had to meet with Cameron and Tristan this morning and I didn't want to wake you," he apologized.

"Why did you have to meet so early?"

"Early?" he laughed. "Sweetheart, it's almost noon."

"What? Are you serious? Jaxon! Why did you let me sleep so late?" I complained.

"You looked like you needed the sleep. I guess I wore you out last night." He smirked.

"Shut up," I grumbled, causing him to laugh again. "Anyway, what was your meeting about?"

"Remember I told you last night that Cameron was showing some pictures to the patrols of the Red Moon pack?" I nodded my head. "Well, we got a hit. One of the patrols recognized two of them. The Gamma and one of their warriors. He saw them with the rogues while patrolling. Now we have our confirmation that Red Moon is controlling the rogues. Tristan is on the phone with Nikolas trying to get the council to hurry up and take action, so we don't have to. For now though, all pack members have been placed on alert," he sighed.

"What does that mean? Placed on alert?" I asked quietly.

"It means no unnecessary travel. Curfew in place. No one outside after dark unless on official pack business. Everyone must travel in groups of three or more. Preferably more. Anyone going into town must be accompanied by a warrior and the trip must be approved by myself or Tristan. Patrols have been doubled. All members capable of doing so, must run at least one patrol a week," he explained.

"Oh wow. What about the children at school?" I asked.

"I have guards setup close to the school. We won't let anything happen to them, plus the school is well within the borders. Anyone trying to get to them will be found long before they get close," he assured me.

"Is it still safe for my family to come visit?"

"Yes, sweetheart. Don't worry. I know it seems like a lot, but everything we've put in place is to ensure the safety of everyone here. It might be a little overboard, but I won't take chances. Not when it comes to our pack and especially not when it comes to you," he replied before leaning down and kissing me softly. "Now then, let's go get you something to eat."

Jaxon and I headed downstairs where lunch was just being served in the dining room. Evie teased me about sleeping in while Tristan laughed when I blushed. I just glared at them and ate my food while grumbling under my breath.

"Bella, can we talk after lunch? I want to go over a few things that we discussed yesterday with my mom," Evie asked as we were finishing up.

"Yeah, of course. As long as we go outside. Someone–cough–Jaxon–cough– promised to take me outside and play in the snow yesterday but he didn't." I playfully glared at him.

"Sorry, sweetheart." He grinned.

After we finished eating, we all headed up to our rooms to get changed to go outside. Deciding my leggings were warm enough, I just added some thick socks, my tall boots, a warm coat, scarf, and gloves. Coming out of my closet, I saw that Jaxon was already dressed to go. He smiled at me before kissing me on the nose and reaching for my hand as we headed downstairs.

We met Evie and Tristan by the back door. Looking out, I saw that there were quite a few kids outside playing, throwing snowballs at each other, and building snowmen. I couldn't help but grin.

Heading out, we passed several adults, men and women, who were supervising the children. After our talk this morning, I wasn't too surprised to see men helping the women. Usually, you only see the women watching them, but with this threat, Jaxon really wasn't taking any chances. We walked over to the far side of the lawn where we could still see everyone, but still have some privacy for our talk.

"Ok Elsa, what do you want to do first?" Jaxon asked with a smirk on his face.

"I don't know. I've never played in snow before. It's so pretty," I gushed.

Jaxon, Evie, and Tristan started laughing at me. Growling quietly, I took advantage of them being distracted and quickly made snowballs. Once I had a small pile of them, I threw one at Jaxon before throwing one each at Evie and Tristan. I couldn't help but laugh at their shocked expressions. They quickly recovered and began to make snowballs for themselves.

We all fell into the same routine. Make a snowball, throw a snowball. Make a snowball, throw a snowball. After a few minutes, we were all covered in snow and laughing hysterically. I looked over to see that the children had all stopped playing to stare at us. I guess seeing the Alpha, Luna, Alpha's sister, and Beta all having a snowball fight was a pretty rare occurrence.

We finally called a truce and decided to build a snowman. We argued back and forth over how to make it before deciding that Evie and I would make our own snowman while Jaxon and Tristan made one. Then we would see who built the better one.

"Come on, Bella. We have to build a better snowman than them!" Evie exclaimed.

"Yes, we do. We both know that they're going to try and make theirs as big as possible, which means it will be sloppy and weak. All we need to do is make ours stable and we win."

Evie and I got to work building the base for the snowman. We quickly rolled some snow into a ball, gradually making it bigger. We made sure to take our time and make sure it was nice and tightly packed. Once the base was big enough, we did the same to the middle section and then the head. Our snowman was about five feet tall by the time we finished building him. Looking over at Jaxon and Tristan, we could see that their snowman was well over six feet tall, possibly even seven feet. And it was wobbly.

Evie and I decided that she would stay and guard our snowman while I went and searched for things to decorate it. I stayed near the edge of the woods where Jaxon could see me so he wouldn't worry. I quickly grabbed a few sticks, some pinecones, and some small rocks.

Hurrying back to Evie, we picked the best branches for the arms and carefully stuck them in the sides of the body. We then used two small pinecones as the eyes, a larger rock for the nose, and the smaller rocks for the mouth. I took my scarf off and wrapped it around the snowman's neck, while Evie took her hat off and placed it on his head.

Stepping back, we surveyed our handiwork. Not too shabby. Hearing a grunt and several curses, we looked over towards Jaxon and Tristan and cracked up laughing. Their snowman had collapsed, covering them both in snow.

CHAPTER FIFTY-FOUR

Jaxon

Hearing my mate's laughter, I couldn't help but smile. Even if I was covered in snow thanks to Tristan. The idiot. Standing up and dusting myself off, I walked over to Isabella and wrapped my arms around her.

Kissing the top of her head I whispered, "I'm glad you're having fun. Even if it is at my expense." She just giggled and hugged me tighter.

"I think we should head in and have some hot chocolate. What do you guys think?" Evie asked, rubbing her hands together. We might have the extra benefit of being warmer than humans, but that didn't mean we don't get cold.

"I agree. It's freezing out here," Tristan said.

As we opened the back door to the pack house, we were greeted with laughing children. All of the kids that had been playing outside, were now inside drinking hot chocolate, and eating cookies.

"Oh Alpha. I'm so sorry. We didn't think you'd be back in so soon.

We'll have the kids out here as soon as possible," Melissa, one of the moms, said.

"Don't worry about it, Melissa. They're fine where they are. In fact, after they finish their snack, why don't you guys take them up to the theater room and turn on a movie for them?" I told her.

"Are you sure, Alpha? We don't want to be a bother."

"Very sure. They're no bother at all. In fact, we're going to go have some hot chocolate ourselves and then head up to my office. So please don't worry about us. Take them upstairs, turn on a movie for them, and relax." I smiled.

"Thank you, Alpha." She smiled, before turning back to the kids. "Who wants to go watch Frozen?" she asked. The children all cheered. The moms quickly gathered them all up and ushered them upstairs while Isabella, Tristan, Evie, and I all went into the kitchen.

"Man, I hope those kids didn't eat all the cookies," Tristan grumbled.

"Shut up, Tristan. You know Cookie always saves extra cookies for you," Evie smacked him. Tristan grinned and rubbed his belly.

Sure enough, once we got to the kitchen and Cookie saw Tristan, she opened a cabinet and grabbed a plate of cookies that she had covered and set aside for him.

"Cookie, you spoil him too much," I complained.

"Oh, you shush, Alpha Jaxon. You know I spoil you just as much." She winked, pulling out a freshly frosted chocolate cake.

"Cookie, I love you," I grinned, reaching for the cake.

She smacked my hand before I could grab the plate. "Behave boy. You better ask that pretty Luna of yours if she wants some first."

"She doesn't. She told me I could have the whole thing." I smiled innocently.

"I don't believe that for a second. Just for that, you have to wait until everyone else gets a piece of cake," she scolded me. Isabella just laughed at me getting in trouble.

"That's not fair, Cookie. Tristan got a whole plate of cookies all to himself and he didn't have to share," I whined. Cookie turned around to glare at Tristan who was quickly shoving the last cookie in his mouth.

"Tristan Xavier Merritt! How dare you eat that entire plate of cookies and not share a single one! See if I make any cookies for you again, you greedy little boy," she yelled at him. I just stood back and grinned.

"Alpha Jaxon, wipe that grin off your face. You're still not getting any cake until everyone else does. Beta Tristan, you aren't getting any cake at all," Cookie scolded us both. At the looks on our faces, Isabella and Evie laughed so hard they had tears rolling down their cheeks.

Tristan and I sat on the stools at the bar and pouted about not getting any cake. Cookie cut big slices of cake for Isabella and Evie. She then poured them some hot chocolate and added marshmallows and fresh chocolate shavings on top. After she was done with that, she finally cut me a slice of cake. I opened my mouth to complain that my slice was way smaller than theirs, but the look on Cookie's face shut me up really quick. I finished my cake quickly, since it was really small. Sitting back in my chair, I drank my hot chocolate and stared at my mate's piece of cake while she ate. I sighed and watched her piece get smaller and smaller. Cookie's chocolate cake was my favorite food in the whole world.

"You can have the last of mine, Jaxon. Now stop pouting," Isabella giggled through our link.

"Thank you, sweetheart. I love you!"

I quickly grabbed her piece of cake and ate it before Cookie could take it from me. I may be Alpha, but that woman runs the kitchen and what she says goes. It didn't matter who you were.

We finished our snacks and Cookie shooed us out of the kitchen so she could finish prepping for dinner. I asked Tristan and Evie to join us in my office.

. . .

"Tristan, have you told Evie everything that is going on? With the rogues and all that?" I asked through our link.

"Yes, I told her everything. I don't want to keep secrets from her," he replied.

"Good. I am sure it will come up in here and I don't want to have to lie to her."

We sat down in my office, Isabella on my lap on one of the chairs while Tristan and Evie sat on the couch.

"When are your parents getting here, Bella?" Evie asked.

"Three days before Christmas. I was thinking maybe we could do the party the day after they get here. That way we aren't doing it on Christmas Eve. I don't want to take away from anyone's family time. Is that ok with you?" she replied.

"Yeah, that sounds great. I was thinking we could do a children's Christmas party first. Have Santa come in, cookies, milk, all that. Then we could announce your engagement. After that, the children can go to bed, and we can have the adult party. What do you think?" Evie suggested.

"I really like that idea. It gets everyone involved. Maybe we can ask Terry if he will be Santa. That way the kids won't recognize his scent and know who it is," Isabella said.

"That's a great idea! Do you think he will do it? We have the Santa suit."

"Of course, he will. He loves doing stuff like that." She laughed. "He always dressed up on holidays for the kids back home. Santa, Easter Bunny, you name it. He has fun with it."

"Perfect. Maybe tomorrow or the next day we can go into town and pick out flowers. We also need to get Christmas trees for the pack house. Jaxon, can you have someone take care of that for us? And have someone get all of the decorations out of storage. We need to make sure that we have everything we need for our color scheme." Evie asked.

"Yeah, I'll take care of it. If you go to town, I want a full guard with you. Grant, Thomas, and both of their teams. No arguments, no excuses. Understood?" I ordered.

"Yes, we both understand. No arguments here," Evie assured me. "Do you want to go tomorrow or the day after, Bella?"

"Let's go tomorrow. That way if they need to order flowers, they have plenty of time." Isabella told her. "Babe, can you have them get everything out of storage in the morning so we can take a look at it before we go?"

"Yes, sweetheart. I'll have them get it all out tonight, so you ladies have plenty of time." I smiled.

"Thank you," she replied, kissing my cheek.

"You're welcome." I smiled at her.

"What is the color scheme for the party?" Tristan asked.

"It's..."

Before Evie could complete her sentence, Cameron burst through the door with a panicked look on his face.

"Alpha! We are under attack! The rogues!" he shouted.

I jumped to my feet and set Isabella on hers. "Where are they coming in from?" I demanded.

"North and East, Alpha. I have scouts watching the West and South. So far, no movement. Everything seems to be centered on the North and East," Cameron replied.

"Isabella, Evie. Get the women and children that are in the pack house and take them upstairs to our floor. Evie, secure the floor once everyone is in there. Tristan, Cameron. You two are with me. Tristan, link everyone and tell them we are under attack and to take shelter. I want all available fighters to head there now. I'll tell the warriors. Let's go. Now!" I commanded.

I kissed Isabella and sent her off with Evie. Tristan and Cameron ran with me downstairs and outside.

"Warriors! We are under attack! The rogues are coming from the North and East side of our territory! Get there now!" I commanded them through our link.

. . .

Once outside, we all shifted into our wolves and ran towards the noise. We could hear the sounds of growling and fighting as we got closer. When we arrived, I couldn't believe what I was seeing. There were hundreds of rogues fighting against us. My patrols were holding their own, but slowly losing ground to them. With a ground-shaking howl, I shot forward into the battle. No one threatens what's mine.

CHAPTER FIFTY-FIVE

Isabella

Evie and I ran out of Jaxon's office and immediately headed upstairs to the theater to help gather the children. When we got there, Melissa and the other moms were rushing around trying to get the kids together and out the door.

"Melissa! This way! We're taking the kids upstairs to the Alpha's floor!" Evie shouted over the noise.

I put my fingers between my lips and let out a shrill whistle. Everyone immediately stopped and turned to stare at me.

"Ok, everyone calm down. Children, line up and follow me. Melissa, you and Evie stay at the back and make sure no one is left behind. I want all other adults spaced out along the line of kids making sure no one runs off. Clear? Good. Let's go!" I shouted.

I quickly led the group towards the stairs as there were too many of us to take the elevator. Once we arrived on our floor, Evie led us all to a room at the opposite end of the hallway from our room. Opening the door, she turned on the light and led the kids inside.

"Alright, I want you all to come in and take a seat on the floor quietly," Evie instructed them.

Melissa took over and made sure that everyone was seated and accounted for. "We have everyone, Luna."

"Thank you, Melissa. Evie, is there anyone else unaccounted for in the house?" I asked.

"Just Cookie. Unless someone told her to come up, she won't know to. Her mindlink doesn't work as well as ours." Evie said.

"Ok. You stay here with the kids. I'm going to go get Cookie," I told her.

"Absolutely not! Jaxon would kill me if anything happened to you. I'll go," she protested.

"Evie, not to be an ass here, but I think we both know that I am the better fighter and stronger wolf of the two of us. Plus, you know how to lock down this floor and I don't. So, stop arguing with me. Lock the door after I leave. There are video screens over there so you can see what's happening. I'm going." I turned and ran out of the room before she could try and stop me.

Heading down the stairs, I made sure to control my breathing and listen carefully. I stopped at the bottom floor and listened at the door. Not hearing anything, I stepped out and looked around and made sure that no one else was around before running towards the kitchen.

In the kitchen, I found Cookie hiding in the pantry. I coaxed her out of there and told her to go upstairs where Evie and the others were. She tried to argue, but I rushed her off. As soon as she was gone, I ran to the back door and outside. Sniffing the air, I found Jaxon's scent and followed it. He was going to be pissed.

CHAPTER FIFTY-SIX

Jaxon

Rushing into the fight, I tore into every rogue that crossed my path. I didn't hesitate to kill each and every one. I could tell that Tristan and Cameron were next to me doing the same. As strong as we were, and we were much stronger than the rogues and better trained as well, we were still struggling. The sheer number of rogues was almost overwhelming.

I tried not to focus on the number of wolves we were up against. I just took it one rogue at a time. I could feel the anger and dread coming through the pack's link. A spark of relief shot through the link taking me by surprise. Pausing for a second to look up, I saw that my warriors had finally arrived. The tides quickly turned, and we overpowered the rogues.

As we were fighting off the last of the rogues, I felt a sharp pain in my back leg. Looking back, I could see that there was no one near me. Panic shot through me as I realized the pain was Isabella's and not mine. I growled loudly, startling the wolves around me.

Sniffing, I quickly found Isabella facing off with Red Moon's Gamma. He was in wolf form, and she was in human form. My wolf and I saw red. I raced forward just as he jumped at my mate. Before I could get to her, she ducked down under him, grabbed his front leg, and yanked hard, flipping him over. She kicked him in the side before pinning him down on his back, immobilizing him.

When I got to them, she had forced him to shift back. I stayed in wolf form when I got to them, ordering Grant and Thomas to come get him and take him to the pack prison. Once they left with him, I shifted back and pulled her into my arms.

"What the fuck were you thinking?" I growled.

"I was thinking that I wasn't about to let our pack fight my battles for me. I was thinking that there was no way I was going to let you come out here and put yourself in danger while I sat there in that room and waited like a good little girl. I was thinking that it would kill me if anything happened to you while I was hiding. That's what I was thinking, Jaxon," she cried. My heart melted and my anger began to seep away at the sight of her tears.

"Sweetheart, it's my job to keep you safe. It's the job of this pack to fight your battles. Your battles are their battles. I didn't tell you to go hide like a good little girl. I told you to take care of our pack members in the house," I whispered against her cheek as I held her tight. "Now, where are you hurt? I felt your pain."

"It's just a scratch on my leg. Nothing serious," she assured me. Not taking a chance, I knelt down next to her and ripped her leggings open to check it out. Sure enough, the minor scratch was already healing. I kissed it softly before standing up. It was then that I noticed that I was still dressed.

"What the hell? How do I have clothes on? I shifted in my clothes, they should have ripped off." I gazed down at them in wonder. Isabella's giggle caused me to look up at her in confusion.

"We mated, Jaxon. Your wolf has taken on some of the properties as mine, like not losing your clothes when you shift," she explained, smiling at me.

"Definite perk." She just laughed at me again. "Come on, let's check on our pack members."

Walking around, I was surprised to see the number of lifeless bodies lying on the ground. I carefully looked over each and every one, relieved when they weren't from our pack. I was beginning to think that we had made it out of the fight without a single life lost when I heard Isabella gasp next to me.

"Oh no. No, no, no." she cried, her hand over her mouth. Before I could ask her what was wrong, she took off running. I quickly followed her, shouting her name. She came to a stop and dropped to her knees, reaching her hands out. What I saw in front of her stopped me cold.

Isabella was kneeling on the ground, crying. She reached forward and brushed his hair off his forehead. Cameron. My Gamma. My friend. How could I face Kayleigh, knowing that her mate died for mine? I couldn't even imagine the pain she must have felt. Hearing a gasp and a groan, my eyes widened. Isabella jerked her hand back in surprise.

"Luna, as much as I appreciate the comfort, could you please get off my arm? It fucking hurts," Cameron groaned.

Isabella jumped up with a squeak. I couldn't help but chuckle. It quickly stopped at the dirty look she gave me. I knelt down next to him and quickly looked over his wounds. They were quite severe. I called out for someone to get a pack doctor. I then looked around for Tristan, wanting to make sure he was ok. Once I spotted him, I waved him over.

When he got to us, I could see the blood on him. Sniffing the air, I knew that a lot of it was his. Before I could ask him if he was ok, he waved me off and smiled, letting me know he was fine.

"Everything ok, Alpha?" he asked before looking down and spotting Cameron. "Holy shit, Cam. You forget how to fight?"

"Shut up, Tristan. You should see the other guys." Cameron grumbled.

"Other guys? What other guys?" Tristan teased.

"Exactly." Cam smirked. His smirk quickly became a grimace as a wave of pain tore through him.

I looked around again, ready to yell for help, before spotting the pack doctor racing towards us. I stood up and stepped back, pulling Isabella with me. Tristan assured me that he would stay with Cameron so Isabella and I could make sure everyone else was ok. Nodding my head, we walked away to check on the others.

Once I made sure everyone else was good, I let my block down to tell the pack that the threat was over. As soon as my block dropped, Evie was shouting in my head.

"Jaxon! Are you okay? Is Bella with you? She better be okay because I am so going to kick her fucking ass when she gets back! Speaking of getting back, rogues got into the pack house. Well, more like I let them in. Don't worry, we're all okay. I managed to trap them in the safe room on the second floor," Evie said quickly.

"We're fine, Evie. On our way back now. Stay where you are!" I ordered.

"Damn that woman!" I shouted.

"What's wrong?" Isabella asked.

"Evie let rogues in the pack house and has them trapped on the second floor. I swear to fuck I am going to kill her," I growled. "Tristan! Come on, we need to get back to the pack house now. Bring some warriors with you. At least ten. Evie has rogues trapped on the second floor and I'm not sure how many there are."

Tristan stared at me in shock before shaking his head and shouting for some warriors to follow us. We all ran back to the pack house as quickly as possible. When we got to the second floor, I ushered the warriors to the front, followed by Tristan. I kept Isabella behind me, just in case. I linked Evie and told her to open the steel door. As soon as she did, my warriors rushed in and subdued the rogues before they even knew what was happening. I ordered them to take the rogues to the pack prison.

Once the warriors left with the rogues, Tristan, Isabella, and I paused for a moment to take a deep breath. We all shook our heads and slowly made our way to the elevator. Time to teach my sister a lesson. Even if she did capture five rogues without leaving the safe room. Damn woman.

CHAPTER FIFTY-SEVEN

Jaxon

Isabella, Tristan, and I headed upstairs to the safe room. I was seriously pissed at my sister. Yes, she caught the rogues, but she never should have taken that risk. What if something had gone wrong? What if they had made it to the safe room with her and all of the kids?

Hearing a growl next to me, I looked over to see Tristan red faced and glaring. Looks like I wasn't the only one that was pissed off at Evie. Maybe I wouldn't need to yell at her after all. Yeah, right. He was her mate. He wouldn't stay mad at her long.

"Jaxon, don't be too hard on her. She did what she thought was best to keep the people in that room safe. Those rogues were going to do whatever was necessary to get in here. She just led them along to where she could trap them. Yes, it was risky, but so was sitting there and not doing anything." Isabella linked me. Always the reasonable one.

"I know, sweetheart. I just hate that she even had to take that risk. I'll try to control my wolf, but he is pissed right now." I told her.

"Just make sure that you tell her that you are proud of how she handled a difficult situation after you yell at her. She needs to hear that," she sighed.

I didn't respond, I just wrapped my arm around her waist and pulled her close to me. Kissing the top of her head, I could feel my wolf begin to relax at her closeness. Damn it. She made it hard to stay mad.

"Tristan, I need you to calm down. Okay?" I glanced over at him as we reached the safe room door.

"I'm not sure I can, Jaxon. My wolf is furious with her." He growled.

"I understand. Mine isn't exactly happy right now. However, as my mate just pointed out to me, she did what she thought was best to keep everyone in that room safe. She made the best decision she could under the circumstances," I reasoned with him. Before he could respond, the door opened, and Evie came flying out and jumped into Tristan's arms.

"Are you okay? What happened? I felt your pain. Oh god, Tris, it hurt so bad. What happened to you?" she rambled, kissing him all over his face.

Isabella and I had a hard time containing our laughter as Tristan just sighed and let Evie continue her ranting and kissing. He finally grabbed her and kissed her hard to shut her up. Gross.

"I'm fine, baby. It's nothing serious. I'm sorry you felt that," Tristan reassured her. "Are you okay?"

"I'm fine. I was so worried," she whispered, holding him tight.

"I know. I'm sorry, baby. I didn't mean to worry you. Right now, though, we need to discuss you letting rogues in the house," he replied, sounding quite stern at the end.

"I know, I know. 'What were you thinking letting rogues in the house? How could you endanger yourself like that? That was highly irresponsible of you. I'm very upset.' Did I cover it all or is there more?" she sassed him.

Tristan damn near fell over in shock at what Evie said. At the look on his face, Isabella and I lost it. We started laughing so hard several of the women in the safe room peeked out to see what was going on. Seeing their Alpha and Luna laugh hysterically, shocked them. Evie just shook her head and motioned for them to go back in the room.

"Okay, if you guys are finished, how about you take a look at the video footage. Then I'm sure you have some rogues to question and some phone calls to make," Evie snapped.

"You're right, Evie. Let's take a look at what you have," Isabella stated, straightening up and heading into the room. I slapped Tristan on the back, and he snapped out of his daze.

"Come on, Tristan. You can't let her get to you like that or she will take advantage of it in the future." I chuckled, following my mate into the safe room.

After watching the video footage, Tristan and I both apologized to Evie for doubting her. We made sure that everyone in the room knew to go back to their homes, with an escort, before heading downstairs to my office to make a few calls.

It was decided that Isabella would call Terry and let him know what had happened and what we had found out. Tristan was going to go check on everyone in the pack hospital and report back to us. Evie said that she would go with him. I was going to call Nikolas and let him know what happened and who we had captured. I knew that the council would want to question them and since we didn't know who had compelled some of the rogues, I wanted Nikolas to be here before the rest of them.

Picking up the phone, I dialed Nikolas' private number. It rang twice before he answered.

"Nikolas, it's Jaxon," I began.

"Hello, Jaxon. How is everything?" he replied.

"Not good. The rogues attacked. Luckily no one from my pack was killed, but we did have several injuries."

"Oh, my goodness. That's terrible news, but I am certainly glad to hear that everyone is going to be alright." Nikolas blurted out.

"That's not all. We managed to capture some of the rogues and take them prisoner. We also captured the Gamma from Red Moon. He tried to attack my mate," I said.

"Holy shit!" Nikolas exclaimed. "We knew that they had something to do with the rogues, but I never thought that they would have one of their top people up there leading them. Where are you keeping him and the rogues? In that prison of yours?"

"Yes, they are all in the prison. We're keeping them in separate cells and Red Moon's Gamma is being kept on a different floor. Just to be safe," I informed him.

"Good, good. That's good," he replied absentmindedly. "Ok, here's what I want you to do. I want you to call the main line and report the attack. I also want you to tell them that you captured a pack wolf with the rogues but say you don't know who he is or what pack he's from. We don't want to give away that we know Red Moon is involved. The council will send a team as soon as they can, probably tomorrow or the day after. As soon as I find out when they are flying out, I will let you know as I plan on getting to you before they do. I want to monitor any and all interactions with the prisoners, especially Red Moon's Gamma. We need to find out who the elder is that is helping them."

"Okay. I'll call the main line as soon as we hang up and I will wait for your call after that. Isabella is on the phone with Terry right now. I'm sure that he will want to come up here as soon as possible," I let him know.

"No! Tell him to stay where he is! If my suspicions are correct, the council will vote to take down Red Moon. I want Terry in place to block them from escaping. Whoever their contact is, will try and warn them. We need someone we can trust to be there," Nikolas argued.

"Okay, I'll tell him. Call me as soon as you know something," I instructed him, hanging up the phone.

I turned to Isabella who was still on the phone but looked like she was waiting for me. I held my hand out and she handed me the phone.

"Terry, you there?" I asked.

"I'm here, Jaxon. What do you need me to do?" he replied.

"I just got off the phone with Nikolas. I'm going to call the main council line and report the attack, let them know that we captured several rogues and what appears to be a pack wolf. We aren't going to tell them who he is or what pack he's from. We're playing dumb on that for now. Nikolas thinks that once the council gets here and conducts their investigation, they will vote to take down Red Moon. We need you and your pack to be ready in case they try and escape. We're going to try and flush out the council mole while they're here. We're sure that he will try and warn them. Are you good with that?"

"Whatever you need, Jaxon. I have a few people that I can send over to keep a discreet eye on Red Moon, so we know what they are up to. Don't worry, Red Moon will never know they are there. When I say people, I mean humans. Not shifters." He chuckled.

"Are you sure you want to send humans to watch over them?" I asked, concerned.

"Positive. These guys are former military, Special Forces. Nothing phases them. I've used them in the past when I need someone more discreet than wolves," he assured me.

"Damn, Terry. That's quite the team," I whistled. "I'm not going to question it. You trust them, I trust you. Send them in as soon as possible."

"You got it. I'll call them as soon as we hang up. Keep me posted with the council," he replied before hanging up.

As soon as I got off the phone with Terry, I dialed the number for the council to report the attack. Filing the report took a very frustrating half hour. By the time I got off the phone with them, I wanted to kill someone. Or at least break lots of things.

Sensing my frustration, Isabella walked over to me and sat down in my lap, resting her head on my chest. I wrapped my arms around her and held her close, breathing in her scent to calm down both my wolf and my human self. Once I felt a little calmer, I leaned back and sighed.

"That bad?" she whispered.

"The council is made up of idiots, I swear. The guy asked me several times if I was sure they were rogues and if I was sure that they were attacking and not just trying to pass through." I growled.

"Are you serious? Did you get the guy's name? We should let

Nikolas know who it was. That's seriously messed up for him to say things like that to an Alpha reporting an attack," Isabella replied.

"I'll let Nikolas know when he gets here. Now, we need to head over to the pack hospital and check on everyone," I said while setting my office phone up to forward to my cell phone while we were gone. I didn't want to miss any important calls. I then texted to Nikolas and Terry to let them know that the report was filed.

Once we arrived at the pack hospital, I was surprised to see that there were only a few wolves being treated for injuries. Cameron was one of them. Even Tristan was being forced to lay down on a bed while he recovered. We walked over to the doctor who was treating Cameron, to get a report.

"Hey, doc. How is he?" I asked.

"He'll live, Alpha," she replied. "The spinal injury will take the longest to heal. But I expect a full recovery. I'd like for him to stay here for at least a couple of days and then bed rest for another week." Cameron just rolled his eyes at that.

"I'll make sure it happens. What about everyone else?"

"Nothing too serious. Cameron was actually the worst. Beta Tristan should be good to go in another couple of hours. Just some fractured ribs and a cracked collarbone. As for everyone else, just the usual. Bites, claw marks, and few broken bones. Very lucky today that there were no serious injuries," she replied.

"Where's your mate?" I asked, looking around.

"Sent him over to the prison to check out the prisoners and the pack members there. Didn't think you wanted anyone dying before you could question them." She grinned. Her mate was also a pack doctor, the one who helped Cameron after the fight.

"Thanks, doc. Keep up the good work."

After talking with Cameron and Kayleigh for a few minutes, we checked in with Tristan and brought him up to date on the phone calls. I told him about the guy that answered the phone, and he was livid. I calmed him down and ordered him to relax until the doctor released him. He agreed to go back to the pack house to rest and we could talk again later.

After leaving the hospital, Isabella and I grabbed one of the snow-mobiles before heading over to the prison. We could have shifted and run over there, but I was tired after fighting and I didn't feel like it. Besides, with the way Isabella squealed when she saw the snowmobile, I knew that she had never been on one before and would want to take it.

CHAPTER FIFTY-EIGHT

Isabella

When I saw the snowmobile, I couldn't contain my excitement. I was so happy that Jaxon said we could take it to the prison instead of running there.

Jaxon handed me a helmet before pulling the snowmobile out of the garage. Once it was in the open, he started it up. He got on first and I sat down behind him, wrapping my arms around him, and holding on tight. He started moving and gave me about thirty seconds to get used to it before he really got on it. Once he took off, it was like we were flying! I had no clue these things could go so fast. It was exhilarating.

Arriving at the prison, Jaxon came to a sliding stop, throwing snow everywhere. When the snow cleared and the guards saw who was there, they all cracked up laughing and shook their heads. I was sure they were used to him doing this.

We climbed off the snowmobile and headed inside. Once we got past all of the security measures and inside, Grant met us and led us down to where the rogues were being held. He said that the doctor was treating the last of the rogues now. Only a few of those captured had serious injuries. One was touch and go. Luckily, they had all of the necessary equipment here at the prison to help keep him alive. We met up with the doctor after he finished with the last patient.

"What's the news, doc?" Jaxon asked.

"Not looking so good for one, but I think if he lasts the night he'll live. It's just keeping him alive for now. He has a brother in here, so we were able to use his blood for a transfusion. I have him in the prison hospital under constant monitoring. I'm cautiously optimistic. As for the rest, they will live. Broken bones, bites, claw marks, the usual. Some will scar, but they will live," he sighed.

"Thank you. You did a good job today. You and your mate," Jaxon assured him.

"Thanks, Alpha. How is Gamma Cameron?" he asked.

"Doing good. He's with his mate. Yours says he has to stay in the hospital for a few days and then bed rest for another week. He'll complain, but he'll be fine."

"That's good news," the doctor replied. "Oh, I injected the pack wolf we captured with some wolfsbane. Not enough to cause harm, just enough to keep him from contacting anyone with his pack link if they're nearby. I didn't want to take any chances that there was another from his pack close enough to link with."

"Good call. Thank you. Go see your mate and get some rest," Jaxon said.

We followed Grant down to where the Gamma from Red Moon was being kept. Jaxon had me wait in a room beside the one he was being kept in. He assured me that I would still be able to hear every-thing and see everything, but that he didn't want me in the same room with him. I frowned, thinking he was being silly, but I didn't argue with him.

I walked into the room and stood before the two-way mirror. I'd be able to see in, but they wouldn't be able to see me. I knew that he'd already seen me, but I didn't want to stress Jaxon out any more than he already was.

I watched Jaxon and Grant walk into the room where Thomas was standing over Red Moon's Gamma. He was an ugly man, deep set eyes, washed out complexion, and a huge scar running down one side of his face. I was quite surprised. Almost every wolf I have ever met has been at the very least, somewhat good looking. Even the scary ones. Not this guy though. Maybe that was why he looked so angry. Jaxon stood staring at the prisoner who was staring right back. After a minute or two, which felt like forever, the man lowered his eyes. Jaxon smirked before taking a seat across the table from the man, directly in front of me.

"What's your name?" Jaxon asked him.

"You know who I am," he sneered. "How's your mate?"

"If you're trying to piss me off, you already accomplished that when you attacked my pack. Now answer the question," Jaxon calmly retorted.

"And I already said, you know who I am," the man scoffed.

Jaxon turned to Thomas and nodded his head. I wasn't sure what was going on, so I watched closely. The prisoner tried to act like he didn't care, but you could see in his eyes that he was worried.

Thomas stepped forward and wrapped his hands around the man's neck and began to squeeze. I couldn't see Jaxon's face, but I could see Grant's and he was smirking. I am not one for violence; I will fight, when necessary, but I'm not so sure I could take a man's life in cold blood, while he's locked up in a prison, chained to a chair. Then again, he did threaten my mate and my pack, so maybe I could.

As Thomas squeezed tighter and tighter, the man's face began to turn red and then purple. Jaxon nodded his head at Thomas once again and he released the man who began to gasp for breath.

"What is your name?" Jaxon asked him.

"Shane," he finally choked out.

"What pack are you with, Shane?"

"You know the answer to that," Shane spit out.

"Thomas." Jaxon nodded.

"Wait! I'll answer your question. Red Moon. I'm the Gamma for Red Moon."

"Why did you attack my pack with a group of rogues?" Jaxon demanded.

"My Alpha ordered me to," Shane replied.

"Why?"

"You have something he wants." Shane smirked.

"And what would that be?" Jaxon growled.

"Your mate. The lost Blackwood girl." Shane smiled, gesturing towards the mirror I was standing behind. Jaxon growled and shook before his wolf finally took over and he shifted. *Oh. Shit.*

THE END. FOR NOW

Read the rest of the story in <u>Blackwood: Book 2</u>

http://bit.ly/BlackwoodBook2

ACKNOWLEDGMENTS

First and foremost, to my family. My husband, Brian, our three kids, and our dog, Panzer. You sacrificed the most while supporting me on this long and arduous journey. I was beginning to think we would never get here. But we did. Thank you. I couldn't have done this without you guys. I love you all.

To my Alpha Reader, and my person, Melissa S. Fucking hell we have been through it, haven't we? From phone calls and video chats about anything and everything to this point right here. You are amazing. I am so lucky to have found you. You. Are. My. Person. I seriously don't know what I would do without you. And I hope I never have to find out. Imagine the hell we will raise when we finally get to meet in person. lol

To my editor, Amy Briggs. Girl. You have been a light in the darkness as I struggled to see this through. Thank you for your insight, your knowledge, your willingness to share both. But mostly, thank you for your friendship. I will be eternally grateful. Drinks on me next time!

To my Wattpad followers who have made it this far. This one's for you! I could not have done this without your support and enthusiasm. Thank you for encouraging me to publish! I really hope you all like the changes that have been made.

To my mom and dad. Who taught me that I could be and do anything I wanted to as long as I put my mind to it and tried my very hardest. I never believed them until now. Now I get it. That same lesson that I am trying to teach my kids. Thank you both for believing in me. I wish you were here to see me succeed.

Made in the USA
Columbia, SC
14 April 2023

15084677R00171